THE LAST CABIN: EMP SURVIVAL

SURVIVAL

JAMES HUNT

❀ Created with Vellum

---

*I*t was a clean kill.

The bolt struck the center of the turkey's heart. It lay limp, its plume of feathers still upright on its backside. Joanna Mercer lowered the crossbow and then emerged from her cover of rocks and bushes.

The sun hadn't risen high enough in the east to fully light the west side of the mountain, but the sky lightened from black to a light grey, and it wouldn't be long before the summer heat was in full swing. Jo collected the bird, then slung the bow over her left shoulder and started her trek back toward the cabin.

The trees provided shade, and a breeze passed through the mixture of oak and maple leaves, cooling the sweat on her tanned neck. Jo had kept her blonde hair short for the past four years, ever since her move off grid. It was practical, comfortable, and she was long past trying to impress anyone.

Jo maintained a leisurely pace on her walk home. She always enjoyed her time on the mountain before sunrise. The scenery was breathtaking. The view of the rolling Tennessee hills in the distance was a wonderful mixture of vibrant colors of untamed and untouched land. Most of the mountain ridge was still asleep, the earth itself still sluggish and still covered with the blanket of fog that provided the Smoky Mountains with its namesake.

And as much as Jo enjoyed the view, she reveled in the mountain's silence. No cars, no phones, no distractions. It was the purest form of living Jo had experienced. But it had come at a great cost.

Today marked the four-year anniversary since Jo had been widowed. Her husband Danny had been driving home when he was struck and killed by a drunk driver. It was a cruel twist of fate that the driver survived. And while her husband's killer was sentenced to prison for life, it didn't replace what their family had lost.

Jo had hoped that the court's conviction would relieve her pain, but it had only fueled an anger that she used to burn down her old life and journey into the wild to start a new one.

Jo sold the house, cashed out all of her investments, and with Danny's life insurance policy, she purchased the fifty acres of untouched wilderness near the summit of Rebel Mountain.

It was here, nestled amongst the trees and dirt at the top of the world, where Jo saw beyond the pain of the moment and the possibilities of a future.

It had gotten easier to remember her husband after all of these years, and Jo saw Danny in their daughters every day. Her youngest, Amelia, carried her father's eternal optimism, while her oldest, Stacy, had his dark eyes and hair along with that inquisitive and reserved gaze that always made it difficult to tell what he was thinking.

A life off the grid had been an adjustment for everyone. None of them had the training for this type of life, and much of it was trial by fire. And while Jo was proud of the home that she had built, it had been a difficult journey.

All of them had left behind the leisure and comforts of the modern world, and the separation from society had raised more than a few eyebrows. The few days of the month that she traveled into town, she was forced to see the community she left behind and the pity she avoided in her retreat.

Most folks referred to her as the Widow in the Woods after she moved, and more than once, she overheard the rumors passed around that detailed the loss of her mind. A part of her thought that was true.

Jo didn't believe that a normal woman would choose to leave her job, her home, and pluck her daughters from their schools and away from their friends.

Looking back on it now, Jo realized how cruel it was for her to change their lives, but it was the only way she knew to survive. The old Joanna Mercer didn't know how to survive without Danny, and so she buried her past with him. And while the girls grieved for their father, Jo had also forced them to grieve for the life that she forced them to leave behind.

The sun had burned away the early morning grey skies by the time she returned, and she moved carefully through the wooded area around her cabin, avoiding the trip alarms that she had installed, which helped ensure that her private property stayed private.

Once past the trip wires, Jo emerged from the dense forest and into the small clearing where she had built her home.

Jo had made the decision to build the cabin on the mountain's south-facing side. It provided the opportunity to enjoy both the sunrise and sunset, and shielded her from the brunt of the winter storms that were blown down from the north.

In addition to the cabin, Jo also had a chicken coop, beehive, and garden that surrounded the cabin in a half circle on the western side.

Jo peered into the coops, finding the hens awake and fed, and the eggs already collected, which was one of Amelia's morning chores.

The garden yielded enough vegetables for year-round consumption, so long as the right seeds were traded out before the seasons changed. Strawberries and green beans in the spring, and melons and squash in the fall. Any excess that they harvested were canned and stored for the winter or hard times.

The bees hummed when she passed them, and Jo smiled. She had always loved bumblebees, ever since she was a little girl, and the bees had been one of the first purchases toward her sustainable, off-grid living to help provide a source of income. In addition to keeping her garden fertile, she also sold the honey at the General Store in the village.

Between the chicken, the garden, the game in the forest, and the shelter of the cabin, Jo had everything she needed right here.

The cabin itself was modest, built from the very trees that had been cleared on this patch of land. It held three bedrooms, a functioning kitchen, and a living room for leisure time.

The roof was lined with solar panels that provided the needed energy to power the few electronics they possessed. A radio antenna protruded from the back of the house, which provided a connection to the sheriff's station via CB radio. And she had been forced to install a satellite dish so the girls could log into their online coursework for school.

Jo curved around the front of the house, checking the rain barrels that collected the water from the top of the roof and funneled it down. The big forty-gallon drums were so full that they had overflowed onto the dirt, creating a muddy circle around them that splashed the muck onto Jo's shin when she planted her boot near the barrel.

There were four barrels total, which provided the needed water for their showering and gardening, and cooking and drinking after it had been purified. And during any dry spells, there were half a dozen rivers that cut through her property, and because she was alone at the top of the mountain, the water remained unpolluted. Jo had wanted to install a toilet in the cabin, but she didn't want to deal with septic issues, so she settled for an outhouse behind the cabin with lime and enzymes.

Jo understood that their way of life looked crude and strange to anyone from the outside. But those people didn't understand the truth of living out here, and that truth was as black and white as anything that Jo had ever known. Out here, on your own, you found out who you really were. And Jo had discovered that she was a survivor.

Walking up the porch steps to the front door, the wind-chimes rang a sweet and peaceful tune. Danny had made them for Amelia's fifth birthday, and she thought of him every time the wind glided through the trees.

Bird and bow still in hand, Jo entered the cabin. "Emmy, you finish the rest of your chores?" She shouted the question as she shut the door behind her, but then stopped when she saw the decorations strung up across the living room ceiling.

"Yup!" Amelia stood beneath her handiwork, smiling so bright that her cheeks had turned red as she rose on her tiptoes. "Do you think Stacy will like it?"

The happy birthday decorations were homemade, the letters crooked and not all the same shape or color, and the streamers and ribbons that curled at the ends swayed from the ceiling next to the banner.

Jo set the bird down on the kitchen counter, flattening the feathers as she walked to her daughter. "Em, you know that Stacy doesn't like to make a big deal about her birthday." In fact, Jo had been surprised when her eldest daughter had called her to tell her that she would be coming up to the cabin for her birthday. She hadn't visited since she left for college last fall, and the pair had barely spoken.

Disappointed, Amelia lowered herself from her tiptoes and slouched. "I know." She looked up at the streamers and the sign that she had made. "Do I really have to take them all down?"

It was clear that Amelia had spent a lot of time on it, and Jo knew that the girl's heart was in the right place. "Why don't we just take down the streamers and leave the sign."

Amelia lifted her chin, that bright smile making its triumphant return. "Really?"

Jo laughed. "Yes. Now get to work." She stood and slapped her daughter's bottom. "You still need to get your school work done before your sister gets here."

Amelia bounced around happily, leaping up and snatching the streamers from the ceiling, returning the paper to the crafts box in the living room.

Jo went to work plucking the bird and kept a close eye on Amelia once she started her schoolwork. The girl was smart, but she had a tendency to daydream, causing the day's assignments to stretch into the late afternoon.

Once Jo finished cleaning the bird, she disposed of the guts in the compost pile out back, then placed the plump turkey in the cooler where it would remain until dinner tonight and descended into the cellar through the kitchen floor.

It had been one of the more challenging projects of the house, carving deep into the earth and rock to remove enough space for the basement. But she was glad that she had taken the time to build it. The food that she had canned and set aside for those rainy days had come in handy more times than she could count.

A hand-powered kinetic flashlight rested on the first shelf, and Jo used it to guide her down the pantry. All four walls were covered with shelves lined with a variety of canned meats, fruits, and vegetables that she had packaged herself. She had enough food down here to keep three people alive for at least a year, longer if they needed to ration. This combined with the game and fish from the wild meant they truly could survive anything save for a direct hit from a nuclear bomb.

Jo plucked some green beans, yams, and stuffing, along with some flour and a jar of apples, cinnamon, and sugar to bake a pie. Stacy had always loved apple pie, and Jo's mother had passed down a recipe to her that would give even the best baker a run for their money. She hoped the gesture would make up for the decorations that Amelia had put up, though Stacy had always been more forgiving to her sister than her mother.

When Jo closed the pantry door in the floor of the kitchen, she set the supplies on the counter and then froze when she heard single gunshot to the south. Someone had set off a trip wire.

Jo hurried toward the door, picking up the crossbow

along the way. "Emmy! Get to the safe box, now!" She paused at the door, loading a bolt into the crossbow as she waited for her daughter to disappear into the safety hatch that she designed should they need a place to hide.

Once Amelia was safe below, Jo donned a small pack that she kept by the front door, which she always did before she left the cabin, and hurried into the woods, chasing the lingering echo of the gunshot that the intruder had triggered.

There was no reason for anyone to have made it this far unless they were looking for trouble. Jo had put up signs and a fence, warning intruders that this was private property and that anyone that decided to trespass would be met with deadly force.

Jo moved swiftly and quietly through the trees, her body trained to remain light and soundless even when she was moving quickly, side effects of hunting for the past three years. The long sleeves of her camouflage jacket and pants concealed the lean and sinewy muscles that were the product of life on the mountain.

Nearing the location of the tripped alarm, Jo slowed, her well-trained eyes scanning the woods, looking for movement between trees.

Heavy footfalls sounded to her left. Whoever was coming wasn't making any effort to hide it, and Jo circled around so she could sneak up on the trespasser from behind. The man never saw her approach, and he jumped when she spoke.

"Don't move," Jo said.

The man froze mid-step and gently placed his hands out on either side of him, and he started to turn. "I'm sorry, I didn't—"

"I said don't move!" Jo barked the order even louder, and the man froze. "Didn't you read the signs on your way in? I'm well within my rights to shoot."

"I'm sorry," he said.

Jo adjusted the crossbow in her hand. "Turn around. Slow."

The man did as he was told, and when the intruder faced her, the man looked more like a tourist than a thief. She got a better look at him, and judging from his attire, she didn't think he was carrying. "What do you want?"

"My car broke down," he answered, babbling and stumbling over his own words. "We're on vacation and— I'm lost, and I can't get any reception on my phone. If you could just let me use your phone or—"

"There's a town a few miles down the road. Talk to Sheriff Turner. He'll help you."

The man smiled and waved a hand. "Thank you. Thank you so much. But um… do you have any water?" He pointed to where he thought the road was. "My family is back at the car, and we had planned on stopping for breakfast, but…"

Jo lowered the crossbow. "I'll follow you."

On the walk back to the road, Jo maintained a safe distance between herself and the man. While he wasn't a threat now, it didn't mean that he couldn't turn into one. But when they reached the road, the car stuck on the street confirmed his troubles. Jo saw the two kids in the backseat and the worried look on the mother's face. They were all nervous, and Jo knew that it had been desperation that had pushed the father onto her land.

Jo offered the water from her pack to the father, and the gesture brought a smile from both parents.

"Thank you." He handed the water to his boys in the backseat, but Jo noticed that the woman remained guarded.

"You live out here by yourself?" she asked.

"No," Jo answered, choosing not to expound on any further information, then gestured to the vehicle. "Did you run out of gas?" She knew that there weren't many stations between the towns that were strung across the mountain, and it was easy for non-locals to find themselves stranded.

"No," the man said, crossing his arms and leaning back up against the car. "The engine just shut off out of nowhere."

"Our phones too," the woman said, then reached inside the car and removed one of the mobile devices which were nothing but a blank screen no matter how many times she pressed the power button. "Even the boys' tablets shut off."

Jo frowned, then looked up and down the road, but she didn't find anyone, which wasn't surprising. The old road was so broken and worn down most folks used the new bypass that went around the mountain instead of over it. But Jo knew that some of the GPS applications would still take motorists down their old country road to save time if the highway was busy.

But the fact that all of their electronic devices had shut off...

Jo retreated toward the woods. "I need to check on something."

The mother frowned. "Do you know what's going on?"

Jo hesitated because she had an inkling of what might be happening, but she couldn't be sure. She needed to check her more sophisticated devices. "I'll be back." She disappeared into the woods before they could ask her any more questions and then sprinted to the cabin.

Dozens of thoughts raced through Jo's mind, most of them circling the possibility of what she thought had happened. And if it did, that meant Stacy would be in danger.

Jo returned to the cabin, quickly retrieving Amelia from the safe room.

"What happened?" Amelia asked.

"I'm not sure yet." Jo kissed the top of her head and then moved into her bedroom, passing by the twin bed and to the pine dresser that she had forged last spring. She opened the top drawer and reached for the mobile device that she kept hidden and charged beneath her underwear drawer. It was an old flip phone, but it still worked. She opened the top and then pressed the on button, waiting for the screen to light up. Nothing.

Keeping the phone in her hand, Jo moved to the living room, where Amelia still stood with a worried look on her face.

"Mom, what's happening?" Amelia asked.

Jo moved toward the CB radio by the back wall living room where the old computer that Amelia and Stacy had done their homeschooling work on rested. A binder sat on top of the radio. It held the step by step instructions of how to use the radio along with the emergency frequencies should she need to contact help. But when she flicked the dial to turn on the radio, there was nothing. Same with the computer.

The dead click of the devices sat heavy in Jo's mind as she gathered her thoughts. Stacy wasn't scheduled to leave the city until mid-morning. She knew that her eldest daughter would recognize what happened, but she didn't know if she would be able to get out of the city before society broke down.

"Mom?" Amelia asked.

Jo looked behind her over her left shoulder. "Grab your go-bag."

Amelia hesitated for a moment, but finally went to her room. Jo went and collected her own bag, knowing that she would have to go into the city to retrieve her eldest daughter, because she knew that if the effects had reached all the way out here, then it had most certainly affected the city. And while Jo wasn't sure how it happened, she was confident that whoever had detonated the EMP would capitalize on their attack.

---

2

*T*he carpet was old, years of prayer wearing the fabric thin. But it was the only item that Muhammed Pathan had kept when he fled his home. When he knelt on his mat, bowing in prayer to the east, he was connected to the very homeland that he swore to avenge.

Once finished with his prayers, Muhammed lingered with his face buried in the carpet. It still smelled of his homeland, and with the familiar scent came a rush of memories. He remembered how Nadia grew red in the face when she had accidently crushed the fresh dates that she'd brought home from the market, and how she started to cry when their father saw. She had expected him to scold her, but instead he brought her onto his lap and wiped the tears from her eyes, reassuring her that everything was all right.

Uzi Pathan had always been a kind man. Muhammed's father never raised a hand to any of his children, choosing instead to use every moment as a teaching tool, to help his children learn from their mistakes and grow into a better person.

"Every day is a chance to become a better person than the

day before. A holier person, a wiser person, someone who inspires others to grow as well."

Muhammed opened his eyes and rose from his bowed position on the carpet, giving him a view of the concrete wall that comprised his tiny bedroom. Cracks crawled over the wall like spiderwebs, and a bucket collected water from a leak in the roof.

The crumbling building where Muhammed and his brothers had taken refuge was no home. No one sang in the evening before supper like his mother had, her sweet voice mixing with the delicious smells of her cooking that warmed their house. There was no laughter here, no joy.

And while Muhammed remembered the teachings of his father, every day it became harder to remember what Uzi Pathan's voice sounded like. It had faded from him like the fibers of the carpet, worn down by time.

Time had stolen much from Muhammed Pathan and, while he had tried denying the truth, he knew that deep down Uzi Pathan would be ashamed of the man that his oldest son had grown to become.

"Forgive me, Father." Muhammed whispered.

Revenge had soaked Muhammed's soul and mind in blood and darkness. It had made him strong, but bitter and resentful. It had sharpened his focus until it could pierce the armor that shielded his enemy. It had taken so long to plot his revenge, to gather the resources, the men, to lay out a plan that would bring the mighty Americans to their knees. But the enemy had not been what he had expected.

The people that Muhammed saw were not fighters, or warriors, or demons. They were weak and small and ripe to be killed. They cared nothing of what happened beyond their small bubble. They only cared about themselves and the preservation of their lavish and obscene livelihood. And for

Muhammed, he believed that to be an even greater sin than any other. The sin of indifference.

Muhammed stood, his knees popping, stiff from the sleepless nights that had plagued him since they arrived in this foreign land. He rolled up his mat, and then propped it into the corner of the room. His hand lingered on top of the fabric. It would be the last time he saw it, the last time that he prayed, the last time that he held onto any semblance of the life that he had known before today.

Because like the day that destroyed his family all those years ago created a perfect and seamless division of what his life was like before that event, and what life was like after that event, today would provide another division from the man he was before he entered this room and the man he would become after he left.

Muhammed had no delusions of making it out of this alive. All he wanted was to kill as many of the infidels as he could before he died.

A knock at the door turned Muhammed's attention to his brother. Zahid was the only surviving member of Muhammed's family, and was only a boy when their family was murdered. And while Zahid was now a man, Muhammed still saw the scared little boy that clung to his leg after they were all alone. It had been the two of them, fighting for each other, protecting one another, doing whatever was necessary to survive.

"The men are ready," Zahid said. "They wait for your command."

Muhammed placed his hands on Zahid's broad shoulders. "Today we will strike back into the heart of those that wronged us. Today we will reap the harvest of the seeds that we have dutifully tended to for so long."

Zahid's eyes watered. "Today, we shall have our vengeance."

"Yes." Muhammed reached for the gold medallion that hung from Zahid's neck. It had been given to Muhammed by their father, but Muhammed gave it to Zahid after the bombing. It had belonged to their family for generations, passed down from father to son. He touched his forehead against his brother's, and the pair closed their eyes. "Today we will strike fear into those that would try and destroy us. Today we will spill their blood into the streets, just as they did in our home."

The pair lingered in silence, understanding the consequences of what came next. It was the end of their journey of this life and the beginning of a new one beyond this mortal world.

"From flesh to the dust that drifts to the heavens," Muhammed said.

Zahid inhaled sharply. "To the heavens."

Muhammad pulled back and then led his brother to the front of the small two-bedroom apartment where they joined ten other men. Hands worked deftly over rifles, cleaning the weapons in preparation for their mission.

There were dozens of cells just like Muhammed's placed all over the country, both in cities and along the countryside. Most of the fighters had snuck through the Canadian border to the north with falsified documents, like Muhammed and his men.

Every cell had their own mission, and while most of their organizations were focused on the denser metropolitan areas, Muhammed would lead his men through the mountains, cleansing the rural areas of their enemy.

Muhammed checked the time and then stared at the television, eagerly waiting for the signal. The room was barely furnished save for an old couch and a few chairs that were used at the square, collapsible table where they took their meals. They had no working air conditioning, and the water that spit from the tap had a metallic taste to it. The television was their only luxury.

As the rest of the men finished assembling their weapons, one by one they turned their own eyes to the TV that played a local news station.

None of them cared what the news said, or the fact that a woman sat behind the news desk where a man should be, but they all watched her with bated breath for the beginning of the end. And when the television screen went blank, silencing the room, Muhammed led his men out of the door. Now, after all these years, he would have his revenge.

3

The pounding in Stacy Mercer's head was followed by the sudden urge to vomit. She rolled from her side and onto her back, her arm bumping into something fleshy that made her recoil. She sat up in the bed and stared at the sleeping boy next to her.

The headache intensified, and Stacy glanced down at her own nakedness, her memory shaky from the night before. She had come to a party off campus last night, invited by the boy who lay next to her. She had thought that he had liked her, and last night those suspicions were confirmed.

Not wanting to wake him, Stacy quietly slipped out of the bed, dressed, and just before she was about to leave, the sudden impulse to vomit flooded through her and she rushed toward the bathroom.

Stacy shut and locked the bathroom door, then dropped to her knees just in time to puke into the toilet.

The vomit burned her esophagus, and the mixture of all the alcohol she consumed the night before was emptied in three gut-wrenching heaves. Her stomach cramped when she

THE LAST CABIN: EMP SURVIVAL

was finished, and she leaned against the bathtub and shut her eyes.

Last night had been an attempt to celebrate her nine-teenth birthday and forget the fourth anniversary of her father's death. She hadn't celebrated since before her father's passing, but for the first time since his death, she could drown her pain until the memories were blurred and she was numb.

Now, she was paying the price for her debauchery, and she lingered on the cold bathroom tile until she was sure the lurching in her stomach had passed.

Stacy didn't dare look at the contents of the toilet before she flushed, already turned off by the sour stench that filled the bowl. She closed the toilet, flushed, and hovered over the sink, which she gripped on both sides, head hung low, eyes shut as she tried to get her bearings.

"Tequila. Bad." Stacy spat into the sink and then turned on the faucet, cupping her palm beneath the spigot, but instead of water, there was nothing but a groan from the pipes. She frowned and then tried the hot water nozzle. Still nothing.

Stacy grimaced and smacked her lips, the sour taste of vomit still on her tongue.

"Stacy?" The voice was soft like the knock that followed. "Are you all right?"

"I'm fine. I'll be out in a minute." Stacy turned back to the mirror, almost not recognizing the haggard, tired face staring back at her. She took a few breaths and then stepped out of the bathroom, finding the boy sitting on the edge of his bed in his boxers. "Hey."

"Hey." The smile he wore was genuine, and he extended a bottle of water to her. "I keep all my water at room temperature for hangovers. I learned last semester that cold water doesn't sit well with an already uneasy stomach."

Stacy took the water, but didn't reciprocate the smile. "Thanks." She drank half the bottle, feeling a little better after she did.

"So," the boy said, rubbing the back of his head awkwardly. "Would you want to go and grab some breakfast or something—"

"I actually have to go," Stacy said. "I'm meeting my family."

"Oh." The boy shrugged it off, pretending that it didn't hurt. "Of course."

Stacy kept the water and left the room. Once she was out of the apartment, guilt flooded her veins from her hasty retreat, but sleeping with him last night was only to provide a distraction.

Outside, Stacy squinted from the harsh brightness of the sun. And even though it was still morning, the heat was already sweltering. The concrete would bake them all by mid-afternoon.

With her head still pounding, Stacy regretted promising Amelia that she would come up to the cabin for her birthday. She hadn't spoken to her mother since the beginning of the year, and the thought of seeing her again only made her anxious. Her birthday had always been bad luck.

It felt wrong to be mad at her father for dying on her birthday, after all, it wasn't his fault. It was a freak accident. Some guy got drunk behind the wheel and then decided that he could make it home without any trouble. But he was wrong. A few miles down the road and one red light later and he t-boned the driver's side of her dad's truck. Her father was killed on impact.

Stacy remembered how her mother looked when she got

home. She had expected to find her father at the door, so many balloons in his hand that she couldn't even see his face. It was one of her father's birthday traditions for the girls in his life. But there were no balloons that day.

Joanna Mercer walked through the door alone that evening. The color had drained from her cheeks, her hair frizzy and greasy and raked back from all the times she had run her hands through it the way she did whenever she was overwhelmed.

Jo moved through the doorway like a ghost, leaving it open behind her. She walked toward Stacy in a trance, mumbling nonsense over and over to herself.

Stacy had to stop her mom from walking right into her. She remembered how light she felt in her hands, as if her mother would dissolve right between her fingers. Finally, Jo looked Stacy in the eye, and a cold chill caused her heart to thump three heavy beats, and she thought it stopped for a second when she said: "he's dead."

And with those words, Stacy would never again think of happiness and balloons on her birthday. Instead she would only remember the trip to the hospital with her mother because Joanna Mercer couldn't bear to identify the body by herself. She remembered looking at the mangled corpse on the steel table and thinking to herself, that's not my father. That can't be. My father doesn't look like that.

But it was her father.

Stacy nodded to the officers, and Joanna Mercer only shivered, unaware of anything that was happening around her. For the first time in her life, Stacy got a taste of what it was like to be a parent, having to take care of both her mother and her sister until her aunt arrived the next day to help.

Stacy spun around and glanced past the downtown

skyline and toward the mountain ridge that had once been a prison for her. Even now, staring at the earthy greens and browns of the mountains rolling toward the horizon, a sense of dread gripped her.

Dread from seeing her mother, and returning to the cabin.

Stacy kept her head down on the walk back to campus, staring at the pavement to shield herself from the harsh reflections of sunlight in the storefront windows that she passed. She searched for any restaurant that was open, but most stores were still closed. Her hangover demanded food, but she would have to wait until she returned to her dorm and hoped that Melissa hadn't eaten all of the snacks.

When Stacy reached a crosswalk, she found the button on the light pole and pressed it, but when she glanced across the street, she saw that the walking sign was blank. She frowned, then pressed the button again. Still nothing.

Stacy checked both sides of the street, looking for any cars, and found two. Both of them were stopped in the middle of the road, hoods up, the drivers staring down into the engines and scratching their heads.

Stacy glanced up at the streetlights and saw that they were blank just like the crosswalk sign. "What the hell?" Staring at the stranded motorists, she crossed the street and removed her phone. It was dead.

A thought pricked in the back of her mind. Something that her mother had told her long ago, something that had sounded crazy at the time.

"No." Stacy shook her head defiantly. "No, that can't be it." But despite the denial, she hastened her pace back to campus. She needed to be sure before she let her imagination run wild.

But along the way, Stacy noticed other things, little

things. There was no buzz of electricity coming from the power lines along the roadside. She heard no hum of A/C units from between the buildings of the businesses that she passed.

Twenty minutes after Stacy left the apartment building downtown, she stepped beneath the brick arch of the university, but not before quickly glancing back to the city behind her, a town that had grown eerily calm and still, even for a Sunday morning.

The campus was barren and empty, most students gone home for the summer after the spring semester ended last month. With the students gone, the old brick buildings looked more like ruins of some abandoned civilization than a school.

For those that stayed, it was still early enough on campus for most folks to still be asleep, nursing their hangovers, or still drunk from a night out. Sundays were always sleepy days on the campus, even during the spring and fall semesters. It was her favorite time of the day.

Because as much as she loved being around people, having friends again, and being able to use the internet whenever she wanted on her phone, the past three years on the mountain had shifted Stacy's heart just a little bit toward isolation.

The residual effects of that off-grid lifestyle didn't completely wash away. Because on those lazy Sunday mornings, when most of the campus was still sleeping, she would walk out to the courtyard at dawn with a book or some assignment that she was working on and just enjoy the silence and the architecture of the campus.

It was a beautiful place, and sometimes that was lost amongst the vapid conversations between students about parties, boys, girls, sports, and the latest social media craze.

All these people sticking their arms out into the air to snap a selfie or send a snapshot or do whatever the hell all of those apps were capable of.

Stacy had tried to get back into all of that when she returned to college, but so much of it felt empty. What was the point? Why did she need to take so many pictures of herself? Who cared what she was eating for lunch?

But when the campus was quiet on those Sunday mornings, Stacy would bask in the glow of what she thought college would really be like; learning, growing, surrounded by people who wanted something more with their lives, providing a better future for them that they couldn't have accomplished had they not come to this institution.

However, the image of college life that Stacy had constructed in her mind didn't exactly match up with her first-year experiences.

The teachers weren't as inspiring as she hoped. Her peers weren't as cultured as she expected. And the boys weren't as experienced as she thought they'd be.

It was the second month into fall semester when she had lost her virginity. She had been drunk. So had the boy. She had been so nervous, but when she touched him, she felt him tremble just as much as she did.

It was a fumbling, awkward slapping of body parts that started quickly and ended even quicker. After he had finished, he flipped onto his side and fell asleep, but Stacy was wide awake, contemplating what she had done.

She had never been one of those girls that fantasized about what her first time would be like, about finding the "one" to sleep with. That had probably been the most important lesson her mother had taught her, explaining the reality of sex and love and relationships.

Still, it didn't calm the nerves from that first time, and

that's why she had insisted on those three drinks before she worked up the courage to follow him into the bedroom. She remembered the door shutting with a distinctive thud that muted the sounds of the party still going on outside.

Since then Stacy had dated two other boys casually, but there was no real connection between them. It was nothing more than a sexual attraction that dulled after a few months when the excitement ran out. Like the boy from last night.

Stacy reached the three-story dorm building and took the stairs to the top floor. She removed her keys and fumbled them into the lock, swinging the door open so fast that it cracked against the wall and caused Mellissa to wake from her slumber.

"Ugh." Melissa groaned and then buried her face deeper into her pillow. "Don't be so loud."

Stacy flicked on the light switch. Nothing. She saw the digital clock by her nightstand blank. She listened for the air conditioning unit, but heard nothing. Panic was slowly replacing her hangover.

"Melissa." Stacy walked to her friend's bed. She rattled her shoulder. "Melissa, wake up."

Melissa groaned again but finally rolled over, eyes squinted. "Why won't you let me die in peace?"

"I need you to check your phone." Stacy hurried to her computer desk and pressed the power button on her laptop. She prayed that she was wrong and hoped that this was all just a coincidence. After all, her phone could have died, they could have had a power outage, something wrong with the campus utilities, but as her computer screen remained black, that hope vanished.

"My phone's dead," Melissa said.

"Oh God." Stacy pressed the heels of her palms against

her temples, pushing harder and harder against her skull. She shook her head. "This can't be happening."

"Are you going to throw up?" Melissa asked. "Do it in the trash can if you are."

"No." Stacy lowered her hands and took a deep breath. "But we need to go."

Melissa tittered. "You can go wherever you want, but I'm going back to sleep."

Stacy moved to her closet and then opened the door, which acted as a full-length mirror. "You need to pack some clothes and grab any food, water, and medicine that you have." She pushed aside her clothes and junk and reached into the back of the closet, stretching her arm into the abyss of the darkness, and felt around for the strap of her backpack. She hadn't touched it since she arrived at school, but she knew everything inside would still be useful, maybe save for the food rations.

Melissa was sitting up now, shaking her head in confusion. "What are you doing?"

"It was a care package from my mom." Stacy dusted off the top and then opened the main compartment, then lowered her voice. "At least as much of a care package as someone like her could give." She reached inside and removed the small camping pack that would provide shelter and a means for her to create a fire. But the only thing that she wanted to find was nestled at the bottom, encased in a leather sheath.

"Oh my God." Melissa stepped closer to get a better look. "You've had that in your closet this whole time? What the hell do you use it for?"

Stacy rotated the five-inch survival blade in her hand. It had a nice weight to it and was a full tang blade, so there was never a fear that the knife would fall apart. The grip was a heavy-duty composite with ridges along the finger holds, so there was less chance that the blade would slip. And Stacy didn't have to touch the edge to know that it was sharp.

"Can I touch it?" Wide-eyed and curious, Melissa stretched out her hand, but Stacy sheathed the blade before she got close.

"No." Stacy returned the contents of the pack to the main compartment and zipped it up, but clipped the blade to the belt loop of her jeans. "Do you have any cash on you?" Stacy knew that there were five twenty-dollar bills hidden in a secret compartment in the bag.

"Um, I think so." Melissa grabbed her purse off her desk and counted the bills in her wallet. "I've got like thirty bucks and some change." She shook her head, tossing the purse on the bed. "So, are we not going to talk about why you have a serial killer blade in some secret Army backpack hidden in your closet?" Her eyes widened with fright. "Are you going to kill me? Is this some kind of long con, some secret under-cover mission? Do you work for the government?"

Stacy grabbed Melissa's shoulders, and the girl stiffened beneath her grip. "Melissa, something has happened. Something awful. Now, I know that your parents are in Connecticut, so there is no way that you're going to make it that far, but you can come with me to my mother's cabin."

Melissa shrugged Stacy's hands off of her. "Your crazy survivalist mom? Are you nuts? I thought you said you hate her?"

Stacy hadn't realized how much she'd told her roommate over the past year, but she realized that it might have been too much. When she first came up here, she was still bitter, and the freedom and booze had given her loose lips.

"The power is out." Stacy pointed to the phones and her computer. "We don't have any more communication, and pretty soon people are going to start freaking out once they realize the power isn't coming back on."

Melissa frowned. "What do you mean the power isn't coming back on? It's probably just—"

"Melissa." Stacy stepped closer, her voice dropping an octave. "The world is going to start collapsing soon. And if we don't leave the city now, we'll be buried under the rubble."

Melissa swallowed. "What do I need to bring?"

Stacy helped Melissa pack, keeping the girl to the essentials and what she could only store in her backpack.

"Why can't I take my duffel bag, or my suitcase, or—"

"We're going to have to hike all the way to the cabin. It's at least half a day, and you won't want something in your hands to slow you down." Stacy had gone on enough hikes with her mother to know that was true. "A few pairs of clean clothes, hiking shoes if you have them."

Stacy walked to the window of their dorm room and peered out into the early morning dawn of the campus. Hardly anyone was awake. And if she were lucky, it would stay that way. Because once the bulk of the city realized that their phones and cars didn't work and that the food in the fridges would spoil within a few days, and when their toilets wouldn't flush anymore, the shit and anger building up in their homes would spill into the streets. And then the real chaos would start.

And for the first time since her father died, Stacy was gripped with fear. Not the childhood fears that most people outgrew. Real fear. The kind that hollowed you out, the type that ate away at your consciousness, leaving you susceptible to attack. It was paralyzing.

"She was right," Stacy said, still looking out the window.

Melissa continued to pack, only half-listening as she

fought between which blouse to bring with her. "Who was right?"

"My mother." Stacy's own words were flung back at her by the window. She turned back to Melissa. "We need to go."

"Okay, just hold your horses." Melissa finished packing her clothes, and Stacy had her bring all of the water and snacks that she had stored in the room.

"Do you have tampons?" Stacy asked.

Melissa blushed. "I'm not on my period—"

"If you have them, bring them." Stacy lifted her pack from the ground and slipped her arms through the straps. "You might not be able to find any more where we're going." And following her own advice, she plucked a packet of tampons from her drawer and then headed into the hallway.

"Will you slow down?" Melissa asked, jogging to catch up with Stacy as she reached the stairwell at the end of the hall. "Stairs? Really?"

"Power is out," Stacy answered. "Elevators won't work."

The stairwell echoed from Stacy's footsteps on her descent, and again she waited at the bottom of the stairs for Melissa, who was already out of breath. Stacy opened the door, but then Melissa groaned from the sunlight spilling inside.

"Oh, I left my sunglasses upstairs," Melissa said.

Stacy kept the door propped open. "We don't have time for you to run back up and get them."

Melissa flapped her arms at her sides, exasperated. "So what do you want me to do, just walk all the way to your cabin with my eyes closed?"

"Melissa, enough!" Stacy spun around, the door closing behind her and stomped her foot on the ground. "We have a long way to go, and I'm not going to be able to stand you complaining the entire way."

Melissa glanced down at her toes, twisting at the waist. She looked like Amelia whenever she was upset about something. "I'm just not used to all of this."

Stacy exhaled, realizing that she was letting the nerves and the sledgehammer-like pounding of her head shorten her patience. "I'm sorry. I didn't mean to be so—"

"Bitchy?" Melissa asked, her words poignant, but the grin that followed softened the blow.

Stacy reciprocated the smirk. "I was going to say irritable, but fine. Yes, bitchy." She slackened her smile. "I know it's hard to understand what's going on, but my mother always told me that if an EMP were detonated that people would lose their minds. I'm beginning to think that she might be right."

"What's an EMP?" Melissa frowned.

"Electro-magnetic pulse," Stacy answered. "It's an invisible blast that fries electronics within its blast radius. You can't see it, or hear it, or feel it, but you're able to see everything that it does to the world once it's finished. Like now." She opened the stairwell door. "Listen."

After half a minute, Melissa shook her head. "I don't hear anything."

"Exactly," Stacy said. "No cars. No planes. No hum of power lines. It's all gone."

Melissa's complexion lightened. "Jesus."

Stacy glanced out the cloudless sky and then gestured up the stairs. "Get your sunglasses. I'll wait for you down here."

Melissa didn't smile like Stacy thought she would, and instead turned around with that stoic stare and hurried up the steps.

Stacy lingered at the stairwell, still in awe of the deafening silence. It reminded her of her time on the mountain, though at least there she could hear the wind through the trees, birds chirping, and the wind chimes on the front porch. As much as she begrudged her mother about leaving her friends and their entire way of life in the rearview mirror, she never told her mother that she had grown to enjoy the nature and solitude of the mountain.

But she let her pettiness get in the way of reconciliation, and even now she was still too bitter to admit to herself that she had treated her mother too harshly. But she made excuses for herself. Her dad dying on her birthday went a long way.

Melissa returned, wearing her shades, the sun reflecting in the black mirrored lenses. "Okay. Now I'm ready."

Stacy smiled at Melissa. It had been a long time since she had been able to have friends. Surprisingly, not many teenagers wanted to come up to the forest and visit a cabin that had no power, no television, and no real forms of modern conveniences. Compared to a sixteen-year-old girl who owned two phones, a car, and had access to daddy's credit card, the cabin might as well have been on the moon.

"Let's go." Stacy opened the door, but only made it one step out of the stairwell when three quick pops echoed in the air, freezing both girls in their tracks.

The sound was distant, ricocheting between the buildings of downtown and onto the open air of the campus.

Melissa stepped forward, frowning. "What is that?"

The noise hollowed Stacy's gut. She had spent enough time hunting with her mother to recognize those sounds.

When the gunfire popped again it was closer, and Melissa stepped backward, reaching for Stacy's hands as her breathing accelerated from fear.

"Stacy?" Melissa asked.

"We need to move," Stacy answered. "Now."

Both girls broke out into a jog, the gunfire growing more

frequent, and it didn't take long before screams pierced the silence between gunshots. The cries were distant like the gunfire, but their anonymity provided an added element of horror. Like being locked in a room and hearing someone tortured through the walls. She wanted to get out of this place. She wanted to leave.

But when the first explosion echoed from downtown, Stacy was afraid that it was already too late to escape.

4

---

*J*o adjusted the rifle on her shoulder. She had
chosen the gun over the crossbow for the trip. It
was more practical to defend herself with than
the bow. In addition to the weapon, Jo had her day pack on
her back, filled with rations, a first aid kit, and other necessi-
ties should her trip take longer than she expected.

The walk to the village was slower than Jo wanted. The
family of four that had hitched their wagon to her caravan
wasn't used to traveling so far on foot. Especially the boys,
both of whom looked barely out of kindergarten.

But Jo swelled with pride as Amelia was able to keep pace,
and she did an excellent job helping keep the boys distracted
on their walk.

Hearing the way that Amelia was interacting with the
other kids, Jo couldn't help but feel that she robbed her
daughter of a real childhood. Instead of playing with dolls
and having sleepovers, Amelia was learning about gun safety
and how to reach the proper acidic levels to preserve meat in
jars.

"Hey." Tim appeared alongside Jo, snapping her out of her

regrets. "How much farther?" Sweat filled the creases of his furrowed brow as he squinted from the sun. His attire wasn't designed for hiking. None of his family were prepared for the long walk.

"Not far," Jo answered, keeping her eyes forward and her rifle at the ready.

"Okay." Tim faced forward again and plucked the sweaty collar that was glued to his skin. "I can't believe how hot it is already."

"It's summertime," Jo said.

"I know it's just…" Tim laughed. "I thought I'd be at the river by now. Tubing or something." He smiled at Jo, but she didn't return one to him, and he cleared his throat. "So, do you know what's going on? Why phones won't work? Why the car wouldn't start?"

"I'll know more when we reach The Village," Jo answered, ending the conversation.

It was another thirty minutes before Jo saw the rooftops of the small cluster of buildings that comprised The Village. It was one of three communities along the mountainside, and it had been where Jo had raised her family until her husband's death.

The Village was of three tows that had survived the collapse of coal mines in the nineties. It wasn't until ten years ago that the tourism trade boomed, bringing people from all around the country to their sleepy mountain. It had sparked a renaissance of sorts, breathing life back into the struggling townships.

But it also brought people. More people than Jo had wanted to deal with, and there were more showing up every season.

And while Jo wished that the tourism trade would slow down, she hoped that when she turned the final curve of the mountain road that gave her a clear shot into town that she would find everything still in its proper place. Because while the tourists were inconvenient, an EMP was deadly. When the rocky side of the mountain finally cleared, Jo slowed to a stop at the sight ahead.

Cars were stopped along the small two-lane road that ran through the heart of town, everyone out of their cars and checking their engines. Some of the vehicles had knocked into one another, but the damage was minimal.

From the crowded street, it looked like every resident of The Village had come outside, everyone asking the same question that Tim had asked her on the way down. What happened?

Jo stopped the group, instructing Tim and his family to rest under the shade. "I'm going to speak with the sheriff." She then turned to Amelia. "C' mon, Em, let's go."

"Can't I stay with them?" Amelia asked, a slight whine in her voice.

"We really don't mind." Nicole, Tim's wife, stepped forward. "Honestly, she's been a lifesaver with the boys."

Amelia smiled hopefully at her mother, but Jo shook her head. She wasn't comfortable leaving her daughter with strangers, no matter how friendly they seemed. "No. C'mon Amelia."

"Okay." Amelia hung her head low, waving goodbye to the boys on her way past. "Bye, Colin. Bye, Freddy."

Both boys waved in unison, speaking at the same time. "Bye, Amelia."

In town, Jo kept away from the crowds, not wanting to draw attention to herself, but a few of her old neighbors had spotted her, whispering to one another about the famous Widow of the Woods.

After isolating herself from the communities, she had

developed a reputation on the mountain as a bit of a snob. Because she left, people assumed that she thought she was better than everyone else. But that wasn't true. Jo had only wanted to be alone with the family that she had left.

The Village was highest community on the mountain, and the most populated due to the beautiful scenery that the elevation provided. And despite the tragedy that forced Jo to move from the area, there were times, though few and far between, where she missed the life that community offered.

It was a quaint town, the picture-perfect image of what small-town America looked like on a postcard. And despite the steady influx of visitors that Rebel Mountain received each year, those charged with the preservation of the mountain had done a fine job.

The core of the original town structures remained in place, and all of the shops, businesses, and bed and breakfasts that had sprouted from the economic boom stretched the length of the mountain road. And while it now had all of the modern businesses of a much-larger town, it had maintained that quaint, small-town look.

All of the new construction that happened had to meet a certain style requirement, and the board that oversaw the efforts had chosen The Village to resemble that of a village in the Alps, with the cottage-esque style pitched roofs and windows.

Boardwalks lined either side of the road and the storefronts as people passed shops, businesses, and small bed and breakfasts.

The crown jewel was the picturesque church at the town's center, complete with large bell tower that protruded high above. It was one of the first structures built when the town was founded.

The church had been restored and had become a popular

location for destination weddings. It was where Jo and Danny had gotten married. Just one more reminder that Jo couldn't take any longer after her husband passed.

"They're not dangerous," Amelia said as they neared Mags' store.

"What?" Jo asked, eyeing three people she didn't recognize across the street. They'd been following her since they entered the town.

"Colin and Freddy," Amelia said. "They're just scared is all."

Jo glanced at her daughter, who stared up at her with those big, beautiful brown eyes, long eyelashes that could flick away worry with a single blink.

"I know they're scared." Jo knelt and brushed Amelia's thick bangs off her forehead. "And that's sweet of you to try and help them. But remember what I always tell you?"

"We have to take care of ourselves before we can take care of someone else," Amelia said, repeating the mantra that had been drilled into her head.

"That's right," Jo said. "We do, and that means making sure that Stacy is all right."

"Okay."

Jo entered Mags' store, finding the friendly woman in the same place where she would always be at the start of her business day, sitting behind the counter with her old, manual cash register, the kind that still had the lever and forced you to add things manually, unwrapping her bills and getting ready for her customers.

Life after Danny's death had been difficult, even after Jo had moved her family off grid. And while most of the town had forgotten her, Maggie Johnson had remained a close and loyal friend. During her early days at the cabin, it had been through Mag's store that she was able to have supplies delivered, and it was also where she was able to sell her honey.

"Jo!" Mags grinned from ear to ear, creasing dozens of smile lines along her face, the kind that so many women her age tried to hide. But at fifty-eight, Maggie Johnson had no issues with her aging body. She'd always said that it was a privilege to grow old, and the scars and wrinkles received along the journey provided stories to tell. "What brings you down the mountain?"

"I wanted to ask if Em could hang out with you for the day," Jo said. "I need to head into the city and check on Stacy."

Mag stopped counting the money and looked up at Jo, those smile lines transformed into a frown. "Everything all right?"

"Is your power out?" Jo asked.

Mag nodded. "Here and the house. Figured something happened to the station in the valley. I keep telling Mike that he needs to talk to the utility company about getting some of our lines replaced."

Mike was their county's sheriff, whose station happened to be headquartered in The Village.

"Is your car still parked around back?" Jo asked.

"Same spot as yesterday." Mags stuffed the rest of the bills in the register, finished with her counting. "You need a ride?"

"No, but I want to check something."

"C'mon." Mags slid off her stool and walked toward the back of the store. "I'll keep the closed sign flipped for a little while longer. Won't hurt anything."

Mag had an old Thunderbird that had belonged to her father. After he passed five years back, Mags inherited the vehicle. She had restored the car from top to bottom but stayed true to the original components. Components that Jo didn't think would be affected by the EMP.

"Here she is." Mag flipped the blue tarp off the vehicle, exposing the red and white Thunderbird, the large tail fins sprouted up in the back tipped with red lights. Compared to some of the other sedans on the road, the old Ford was more of a tank.

Jo grabbed the keys and opened the heavy metal door. She sat down on the red leather seat and placed the key in the ignition. The engine cranked, and after kicking a half dozen times it finally caught, the big V8 rumbling and sputtering smoke from its dual exhaust.

Satisfied, Jo turned the car off before it drew too much attention. She knew that working vehicles were going to be valuable in the coming months, and people would kill for it. She climbed out, shutting the door, and then helped Mags cover it back up with the tarp.

When they were finished, Mags met Jo at the hood, her left eyebrow raised in question. "So are you going to tell me what's going on? Or are you going to make me guess?"

"The power's not coming back on, Mags," Jo answered.

Mags waited for more, but when Jo said nothing, her face slackened from shock. "Well, that's going to cause some problems."

"I need to talk to the sheriff before I leave, tell him what I know."

"And what do you know?" Mag leaned in, more curious than ever.

"I think we were hit by an EMP. It's a blast that usually follows a nuclear detonation, but some have theorized that you could isolate the EMP component and set one off, rendering all electronics useless. And no electronic microchips means no basic utilities like water and power, sewage. No refrigeration to keep your food cold. No transportation, no communication, nothing. It's like living in the Stone Age."

Mag studied Jo for a moment, the old timer waiting to see if Jo was pulling her leg. But when there was no punchline, she only nodded.

"When I come back from the city, I'll make sure you're taken care of for looking after Amelia." Jo reached for Mags' hand. "You have my word."

Mag regained some of her optimism and gave a firm squeeze back to Jo. "Don't you worry about me. I've survived on this mountain for longer than you have. Granted, I don't live all the way out in the bush like you, but I've gotten through hard times before."

Jo had no doubt that the woman was a fighter. But even Jo was worried about what came next, and this was something she had prepared herself for a very long time.

"I should be back by nightfall," Jo said, and then turned to Amelia, giving her daughter a hug. "You behave yourself for Mags, okay?"

"I will," Amelia said, squeezing her mother tightly. "Be safe."

Jo planted a big wet kiss on her daughter's cheek. "I love you."

"Love you too, Mom."

Jo returned to the street, knowing that Amelia was in good hands. She trusted Mags, and that wasn't something many people had earned.

On the way to the sheriff's station, Jo passed Rusty's auto shop, and she saw the big wrecker sitting on the side of the sagging garage.

Jo turned back and knew that Tim and his family were still in need of help with their car. If Mags' old Thunderbird still worked, there was a chance the ancient wrecker might still be able to fire up, and she turned into the garage. "Hey, Rusty!"

"Yeah!" The gruff answer came from somewhere in the back, and Jo saw the hunched back of the station's owner behind a stack of old tires.

"It's Jo."

"Hey, Jo!" The gruff nature of Rusty's voice remained, but she heard the smile behind the greeting as he remained behind the tires. "Everything all right—GARSH DANGIT!" Rusty straightened up quickly, his face red and sweaty, shaking his left hand and then examining the thumb. "Stupid tire." He kicked the rubber, and his leg bounced back harmlessly.

Rusty Behr was one of the few residents of The Village that had been born here and would die here. He came from a long lineage of mountain blood, a point of pride for the man. His family was one of the original founding citizens, and they had stuck it out for generations, through the good and the bad. He was the youngest of four brothers who offered hunting and horseback riding expeditions on the mountain.

Rusty stepped around the stack of tires, dressed in his usual blue jumpsuit, the clothes permanently stained like the man's hands. No matter how hard he tried to scrub off the grease, he just couldn't get rid of all of it.

"What's up, Jo?" Rusty pushed up his hat, exposing the receding hairline, and planted his fists on either side of his rotund midriff.

"How old is your wrecker?" Jo asked.

Rusty scratched his head, squinting. "Pops got her in seventy-three. Brand new back then. Course there's been quite a bit of wear and tear on it since then. You need a tow? I thought you didn't have a car?"

JAMES HUNT

"I don't," Jo answered. "But there was a family that got stranded on the road outside my property. If your wrecker is still in commission, I was hoping you could bring their vehicle into town."

"Of course!" Rusty smiled, pushing his fat cheeks up the side of his face. "Give me a minute here to finish up, and I'll be happy to take care of it."

"Thanks, Rusty. The father's name is Tim. And go easy on him. He's not from around here."

"Yes, ma'am."

The rest of the walk to the sheriff's station provided Jo the time to look around the town. It was the height of tourist season, and Jo knew that the big crowds would cause a problem. Anyone visiting on vacation wasn't prepared, and they would put a burden on those that were. Jo hoped that Mike was prepared for what came next.

Sweating by the time she entered the sheriff's office, Jo was greeted with a few concerned citizens chatting up Deputy Moynihan, who looked ill-equipped to handle their complaints. He was the newest deputy, and the youngest.

"And how come my daughter's computer doesn't work?" The woman was Riley Cantz, a woman as rough as her last name sounded. She was dressed in socks and sandals, short bottoms that weren't doing her any favors, and a tank top that looked one wrong jiggle away from the deputy slapping an indecent exposure on her. "It's a laptop! It doesn't need to be plugged into the wall to work, and it had a full charge last night."

Moynihan was clean-cut, his face freshly shaved and his hair buzzed down to a nub. When he held up his hands to try and calm Riley down, Jo saw his underarms were already drenched in sweat. And so long as the temperature continued to rise, so would people's tempers.

42

"Mrs. Cantz, we're trying to get in contact with the utility company, and we apologize that your daughter can't watch her Sunday morning cartoons, but right now—"

"And my phone doesn't work either!" Riley waved the impotent device around in the deputy's face, the fat at the bottom of her arm wiggling from the movement. "How am I supposed to call my brother in Knoxville to make sure he gets his medication—"

"Riley!" The voice bellowed with authority, and Sheriff Mike Turner stepped from his office. He was a tall man, a few hairs over six feet, a wide jaw that was currently clenched in frustration, and a pair of ice blue eyes that bore right into Riley Cantz's soul. "I swear on my mamma's grave that if you don't calm down, I will throw you in a cell." His voice boomed throughout the precinct, even startling Moynihan, but it produced the desired effect of piping Riley down.

The heavyset woman pocketed the phone and tilted her chin up, indignant. "Fine. But I expect something to be done by tomorrow or you won't be counting on my vote for re-election next year, Sheriff." She turned, arms swinging as she practically goose-stepped her way out the door.

Moynihan exhaled and slouched. "God almighty, that woman is one hot bag of air."

"She's all bark." And just like the flick of a switch, Mike had calmed, his demeanor no more menacing than a crate full of puppies. When he saw Jo standing inside, a smile graced his lips, and it grew wider as he walked toward her. "Jo, what are you doing down here?"

"I need to talk." Jo walked past him and headed toward the office. Mike's heavy footsteps followed and then closed the door, sealing the pair in privacy.

"You wanna sit down or—"

"I don't have time," Jo said. "I think the country has been attacked."

Mike walked by his desk, but stopped. He crossed his arms, frowning. "Attacked by who?"

"I don't know," Jo answered. "But I know what they used."

Jo gave Mike the short version, making sure that he understood what was happening and how people's complaints about laptops and phones were about to be the least of their worries.

"This isn't something that's going to be fixed in a week, a month, or even a year," Jo said. "And if this was a nationwide strike, it could mean a complete collapse of the government, infrastructure, and the rule of law."

Mike's stare hardened. "Not in this county."

"It might not be up to you." Jo stepped closer to him, and she caught the scent of his soap. He smelled nice. "You need to get people ready for the long haul. First priority will be food, water, and any medications that people might need. Talk to Mags down at the general store, I left Amelia there with her, she should have some supplies stockpiled. But people will start to panic if they think this will last for a while and—"

"And then they'll start to loot." Mike nodded and ran his big palm beneath his jaw. "Well, it explains why all the systems are down, and our squad cars."

"Any vehicles that were made before 1980 should run," Jo said. "That was before fuel injection had processors in them to make them more fuel efficient."

And it seemed that for the first time, Mike noticed the pack and the rifle. "What's all this?"

"I'm heading to the city," Jo answered. "I need to get Stacy out of there before things get worse."

Mike raised both eyebrows. "You're going alone?"

Jo tossed him a sideways glance. "I can handle myself."

"Jo, it's not about that." Mike closed the rest of the space between them, cupping his hands beneath her elbows with the lightest touch. "You don't have eyes in the back of your head."

A lump caught in Jo's throat, but she quickly cleared it and took a step back. "I'll be faster on my own." She turned for the door and then opened it, finding Moynihan pretending like he wasn't just eavesdropping. But she turned back to Mike, and her eyes watered. "Watch out for Amelia?"

"Of course," Mike answered. "You have my word."

And like Mags, Mike's word was another she trusted.

5

*M*ike had gathered his deputies in his office, wanting to make sure that when they faced the mob gathering in the streets outside of the station doors, they had a united front.

Mike had three deputies under his command. His most trusted deputy was Janet Donoghue, who had her arms crossed beneath her chest. She was a practical woman, wearing her brown hair buzzed short, which accentuated the rich dark brown of her eyes. She and Mike had been hired by the previous Sheriff around the same time. They worked well together.

Deputy William Furst was a former Marine, though he only served one term and didn't see combat. From his clean-shaven crew cut to the fine creases of his uniform, the man was no nonsense from head to toe.

Deputy Gus Moynihan was the newest recruit. Like Mike, the young man had grown up on the mountain, and would most likely die here. But hopefully not for years to come.

"Food, water, medicine, and protection," Mike said, rattling off the words like he was reading off of a grocery list.

"We have a lot of visitors up here this season who'll need food and water until we get a better handle on the situation." He turned to Jan. "I want you to head toward all of the bed and breakfast joints in town and make sure all the owners are on board to handle a prolonged stay. Get an idea of their supplies, and make a list." He turned to Furst. "I want you to head down to Jed Meyer's practice and check on his medical supplies. See what he has in stock, and make sure that it's protected under lock and key."

"We should consider deputizing more men," Furst said. "It'll help with crowd control."

"Hopefully we won't need it." Mike looked to Gus. "Your brother is down at the Army Reserve base at the bottom of the mountain for his monthly training, right?"

"Yeah, he left Friday," Gus answered.

"I want you to go down there and have him send men back up with you," Mike said. "He also might be able to tells us about what's going on around the rest of the area, and I want to know what he knows. Go to the Behrs' stables, they will let you borrow a horse."

"You got it, Sheriff," Gus said.

Mike nodded, glad everyone understood their assignments. "The most important thing we can do now is to keep people calm."

Furst snickered. "Easier said than done in this heat."

"We are the law," Mike said, hardening his voice. "It's our job to protect people. So let's get to work."

On an average day in the middle of summer, Sheriff Michael Turner would be able to walk from his office at the west end of Main Street all the way to Mags' General Store for a pop and a sandwich in less than three minutes. Today, that journey was slowed by the hordes of residents and tourists who wanted to know what in the hell was going on.

The questions were fired at him quickly, the faces around him multiplying. Some were faces he knew, others were just folks that had come to their sleepy little village for some vacation and a little R&R. Mike thought it was funny how these tourists had wanted to be here so much until they realized that they couldn't leave. Humans were always fickle.

The roar of questions became so loud and so heavy that Mike placed his thumb and forefinger in his mouth and whistled, the noise so high-pitched and loud that it silenced the endless inquiries into their precarious situation.

"All right," Mike said, letting the crowd take a step back and giving him some room to breathe. "I know everyone is concerned, and you all have a right to be. But the fact of the matter is that this might be something that we're dealing with for a while."

Groans and whispers hurried through the crowd, folks turning to one another.

"How long?" A voice shouted from the back of the crowd.

"I don't know," Mike answered.

More worried groans collected in the air, growing like a storm cloud on the horizon.

Mike raised the volume of his voice. "I may not know how long this is going to last, but I do know that the longer we stand here and squabble amongst ourselves, the less time that we have to prepare. Now, our first steps will be to make sure that we have enough food and water to last us through the week. I'm going to have my deputies come around and grab a list of any essential items that you need such as medications. But right now, I need everyone to return to their homes, or their places of current residence, and take stock of your resources. Thank you." He nodded curtly, and the crowd parted, breaking apart.

After the streets had cleared, Mike continued toward

Mags' store and saw the door propped open. He removed his sunglasses before he stepped through the entrance, tucking the gold aviators in his breast pocket, smiling at the friendly old woman that used to give him free candy before he could even see over the counter.

"Sheriff," Mags said, smirking as she said it.

"You should probably lock that door," Mike said, gesturing to the open entryway. "You never know what kind of trouble might blow through."

"You're never trouble." Mags stepped from around the counter and pecked a kiss on his cheek. "Jo come to see you?"

Mike nodded.

Mags sighed and then looked out the door to the crowds gathered around the deputies. "Anything that can spook that woman isn't anything that I want to play around with."

"She said that you're watching Amelia while she goes to the city to grab Stacy?" Mike asked, not seeing the youngest Mercer in the store.

"She's out back in the Thunderbird," Mags said, then smiled. "She likes to pretend she's driving."

"It is a very nice car," Mike said. "And my offer still stands to buy it from you. Seems like now might be a good time to sell it."

"HA!" Mag slapped Mike on the arm, and then returned to her stool behind the counter. "Nice try."

"I thought it was worth a shot." He smiled, and then he walked over and placed his hand on the counter. "I need to know how much medicine you've got in the pharmacy."

"Well, most of my regular folks come and pick up their medications on Monday, but seeing as how the world is falling apart, I'm inclined to believe that a few of them might show up today." She shrugged, shaking her head. "Most folks have enough to last them a month, but that's about it."

JAMES HUNT

A month was better than a week.

"But we'll have a problem with some of our diabetics," Mags said.

"What do you mean?" Mike asked.

"Insulin needs to be refrigerated to stay potent," Mag said. "And because we don't have any power—"

"No refrigeration," Mike said, nodding along. "We have some old gas generators in the station's basement. Once my deputies are done getting a head count, I'll wheel them out and start hooking them up to your coolers." He turned and got a better look at the layout of the general store.

It wasn't a big place and only had three aisles filled with snacks and other items that folks might find they need to grab on the go. The outer walls were lined with the coolers that were slowly warming, and while she had water bottles and soda, it wasn't enough to last the town more than a day or two.

Mike knew that what he was going to ask Mags was more than he had the right to, but he didn't know what else he could do without letting the town fall to pieces. "What's your inventory look like for perishables and water?"

And while Mags had every right to tell Mike to go screw himself, she only nodded, giving the question the serious thought that it deserved.

"Two pallets of water in the back," Mags said, glancing out to the aisles of her store. "A lot of junk food. Not too many fruits and vegetables. It might not be healthy, but it should keep them alive."

"Alive will have to do for now," Mike said. "You have a lock for your storage door?"

Mags nodded. "And only one key." She patted her left jean pocket and then reached beneath the counter and removed the .38 special revolver that was hidden underneath. "And I've still got the snub nose if things get hairy."

"Hopefully it won't come to that." But even as he said it, Mike remembered the fear and anger in the voices of the crowd that had stopped him. When the mob mentality took over, he knew that no amount of reason or logic could prevent them from rioting.

Mike turned back to Mags. "Mind if I head out back?"

Mags smiled. "You think you're ever actually going to get the courage to Amelia's mother out on a date?"

Mike blushed and stared down at his boots. His ears glowed a hot red. "Mags, I—"

"Go on," Mag said. "Your secret is safe with me."

Mike opened his mouth to speak but then chose to remain silent as he walked toward the back of the store. It wasn't so much a secret that he was in love with Joanna Mercer as much as it was a well-known fact.

Mike had known Joanna for a long time, both of them having grown up on the mountain together. But Jo had always been in love with Danny, and Mike had never caught her eye. And so they grew apart, but remained friendly acquaintances.

Mike never married, devoting himself to his work. He dated a few women, but nothing ever stuck. And while he had considered asking Jo out, it never felt like the right time, and when Jo finished grieving the death of her husband, she had withdrawn even further from the world. She had chosen a life of isolation, shunning the world that had killed her husband.

But despite all of that, Mike still held out hope because the pair had gotten to know one another well over the past three years. Jo didn't let many people into her circle, but Mike had earned her highly-coveted trust. He would never take advantage of that, but he also sensed that Jo wanted something more from him. She just wouldn't open that door.

"Hey, Em!" Mike smiled when he saw Amelia behind the wheel of the big Thunderbird, barely able to see over the dash.

"Look out, Sheriff, I almost ran you over!" Amelia kept both hands on the wheel, jerking it back and forth on her pretend chase.

Mike jumped out of the way, clutching his heart and joining in the play. "Sorry." He walked around to the passenger side and sat down, Amelia barely noticing him as she concentrated on the make-believe path ahead. "Where are we going?"

"To save the people in the city," Amelia said, holding the same fiery and determined gaze as her mother. "They're in trouble."

Mike smiled. "Think you can put it in park for me so I can bend your ear for a minute?"

Amelia sighed, taking her hands off the wheel. "Okay. What's up?"

Mike leaned against the Thunderbird's hood, thumbs hooked in his waistband. "Do you know what's going on? What's happening and why your mom left to go and get your sister in the city?"

Amelia nodded. "The EMP."

Of course Jo had told her nine-year-old about the effects of an EMP. The woman had hardened both herself and her girls. She wanted to prepare them, no matter how old they were. Amelia was probably more prepared to handle the crisis than some of his deputies.

"I want to make sure you stay close to Mags and the store," Mike said. "I know that you can handle yourself, but people are getting nervous, and when they're nervous, they do stupid things. And I don't want you to get caught up in the crosshairs of that stupidity. K?"

Amelia didn't acknowledge him at first, her big brown eyes just staring into his blue ones. And when she spoke again, the answer surprised him.

"People are going to die," Amelia said. "I know that. But I'm not. I'm ready."

Mike reached for the girl's hands. "Yes, you are." He bent over and kissed her forehead. He walked back toward the store, glancing behind her and pointing to the open patch of grass in front of the Thunderbird. "Better hurry to get down there so you can save all of those folks."

Amelia placed both hands back on the wheel and then faced forward, that steely gaze returning as she did, but then stuck her head out the window. "Hey, Sheriff?"

Mike turned around. "What's up?"

Amelia stared at him with a curiosity that typically followed questions that adults didn't like to answer. "Are you going to marry my mom?"

Heat flushed Mike's cheeks, and again he felt his ears burn hot. "I think to marry someone, you need to go on a few dates first. That's something your mother and I haven't done."

"Why not?" Amelia asked, continuing to press the issue.

"Well," Mike said. "I haven't asked her."

"How come?"

Mike laughed, shaking his head. "Why are you so interested in your mother and me? You trying to play matchmaker or something?"

Amelia lowered her head and stared at the ground, giving the question considerable thought before she looked back up at Mike, her eyes squinting from the sun. "I just think that you guys look good together. And… I think she likes you."

Mike brushed the girl's sweaty bangs from her forehead and smoothed out the curly waves on her scalp. "Well, why don't we think about that after things calm down?" He turned away but looked back over his shoulder at her. "Don't run anyone over on your way down the mountain."

"You got it, Sheriff!" Amelia offered her hardiest salute and then ducked back behind the wheel, slamming on the accelerator and weaving around the dangerous curves of the mountainside.

And while Mike understood the hard times that lay ahead and the difficulties that they all faced from the sudden erosion of society, he couldn't wipe the smile from his face as Amelia's words lingered in his head.

---

6

*O*nce The Village was behind her, Jo veered off the paved road and into the woods. It was her terrain, and she felt safer in the thick foliage. She knew that with cars broken down, most people would be walking along the road, and she wanted to avoid the crowds.

Now that law and order were in jeopardy, Jo knew that it was only a matter of time before society's thin veil of civility was torn down. She was confident that she could handle trouble, but the first priority for survival was evasion.

It had only been a few hours, but the summer heat was already working against her. Jo forced herself to hydrate, knowing that the sweat collecting in her clothes would take its toll on her, and with the level of exertion from the trip down, Jo had to fight against fatigue as much as her own worry.

The trees helped provide shade, but Jo still applied sunscreen on any exposed areas, reapplying when she could. Because in a world without medicine, or clean water, or food, Jo knew that exposure would kill more people than bullets.

Jo moved deftly down the mountain, sure-footed even with her quick pace. But she struggled to keep her mind present. It was difficult not to think of her daughter, not to worry about the danger that might have befallen her. But the farther Jo descended the mountain, the harder it became to ignore the scenarios running through her imagination.

When the forest started to thin, Jo knew she was close to the outer suburban areas of Knoxville. She'd have to cross the river into downtown to get into the campus, and she hoped that the bridge was still standing.

Up ahead, the trees cleared and Jo saw a bluff that provided a clear view of the city below. But when she finally saw the carnage, the color drained from Jo's face.

Thick black plumes of smoke rose from the city, fires raging as hot as the sun above. The stacks were scattered through the streets. The distinct pop of gunfire rose from the city in unison with the smoke, though the distance made it sound like nothing more than firecrackers on the Fourth of July.

Jo removed the rifle from her shoulder, using the scope to get a better look at the situation below, and the lens thrust her into the chaos.

People scurried between buildings, and at first Jo thought their frantic pace was the evasion of the fires, but she saw masked men with rifles, firing their automatic weapons, leaving corpses and blood in their wake.

Jo pivoted the scope toward the campus, her palms slick with sweat. She saw no fires at the university, but her heart skipped a beat when she saw the masked men roaming the campus.

Jo shouldered the rifle and then continued her trek down the steep decline of the mountainside. Mountain travel was always deceptive. No matter how close something looked, it was always farther than you thought.

The thinning forest allowed Jo to see the road through the trees, which was clogged with broken-down vehicles, transforming the roadways into parking lots.

The drivers were too distracted with one another and their busted vehicles to notice Jo, and as she listened to their frustrations and fear, she pitied them. None of them understood what had happened, none of them understood the challenges of what came next. All of them were vulnerable.

With the crowds growing thicker, Jo kept a close eye on the road. Everyone's voices blended together, drowning out the sounds of the forest.

The gunfire grew louder too, and it no longer resembled the childlike pops of firecrackers. Every gunshot thundered with a dense timbre that sent shock waves through her own body. It was the beat of a war that Jo never wanted to be a part of. But she didn't need to win the war. She only needed to survive it.

The rocky terrain leveled and allowed Jo to move faster through the woods. And with the increased speed came added noise from the debris on the forest floor. Dead leaves, branches, rocks, all of it crunched beneath Jo's boots as she moved as fast as she could through the fallen foliage, but the journey came to a sudden and abrupt stop when she saw movement ahead.

Jo stopped and removed the rifle from her side, aiming it at the person she saw retreat back behind the trees. "Come on out!"

"Don't shoot!" The request was followed by a pair of hands that stuck out from behind a tree, and then a man emerged from the cover. "I'm not armed."

The man was only fifteen yards out. It would be an easy

shot if it came to that, but she hoped that it wouldn't. Killing an animal was one thing, but the idea of killing another person… Well, she hadn't thought of that since Danny's killer was sentenced to prison.

The man emerged from the cover of the trees with his arms raised. He was on the shorter side, dressed in shorts and a graphic t-shirt with a design that she didn't recognize. He was balding, a little heavyset, and wore glasses.

"You following me?" Jo asked, keeping the rifle aimed at him.

"No." The man shook his head, his jowls wiggling from the movement. "My car broke down, and I just wanted some shade from the sun."

Jo studied the man more closely. He was shaking. Just a babe lost in the woods. She lowered the rifle but didn't shoulder the weapon, keeping it at the ready. "You should head back to your car, walk to shelter if you can find it."

"Do you have a phone?" The big man gulped. "Mine won't work."

"No." Jo walked around him, keeping eyes on him as she slowly turned to follow. "Go back to your car. Grab what you can carry and then head for the nearest town."

"What about the city?" the man asked, shouting through the woods.

"The city's already burning," Jo answered.

---

7

*T*he campus was crawling with masked men, more than Stacy could evade, but she had realized it too late after she and Melissa had started running. And from the sight of the plumes of smoke in the city, the fighting had spread everywhere.

Stacy knew that her mother would realize what happened soon, if she hadn't already. And despite everything that they'd gone through, all of the angry shouting and name calling, deep down she knew that her mother would come and find her. And because of that, she steered Melissa toward the nearest building to hide.

"I can't—" Melissa drew in a breath. "Keep—" Another sharp inhale. "Going—" Sharp wheeze.

Stacy grabbed hold of her friend's hand, pulling Melissa with her. "We can't stay out in the open!"

More gunshots, closer, triggered a panicked urgency for both girls, and Stacy's mouth went dry. Finally, she saw the library less than fifty yards away. It was their best shot.

Stacy reached the doors first, yanking them open and then shoving Melissa inside. "Hurry." She swung the door shut behind her and then glanced out the window, watching a few other classmates be gunned down in the courtyard that they had just passed through, and Stacy quickly backed away from the glass.

Melissa stumbled until she collapsed onto a nearby chair in the lobby. "We're going to die." Her voice was on the edge of panic. "They're going to kill us. God, what the hell is going on?"

"We're not in any immediate danger. Not yet." Stacy slowly retreated into the darkness of the library. "C'mon, Melissa, we need to move."

The girl only shook her head, hyperventilating. "I can't move. I can't even breathe." She gasped and the color drained from her cheeks. The sweat beaded on her face, causing the make-up she wore the night before to run.

Stacy knelt by her friend's side and grabbed her hand. "Just breathe with me. In..." She drew in a breath for four seconds, "...and out." Then she exhaled for four seconds, repeating the process until Melissa calmed. "Better?"

Melissa nodded tentatively. "I think so."

"Good," Stacy said. "C'mon."

The library reception desk was unmanned, as it always was on Sunday mornings. But the library allowed twenty-four-seven access to all students.

The place smelled of mildew, but it was already warming. She walked past the front foyer, which had tables and chairs stacked and a small cafeteria where you could buy coffee and snacks. It was also unmanned.

"I don't want to die, Stacy," Melissa said, her voice quivering. "I-I r-really don't w-want to d-die." She sucked in her lower lip, animalistic whimpers escaping her throat.

"Hey." Stacy grabbed Melissa's shoulders and forced her friend's eyes on her. "You're not going to die." She placed her arm around her friend and then guided her deeper into the quiet library. "We'll just hang out here. Catch up on our reading."

The library was a massive structure. Four stories, each level corresponding with a specific set of scholarly needs.

A mixture of small cubbies and large tables were stationed near the books where students would sit with their laptops and their books, headphones plugged in and focused on their projects. Stacy had come here often, seeing as how it was much quieter than her dorm room.

During the fall and spring the library was always filled with students, making it hard to find an open spot where she could study, but seeing the space so empty now suddenly reminded her of the cabin.

"Stacy." Melissa's voice was a sharp whisper, and she quickly tugged on Stacy's sleeve, pulling it with three hard yanks. "Someone's back there."

Stacy followed Melissa's line of sight, her eyes fixated on a row of books a few aisles down from where they stood near one of the tables. She listened, but she heard nothing. "There's no one here, Melissa—"

A creak came from somewhere amongst the books, and Stacy recognized the noise. The building was old and still had much of the original flooring, which groaned for even the softest steps.

Stacy placed her hand on Melissa's shoulders and instructed her to stay put. She moved slowly, carefully, praying that the floor wouldn't give away her position as she approached. She unsheathed the blade and held a firm grip around the handle.

Knees bent, arm raised, Stacy's pulse quickened. The three years of training that her mother provided to her in the woods returned on instinct.

Stacy heard her mother's whispers, telling her that if she couldn't see something, then there was no need for her eyes, and she closed them. She focused on her other senses, listening, feeling, smelling the air. The old library floor groaned again, this one louder and closer than before, and Stacy opened her eyes.

Stacy pivoted around the corner of the aisle, the blade raised high in her right hand, and her left stretched out to grab hold of whoever was in her path. She touched flesh and muscle and grabbed it tightly, pinning her prey to the floor.

"Don't kill me!" The boy raised both hands and turned away from the tip of the blade that was only inches away from his cheek. He was a student.

Stacy let him go and stood up, but kept the blade out so he could see it. "What the hell are you doing?"

Still on his back, the boy slowly opened his eyes and looked up at her with a look of surprised indignation. "What am *I* doing?" He propped himself up on his elbows and then scooted backward. "You're the one with a knife in your hand."

Stacy flexed her grip on the weapon but kept it at her side. "I thought that you were one of the—" She shook her head, knowing that if the terrorists were to barge in here, they wouldn't be sneaking around. "I'm sorry."

The boy awkwardly got to his feet. He was tall, lanky, with a mop of tangled black curls. His face was planed with sharp edges along his cheeks and nose, and a pair of small but intelligent eyes hid behind the glasses that he adjusted on his face. He was dressed in a shirt, cargo shorts, and sneakers.

"You know what's going on out there?" the boy asked.

"Something happened to the city," Stacy answered, finally returning the blade to its sheath.

"Yeah," the boy said, his tone erring on the side of petulance, but he omitted the 'no shit, Sherlock.' "Is your phone working?"

"Nothing is working," Stacy answered.

"It doesn't make any sense." The boy stared at the floor in frustration. "I mean what kind of device could do this? And why would anyone do this—"

"Are you alone?" Stacy asked, trying to cut the kid off before his brain exploded from an aneurysm.

"No," the boy said. "I was part of a study group. We were on the fourth floor when the power cut out. Some of them left, but a few of us stayed, thinking that the power was going to come back on soon. But then when we heard those explosions and gunfire…" He stared at the floor again then shook his head. "It just doesn't make any sense."

Stacy retreated a few steps from the aisle and then turned to find Melissa still at the table. She looked back to the boy. "How many are with you?"

"Five, including me," the boy answered, and then peeked through the stacks of books and saw Melissa through the space. "Is it just you and your friend?"

Stacy nodded. "You guys need to get off the fourth floor."

"What? Why?"

"Because if those gunmen come in here, then you're going to need a quick escape, and this building only has one stairwell." Stacy arched both of her eyebrows. "It's a kill zone."

The boy nodded. "Right, yeah, like in Call of Duty." He smiled, but Stacy didn't reciprocate it, and he cleared his throat. "I'll, um, go and get the others, tell them to come down."

When he turned to leave, Stacy called after him. "Hey, do you have any food and water?"

The boy nodded. "I brought some snacks, but most of them are gone."

"Bring anything you have left and save it," Stacy said. "You might need it."

"Right." The boy lingered for a minute, and Stacy caught him giving her the once over. When he realized that she noticed what he was doing, he blushed and then scurried away.

Stacy rolled her eyes. Even when the world was falling apart, boys were still thinking about getting laid. She returned to her friend, who was still shaking from the fear of whatever was waiting for them beyond the darkness.

"Who was it?" Melissa asked, staring up at her like Amelia used to do whenever she was scared.

"A boy," Stacy answered, looking back to the aisle where the pair had met. "He's a student. Said he was with a study group on the fourth floor. They're coming down to join—"

Gunfire permeated through the library walls, and Melissa immediately melted into a puddle of shivers and whimpers, making no effort to be quiet.

Stacy placed her finger to her lip, pushing her friend, and then grabbed her arm, pulling her away from the table and deeper into the library. They ducked down one of the aisles as they heard the front doors open and the gunmen entered.

Stacy led Melissa to the end of the aisle, making sure that they were hunched low as the gunmen's voice carried into the building.

Keeping as quiet as possible, Stacy grabbed hold of Melissa's face and pulled it within inches of hers. "Don't speak, and follow me wherever I go. Nod if you understand." Melissa nodded, and Stacy pushed her friend behind her, waiting to see what the gunmen would do.

Between the stacks of books, she saw their rifles. They exchanged a few quick and hurried words in their native language, and then fanned out to search the aisles.

Before the gunmen neared the end of their aisles, Stacy pulled Melissa toward the back of the building. They weren't near any of the exits, and the nearest one would take them past the terrorists combing the aisles.

Stacy knew that their best chance was to hide, to keep moving, using the maze of book aisles to their advantage. She kept a close eye on the enemy, keeping both herself and Melissa out of harm's way, but they were slowly running out of space.

Finally, Stacy and Melissa backed into the stairwell door, the enemy moving closer. Stacy was about to take a step up the aisle, but the door swung open behind her, and she turned to find the boy leading the other four students onto the first floor. He was in midsentence when Stacy clamped her hand over his mouth to keep him quiet. But it was too late.

The gunmen hurried toward the stairwell, two at the front of the aisles of books and one in the back, blocking all of their potential exits and leaving her exposed and in the open. They wouldn't be able to dodge them. They had to go up.

Stacy grabbed hold of Melissa's hand and then yanked her into the stairwell and shoulder-checked the boy. She passed the cluster of frightened faces staring back at her, all of them standing still.

In the end, it was the shouts and gunfire from the terrorists that triggered the stampede up the steps.

They made it to the second floor when the terrorists barged into the bottom of the stairwell. Knowing that they wouldn't survive in the stairwell, Stacy pulled Melissa toward the second-floor exit door while the others continued their frantic sprint upward.

The door swung shut behind them, and Stacy guided

Melissa directly away from the staircase opening and to the left as fast as she could.

Stacy shoved Melissa back behind the nearest wall of books and ducked low. The pair of girls huddled close together, and Stacy covered Melissa's mouth as the door opened and one of the gunmen entered the second floor.

The door closed behind the terrorist, muting the sounds of the foot chase in the stairwell. It was quiet for a little while longer before she heard the terrorist move.

The terrorist walked forward into the room instead of taking that immediate left like Stacy and Melissa had done. He moved slowly, methodically.

Melissa trembled, rattling quick breaths into Stacy's palm. Stacy placed her finger over her lips, miming for Melissa to keep quiet, and the gesture was enough to stop the panic attack before it started.

Those old wooden boards groaned with the terrorist's every step, and it grew louder the closer the gunman moved toward Melissa and Stacy.

Almost on instinct, Stacy moved her hand toward her blade's handle. Because as frightened as she was, she knew that if this was her end, then she refused to go quietly.

The boards groaned louder, the gunman less than three feet from the short wall of books, and Stacy tensed. She lowered her hand from Melissa's mouth so she had the use of both hands. She shut her eyes and gathered her nerves.

Prepared for death, the terrorist hunting them suddenly stopped at the sound of muted gunfire from above. He hurried back toward the door, disappearing into the stairwell.

When the door closed, both girls exhaled, and Stacy slouched from exhaustion while Melissa squirmed on the floor, kicking her feet as if she were trying to stand up, but couldn't muster the strength to do it.

"We're going to die," Melissa said, shaking her head. "We're going to die. They're going to kill us. We're going to die."

Stacy kept her eyes peeled on the door as more gunfire echoed from upstairs. Every beat that she heard stabbed another knife into her gut. She didn't know those people. The campus was too big for her to recognize every face. But they were students, like her, and now they were dead.

"We're going to die," Melissa said. "We're going to die!"

Stacy spun around, grabbing Melissa's face and pulling it toward her. "Hey! We are not going to die. We just need to be quiet until they leave." Stacy's voice cracked, and her own resolved started to dissolve. "Please."

The gunfire was sporadic and quick. Once it ended, the silence that followed was deafening. Stacy kept her eyes locked on the door until the sound of footsteps echoed down the stairs.

Stacy ducked low, praying the gunmen would pass their floor and leave the building. She held her breath when they neared the second floor, and she shut her eyes. And while it felt like the moment dragged on forever, their door remained closed.

Stacy lingered in the same spot for a while, making sure that the gunmen weren't just trying to trick her and lure anyone else out that still might be in the library. But after ten minutes and no sound, Stacy emerged from cover.

She crept toward the door, peeking through the narrow glass window and into the darkened stairwell. She saw nothing. She hurried back to Melissa and tried to get her friend up. "C'mon, we need to leave."

"No," Melissa said, shaking her head. "No, I'm not leaving."

Stacy grabbed hold of Melissa's hand. "C'mon, we need to go now."

"I said no!" Melissa yanked her hand back and moved out of reach so Stacy couldn't grab her again. She stood, her cheeks a bright cherry red. "This isn't right! None of this is right!" She was hysterical, screaming.

Stacy rushed toward her friend, grabbing her wrists and keeping her from thrashing about. She was stronger than Melissa, and the girl finally subdued her movements. "Hey! Shut up. *Shut up!*"

Melissa finally kept still and quiet, looking up at Stacy through the bangs that covered her eyes.

"We're alive," Stacy said. "Okay? And the people who tried to kill us are gone. But if we don't keep our heads on straight, that's not going to be the case for much longer. So keep it together."

Melissa stood there, shaking. Her lower lip quivered, but she didn't cry again. She only gave a slight nod of her head, but her breathing slowed, and her cheeks weren't as flushed as they were before.

"Sorry," Melissa said, and then quickly dropped her arm. "What do we about…" She lifted her gaze to the ceiling.

Stacy cleared her throat, glancing to the ceiling too. "We can't do anything for them. They're gone." She led Melissa back to the stairwell, and even though both were sure that the threat had left, they moved quietly.

But when Stacy entered the stairwell, she remembered what the boy had said. They had food and water. Supplies that she could use. Stacy glanced up the steps, and Melissa looked up as well.

"What?" Melissa asked, her voice shaking. "Do you hear something?"

Stacy hesitated, but finally shook her head. "They said they have food. And water. If the terrorists didn't take it, then we'll need it."

"You want to go up there?" Melissa asked.

"Want doesn't have anything to do with it," Stacy answered.

Stacy placed one foot on the next step up, but couldn't stop shaking. She hadn't been this nervous since her father had died and she had to go to the funeral. She remembered standing outside the entrance to the church, frozen, paralyzed.

Melissa followed, and when they reached the top floor, Stacy paused outside the door. She shut her eyes, grabbed the handle, and then pulled the door open to step inside.

The scent of death hung in the air, along with the metallic taste of lead and smoke from the bullets. Without the air conditioning working, everything hung in the air like dirt on sweaty skin.

"Stacy," Melissa said, grabbing her friend's arm. "Look."

Stacy opened her eyes and followed Melissa's finger to one of the clusters of desk cubbies where an arm stuck out from view. The furniture blocked the rest of the body from view, but Stacy forced herself to walk around and see the corpse.

It was a girl. She was dressed in short workout bottoms and a baggy shirt. She wore sandals, the left one off her foot while the right clung between her toes even though the rest of the foot was removed entirely from it. The girl lay on her side, motionless.

The next body they came across was a boy who lay face down on the floor between two book aisles. Stacy wondered if the boy had tried to run and how far he'd gotten before a bullet to the back knocked him flat.

The third body was one that Melissa found, and she gasped. The boy had died from a head shot. Behind him, little bits of bone and brain matter spread out on the floor.

The scent of death was overwhelming, and Stacy knew that the bodies would rot quickly from the heat and moisture.

"Have you ever seen a dead body before?" Melissa asked, staring down at the boy.

"Not like this one," Stacy answered.

After Stacy's mother moved their family into the woods, she had grown accustomed to death. She hunted, skinned, and cleaned most everything that they ate, and it had given her an appreciation for life that she hadn't felt before. Because unlike people, nature wasted nothing of the dead. Everything was consumed and returned to the earth so life could go on.

Nature didn't mourn the dead either. There were no funerals, no ceremonies, no tears were shed. Because nature only cared for the living. Only people cared for the dead.

Stacy stopped alongside a bank of computers and saw the fourth body at the end of the row of books where the floor ended and the wall began. The girl had run out of space to flee.

Stacy stood there, not wanting to investigate how that girl died. She didn't want to see another blank face staring at nothing. It wasn't because she was scared or because she thought those faces would haunt her nightmares, she didn't dream or have nightmares anymore.

She didn't want to walk down there because she knew what happened when people wasted too much time on the dead. They became crazy. They lost their minds and sanity.

They moved their children out into the middle of nowhere and away from the only world that they had ever known.

Melissa remained a silent shadow behind Stacy, shaking her head in disbelief. "This is unbelievable. This is… evil."

Stacy nodded. "It is. And we need to collect what we can before that evil comes back."

8

The gunshots were random, popping wildly like firecrackers throughout the city. Jo saw the bodies that had already been slain, lying motionless in the streets and sidewalks.

From what Jo could see in the city, the objective was more to terrorize than to conquer. It wouldn't be logistically possible for an entire army to stay hidden within the United States, not with the type of surveillance that existed.

But several small factions? Groups each comprised of a dozen or so men? Yes, that could be done. And with people still reeling from confusion over the EMP blast, it would be easy to capitalize on the city's distress. They had attacked quickly, probably moments after the EMP had been detonated.

Out of the forest and away from the cover of her natural element, Jo brought the rifle's stock flush to her shoulder. She moved forward quickly and with purpose, her vision focused ahead but always aware of her peripheral.

Jo kept to the roads, the slew of old vehicles providing excellent cover for her if she needed it. She caught movement in the buildings that had windows in the storefronts where people had taken shelter.

They all watched Jo as she moved tactically down the road, pausing at each cross-section, clearing both sides before pressing forward. She wondered what they were thinking of her as they moved through the city. Did they think she was military? Were they afraid that she was one of the terrorists that were wreaking havoc on their people? Either way, no one stepped out from behind their walls and shelter to ask.

Less than a mile after Jo entered the city, the gunfire grew louder, and she dropped behind the cover of a Lexus, its car doors still open.

Jo planted her elbows on the tanned leather seats, which were hot from the sun. She ignored the burn and aimed the scope of her rifle to the gunfire in the north.

A cluster of people ran down the parallel street, heading west. They all glanced back behind them on their retreat, and after they cleared the intersection and were out of view, Jo saw the covered tactical unit that was chasing them down like a pack of dogs.

They moved in a line formation, sweeping through the street with calculated precision. Jo suspected that they were working the city in a grid, going from road to road, making sure that anything that wandered into their path was eradicated from the face of the earth. They were the sweeping scythe of the reaper, adding more bodies for the greedy hooded creature to scoop up and drag into hell.

Jo waited until they passed, and the moment they were gone, she continued her journey east, deeper into the city. All she could think of was getting to her daughter before it was too late, before the monsters that had been unleashed from their cages ripped her apart.

Gunfire shattered the storefront glass to her left, and Jo dropped to the pavement, then backed up against the nearest car door.

More bullets pinged against the vehicle that Jo used for cover, and she felt the vibrations from each strike. She crawled toward the front of the car, knowing that it was vital for her to keep moving, and then darted behind another vehicle.

Jo moved up two more car lengths before she finally stopped to reassess the situation. Between the ache in her body and the ringing in her head, Jo struggled to form a plan. The adrenaline from the fight caused her hand to tremble.

Jo turned back behind her and saw the cluster of people fleeing into nearby storefronts and down alleyways, anywhere that would take them out of the kill zone in the streets.

A woman and her son reached a nearby door. The mother's fingertips touched the door's handle, and just before she pulled it open, a spray of bullets dropped both her and the child to the pavement. The storefront glass shattered and their bodies lay still amongst the shards.

The scene was similar on the other side of the street, and with only a few remaining survivors from the original pack of those that had fled from their attackers, Jo couldn't stand by and watch as the rest of them were gunned down in cold blood.

Jo stood in front of the hood of an old black Honda coup, the paint worn thin by time and the elements, and then raised the rifle. She guided the crosshairs over the enemy slaughtering the innocent. She didn't hesitate when she pulled the trigger, and she thought of nothing else but moving onto the next target once the first terrorist was dead.

Time slowed in the haste of combat, and Jo's senses

heightened. She was aware of the sunlight that gleamed off the vehicles that stood between herself and the enemy. She was mindful of the recoil of the weapon in her hands, the stock of the rifle knocking firmly against her shoulder with every squeeze of the trigger.

The world had narrowed to the view of the scope, and anything that fell into her crosshairs was brought down with the same authority as if she were hunting in her own backyard.

But the terrorists fought back with force, causing Jo to duck back behind vehicles for cover. She glanced to her right and saw four people disappear into a flower shop, safe from the fighting in the streets. And while Jo was glad she was able to keep some people safe, her efforts brought the enemy's concentrated focus solely on her, transforming every vehicle she hid behind into Swiss Cheese.

Ducked behind an old Chevy Silverado, Jo spied a building on the southwest corner of the cross street behind her. Jo readied her weapon to provide her own cover fire, mapping out the path to the door in her mind. Confident she could make it, Jo sprinted toward the building.

The terrorists opened fire on her sprint, but their aim was poor. Keeping her speed up, Jo shouldered the door open and vanished into the darkness, never breaking stride as she found the staircase to lead her to the roof.

Two of the terrorists followed her inside, and Jo rounded the old staircase corners quickly. Lungs and legs burning when she reached the top, Jo found the roof access and sprinted back out into the hot sun. She ran toward the back of the building and then stopped at the rooftop's ledge, which was close to another taller building with a fire escape.

Jo calculated the distance at less than three feet, and then backpedaled to build up momentum for her jump.

The pair of terrorists in pursuit rushed onto the roof, and Jo bolted forward. Bullets and screams chasing her, Jo flung herself from the roof, leaping over the empty space between the buildings, and slammed into the fire railing.

Jo kicked her dangling legs and heaved herself over the side. She found her footing on the grated scaffolding and aimed her rifle at the nearest window, shot out the glass, and then burst inside the room, rolling out of view of the window just as the terrorists opened fire on the other side of the building.

Blinded from the sudden contrast of light to dark, it took a moment for Jo's vision to adjust, but just as she suspected, neither of the terrorists made the jump to the other side. And she heard them curse as they walked away, leaving Jo to catch her breath and let her vision adjust.

It took thirty seconds before the darkness began to take shape, and she was startled by the man huddled in the corner, his body blocking a young woman and a little boy. All three of them were wide-eyed and staring at Jo, looking at her the way she had seen the civilians outside look at the terrorists.

"I'm not here to hurt you," Jo said, her voice a whisper, but she didn't lower her weapon. While she meant them no harm, that didn't say they meant the same.

The father took a step toward Jo, away from his family. "Do you know what's going on?" He was a big man, but he couldn't hide the tremble in his voice.

Jo looked back to the window that she had shattered, the pieces of broken glass lying precariously on the carpet. After the fright she'd given them, answers were the least that she could provide. She told them about the EMP, about the terrorists, and, if they had the means, to evacuate the city immediately.

"Do you have a weapon?" Jo asked.

"I have a pistol," the father answered. "Haven't used it in over a year though."

"It's better than nothing," Jo said. "So long as you don't run into the people that were chasing me, anyone else should be scared off by the weapon if you just flash it." She had stood and walked over to the mother and son, the boy clinging tightly to his mother's legs. He couldn't have been older than four. "Do you have food, anything non-perishable that you can take on the road? Water?"

"Not much," the father said. "Some jerky and whatnot, maybe a few canned foods. We have half a case of bottled water."

"Take everything that you can carry," Jo said. "Move quickly once you're outside. Don't stop for anyone or anything."

The father nodded quickly, and then cleared his throat. "Thank you."

"Good luck." Jo walked to the front door, pausing to look back at the family. She saw how the father held both his wife and his son in his arms, protecting them, a shield against the enemies that wanted nothing but to tear them apart.

And while Jo knew she was better prepared for what came next, she was suddenly envious of that little family holding onto one another in the living room. Jealous because they were complete. Jealous because she wanted Danny to be here, and then guilt flooded her body when she realized that she would have traded all of their lives to bring him back. And then she left the apartment, shutting the door behind her along with those horrible thoughts.

9

*J*o cautiously emerged from the apartment building. Judging by the gunfire that she heard, the fighting had moved farther west. But despite how the fighting sounded, Jo kept her guard up, because terrorists wouldn't be the only enemy.

If experience had taught her anything, it was that people behaved poorly during stressful or dire situations. The moment a person's life was in danger that fight-or-flight switch was engaged, and the rest was history. Because Jo knew that as evolved as society had become, when shit hit the fan, people couldn't deny those ancient instincts, the ones still coded into DNA, the ones that kept us alive and over-rode our rational mind.

And with the world collapsing around her, Jo knew that the average citizen was more inclined to kill her and take her supplies.

Jo picked up the pace, checking the time, and with only a mile until she reached the campus, she stopped to rehydrate. She ducked down an alleyway and behind a dumpster where she was hidden from the main road. She set the rifle down, but kept one hand free to reach for her pistol if she needed it, then removed the water bottle from her pack and drank, slowly.

The water was still cold in the canteen, one of the reasons she had bought the highly-insulated device in the first place.

Drenched in sweat, Jo knew the water wouldn't be enough and she crunched an electrolyte tab, then rinsed her mouth when she was finished.

The enemy had picked an excellent time to attack. People had grown used to their summer comforts: air conditioning, ice, refrigeration. But all of those things were gone, at least by every conventional standard. It was hard to believe, but the reality of the situation was most of the people in this city wouldn't survive to see the fall.

Rejuvenated, Jo slipped her pack on, picked up her rifle, and then double-timed it to the campus. She had only visited the campus once, in secret, the month before Stacy's orientation. She wasn't about to let her daughter go off to a school without Jo knowing the ins and outs of the place. And so, she took a tour of the campus. She had seen the dorm where Stacy would live, and that's where she headed first.

Once Jo reached the campus, she navigated the empty paved walkways and the freshly-cut grass. After the chaos of the city, it was odd to see such a place of grandeur and opulence still standing, but she was thrust back into the reality of the situation when she saw the first body lying on the grass in the middle of a courtyard.

It was a girl with brunette hair, and she lay on her stomach, her face turned away from Jo. Even from this distance, Jo could tell that the girl was also about the same height and weight as Stacy.

Jo moved to the girl like a ghost, her guard down, which she knew wasn't smart, but those motherly instincts had overridden her training. She knelt by the girl, then grabbed her shoulder and pulled, rotating the girl to her back so she could see her face, and then covered her mouth.

It wasn't Stacy.

Jo's eyes watered, the tears running down red cheeks as she kept her hand clamped tightly over her mouth to quiet the involuntary whimpers. She shut her eyes, repeating the same thought in her mind. *It's not Stacy.*

Jo stood, leaving the body at peace, and pressed forward to the dorm rooms. She saw more bodies along the way, the blood kept warm and fresh from the hot sun. And for every murdered student that Jo passed on the campus, her grief turned to rage.

Stacy's dorm finally appeared ahead, and Jo approached wearily, still unsure if the terrorists were roaming the campus.

The air in the stairwell was already hot and stale, and Jo had trouble breathing by the time she reached the top floor. She paused at the door, readying her weapon as she slowly reached for the door's handle. Despite the desire to find her daughter quickly, she needed to remember to move tactically.

Jo swung the door open and aimed her weapon down an empty hallway. Every door was closed, and she moved swiftly down the hall, looking at the names on the doors, searching for Stacy Mercer.

Jo prayed that she found her daughter alive. She prayed that she wouldn't have to approach another body and turn it over only to find her daughter's lifeless eyes staring back at her.

Hinges from a door behind her groaned, and Jo spun around, aiming her weapon into the ghost-white face of a frightened young girl.

"Are you here to help us?" The girl's voice was meek and traveled quietly, practically vanishing by the time it reached Jo's ears.

Jo lowered the rifle. "I'm looking for my daughter. Her name is Stacy Mercer. Do you know her? Is she here?"

"I know her." The girl opened the door a little wider, and then Jo saw another girl appear from behind her, who was much taller. "She's in room three-nineteen."

Jo turned to find the room, but then stopped.

"She's not there," the short girl said, calling out. "We've checked all the rooms. We're the only ones left in the building. It's because it's summer and—"

Jo turned and then rushed back to the girl, moving with force and precision. The short college girl with her hair tied up in a bun and still dressed in her sleeping shorts and baggy, oversized shirt was too tired to try and move.

"Do you know where she went?" Jo asked, her voice steady but stern.

"No." The voice came from the taller girl. She was close to six feet, nothing but knees, elbows, and hair. She crossed her long forearms over her stomach and then nervously chewed on her lower lip.

"When did they leave?" Jo grabbed the girl's elbow, the bone engulfed in the palm.

The tall girl winced. "Like an hour ago, maybe? I-I-I don't know— you're hurting my arm."

Jo released her grip on the girl and then glanced around the room. It was messy and dirty, already hot from the combination of no air and the two bodies that had been huddled inside. It smelled of perfume and detergent and sweat.

Jo looked to the girls, who huddled close, clinging to the idea that they would be safe so long as they stayed together.

But they weren't safe. If the terrorists didn't kill them, then thirst or starvation or exposure would.

"Do any of you have family nearby?" Jo asked.

Both of them shook their heads.

"What about food, water, medicine?" Jo asked.

"I brought some of my snacks from my room on the first floor." The tall girl pointed to a small grocery bag filled with chips and junk food. "And I had some water that I brought up too, but it's not cold anymore."

Jo examined the pitiful amount of supplies and assessed the situation. If Stacy had left with her friend to head to the cabin, then the pair could be anywhere by now. She might be able to pick up their trail once she returned to the mountain, but finding them in the city now would be like searching for a needle in a haystack.

And then Jo thought of all the parents who wouldn't be able to find their own children, and the worry that plagued them. But while their parents couldn't help these girls, Jo could.

"Put on some different clothes," Jo said, glancing to the three girls individually. "Both of you. Something that you can hike in. Do you all have sneakers or hiking boots?"

Both of them nodded again.

"Put them on," Jo said. "Grab enough clothes for three days, along with all of the non-perishable food that you have and all the water that you have. If you have any medications, you need to bring those as well, or if you have Advil or aspirin or ibuprofen, grab those too. Anything that's first-aid related. Pack it all into a backpack."

The girls nodded, but they didn't move, both of them standing entirely still.

Jo clapped her hands. "Let's go! Move it, girls!"

The sound of her voice triggered them into motion, and

they scurried around the room like frantic bunnies, hopping about.

Jo stepped out of the room, letting the girls pack, then the tall girl who lived on the first floor said she needed to grab some more things from her room.

"Come back up here when you're finished," Jo said.

"Thank you," the tall girl said. "Thank you so much for helping us. We didn't know what to do, we don't even know what's happening, and—"

"It's okay," Jo said. "Just hurry."

The tall girl nodded and then sprinted to the stairwell, moving with better coordination than her long, lanky body suggested.

Jo wasn't sure what she was going to do with these girls. Neither of them were prepared for what they were about to face when they stepped out into the city, and even if all of them survived the trip, she didn't know how they would survive the aftermath.

Because the fighting would eventually die down. And then it would be who knew how to hunt. Who knew what to look for and collect in the woods to eat? Who knew how to filter water to make it drinkable? Who could treat injuries and sew up a wound? Who could start a fire or build a shelter, or fire a weapon, or defend themselves against a threat that sought to take everything that they had made to survive the long storm of isolation?

That was where the real fight lay, and Jo hoped that the girls were quick learners. Because she couldn't carry them. She had her own family to worry about. It wasn't fair, but that's the way that it was.

When the girls were finally packed, Jo did a quick inspection of their bags and removed any non-essentials. They groaned as their make-up went into the trash, and Jo had them replace it with more socks and underwear. They'd be thanking her later.

With the packs filled with the best supplies that the girls had available, Jo walked them down to the first floor and then paused in the stairwell before they stepped outside and onto the campus.

"Out there, you listen to everything I say, and you do exactly what I tell you when I tell you to do it," Jo said, glad to see all of them scared. A little fear was good. It kept them alert, aware, and alive. "We will not stop moving unless I tell you. We won't have a lot of time for breaks."

"Where are we going?" the short girl asked. "Are we going to the police, the fire department? Is there a safe place—"

"There are no more safe places," Jo answered. "The only safe place is the one that you create."

The girls piped down. Neither of them had ever found themselves in trouble, not real trouble. Not the kind that would kill you if you slipped up. But she wasn't going to sugarcoat it for them. Jo had learned that watering things down only made people lazy. It was best to be informed and to know what you were getting yourself into in the first place.

"You'll see dead bodies," Jo said. "You'll see things that will make you want to curl up into a ball and cry. But you can't stop moving. You hear me? We have to press forward. We survive by moving on. It will be hard, but hard is better than dead. Or worse."

"Worse than what?" the short girl asked. "What could be worse than dead?" She laughed nervously, but the tall girl stared at the floor, her voice almost a whisper as she spoke aloud the same thought running through Jo's mind.

"Rape," the tall girl said. "Rape would be worse than dead."

The shorter girl shivered.

"Stay close to me," Jo said. "Where I move, you move, got it? You can survive. You can make it. But you have to want it more than the world that's trying to kill you. You have to be stronger, smarter, and faster than the hunter. Or you will die."

Jo let her words resonate with the girls, but she didn't linger much longer in the stairwell. She still had to find her daughter. She turned to the door, adjusted the rifle in her hands, and then glanced down at the light shining through the cracks of the stairwell door. She looked back at the girls, both of them with their hands on the straps of their packs, ready to run.

Jo lowered her sunglasses and then faced the door, reaching for the handle and taking a breath. "Let's go." She swung the door open, light flooding everyone's senses as she led the girls onto the campus.

It wasn't but ten yards from the building that gunfire popped somewhere nearby, and one of the girls screamed, suddenly stopping and shaking her head.

"I can't do this, I can't do this."

Jo turned and saw that it was the short girl. She was retreating toward the door, the tall girl trying to coax her forward.

"No!" She screamed louder, and then Jo heard the shouts of voices of men nearby. It was the shooters. The girl was giving away their position.

Jo rushed to the girl, her voice trembling with rage and hate. Hate for the girl and her weakness, hate for herself and thinking that she could save these little girls that were too stupid for their own good. "You stay here, and you die. Do you hear me? You stay and—No!"

The girl sprinted back into the stairwell, crying as she did it, the slam of the door shutting behind her akin to the nail in the coffin.

Jo looked to the tall girl who had stayed. "We need to move, and quickly." She moved forward, keeping her eyes ahead of her, searching for the threat. She heard the heavy breaths of the tall girl jogging to keep up. They were loud, but it was more about speed than stealth now. They had to get out of the firing range of the enemy. Because while she still couldn't see them, she could hear them, and they were getting closer. It was only a matter of time before they were brought into the crosshairs, and that was more of a gamble than Jo was willing to make.

10

Once Stacy and Melissa collected everything that they could find upstairs off the dead bodies, they returned to the first floor. More gunfire popped outside, and both Stacy and Melissa flinched. The enemy was still swarming outside, but Stacy knew that they couldn't hide here forever. Carefully, she moved toward the window.

"Stacy," Melissa said, her voice a harsh whisper even though they were the only ones in the building. "What are you doing?"

"I need to see where they are to know here to avoid." Stacy ducked low as the gunfire worsened, and now that most of the campus was awake, there was something even more horrifying sounding besides the shooting: screams.

Stacy arrived at the window in time to watch a flood of students sprinting wildly across the campus, no rhyme or reason to their movement other than the fact that they were trying to survive. But that instinct had stolen their ability to think about their next move, and because of that, they didn't have the forethought to know that they needed to run for cover. The only thing that mattered was getting as far away from the people trying to kill them as possible.

One by one, the students were shot. Some of them wallowed, alive but unable to move because of their injury, and others lay still once they hit the ground. All the while, the terrorists marched forward with the slow, steady progression of a parade.

When the gunmen reached the dying, the students stretched their arms up, a final plea for mercy. But their pleas were muted by the final kill shot.

Stacy turned away from the window, keeping her back to the wall. She was angry, and powerless, and fucking scared out of her mind.

Finally, Stacy rejoined Melissa in the darkness. "We need to leave. Now."

"What?" Melissa asked. "But those people are still out there. They're still killing people. They'll kill us if we—"

"We can't stay here." Stacy searched her friend's eyes, hoping to find some resolve, hoping that fear hadn't completely crippled her courage.

Melissa finally nodded. "Okay. So what's the plan?"

Stacy donned her pack. "We'll go out the back, then head toward the north gate and keep the library between us and the bulk of the fighting."

The pair lingered for a moment longer, and then Stacy turned to the door. "Stay close." She held the knife and shouldered open the door, the brightness of the sun causing her to lower her sunglasses.

The gunfire on the other side of the library was louder in the open air, and Stacy heard the screams between the deadly pop of the rifles that continued their deadly rain over the campus.

Stacy maintained a vigilant eye for any random fighters

that might have broken away from the main pack and periodically glanced back at Melissa, making sure she was keeping pace. She was struggling, but she was keeping up.

The more distance they put between themselves and the library, the more Stacy believed that they were going to make it. But that hope came crashing down when she heard the gunfire behind them.

Stacy twisted at the waist to glance behind her and saw three gunmen in pursuit.

Seeing the gunmen, hearing the gunshots, and knowing that those bullets were meant to kill them triggered something Stacy's mind. It shifted the plane of her reality, and suddenly the world exploded with brightness, color, and sensations. She felt the vibrations from her heel striking the pavement, and then the contrast when she moved to the grass.

Death and smoke and pollen graced her nostrils with every breath, and Stacy's heart pumped with the quickened pace of her feet, and before she realized it, she was twenty yards ahead of Melissa, her friend struggling to keep up.

And while other people may have let those instincts abandon their friends, Stacy forced herself to stop, turning around and grabbing hold of Melissa's outstretched hand.

With the enemy closing the gap, Stacy searched for cover. "Over there!" She saw the nearest building, which happened to be the performing arts building.

Stacy pulled Melissa through the building's entrance, the bullets cracking the glass along the entryway. "Into the theater, go!" Stacy shoved the door open with her shoulder and pointed down the aisle toward the stage as Melissa passed through. Stacy shut the door, then engaged the bottom locks. "Get behind the stage!"

Climbing up onto the stage and disappearing back behind

the curtain, Stacy glanced behind in time to see the animals pound on the doors and then shoot at the locks, forcing their way inside.

Behind the stage curtain it was completely dark, and Stacy grabbed hold of Melissa's hand, keeping quiet and praying the enemy would give up.

It was quiet for a minute after the doors had been knocked down, and then the darkness was penetrated by light. Stacy glanced between the curtains and saw the terrorists with lights, walking down the aisle and checking the rows of seats for their prey.

Stacy gripped her blade's handle. She wouldn't go down without a fight. At the very least she could surprise them, drive the blade into one of their chests. Maybe even grab the weapon and shoot the other terrorist before they died.

Through the crack in the curtain, Stacy saw the pair of gunmen gesture to the stage. They walked up slowly, guns aimed at the curtain, and Stacy knew that this was it.

But despite the fear of death, Stacy was calm. Perhaps it was because she wasn't alone. Maybe it was because she had made a choice to try and help when she could have run. Her father had always told her that a clean conscience led to a worry-free life. She always thought there was some truth in that.

Both terrorists were on the stage now. They wouldn't even have to open the curtain to kill them, just squeeze the trigger and tear them to bits. Stacy hoped it would be quick, and she didn't suffer like the dying students she saw on the lawn.

The medics who found her father after the wreck had told her the death had been quick. No suffering. It had been the one silver lining of the accident. And soon Stacy would see him again.

Unable to stare death down, Stacy shut her eyes, waiting for the sound of gunfire and the perpetual darkness. When the shots were fired, Stacy shuddered and Melissa screamed.

But after the gunfire ended, Stacy wasn't sure what happened. Had she died? Had it all ended just like that? Was the afterlife just more darkness?

It was the sound of footsteps that made her open her eyes, and she saw a pair of terrorists on the floor through the crack, their lights pointed back toward the empty audience chairs.

The curtain was pulled back, and the motion was so quick that Stacy raised the dagger to strike as Melissa screamed once more.

But even in the darkness, her eyes straining to see, Stacy knew the woman who stood above her.

"Mom?" Stacy asked.

Jo Mercer stood with the rifle in her hand, the whites of her eyes glowing in the darkness, her breathing heavy and accelerated. And then without warning, she dropped the weapon, fell to her knees, and wrapped Stacy in her arms.

Stacy let go of the blade and squeezed her mother back, the embrace involuntary. It was like a shipwrecked survivor who had managed to find a piece of driftwood to cling to and float. That's what her mother was. A life raft. Stacy didn't have to kick around in the ocean alone anymore. She was safe.

11

The heat had only gotten worse since he left The Village, and despite the cool mountain breeze that graced the roadway every now and again, Deputy Gus Moynihan had already sweated through his uniform.

The horse he rode offered a disgruntled whinny, and Moynihan wiped the sweat collecting on his brow and around his eyes. "I hear that, boy."

The animal's rhythmic clapping against the pavement had become a lullaby that was putting Moynihan to sleep the longer that he was forced to ride. All he wanted to do was pull the horse over and sit in the shade.

But the sheriff had been adamant about getting help, and that he should only stop if it were absolutely necessary.

Moynihan considered taking off the bulletproof vest. It wasn't like he was going to get shot out here amongst his own people. But that had been another one of the sheriff's strict rules, and somehow the sheriff always knew when he lied. It was like the man had a sixth sense, or maybe Moynihan was just bad at lying. It was probably the latter.

Gus steered the animal toward the edge of the road,

trying to catch as much of the shade from the trees along the way as he could. But with the sun at its highest point in the sky, shadows and darkness were few and far between.

Thirsty, Gus reached for the canteen that he brought and cooled his tongue, swishing the water around his dry mouth and letting it linger before he finally swallowed. Like most of the other deputies under the sheriff's command, he had lived on the mountain his entire life, but even after all of those years, he still hadn't grown used to the brutal heat that could plague the countryside.

Along the road, Gus had passed through the other two communities on his way down the mountain, and found that they were having the same kind of trouble as The Village. No power, no communications, and nothing but broken-down cars littering their roadways.

Gus did his best to assure the folks that came up to him that Sheriff Turner was busy making preparations, but that did little to calm their fears. For those that he ran into that couldn't take care of themselves, he pointed them in the sheriff's direction where they would be able to wait out the storm.

Most of the folks that he'd come across were just scared of what might happen to them and their families. They had questions about what was happening and when it would be over. And while Gus couldn't calm all of their fears, he tried to calm as many of them as he could.

Gus tried not to lie, but he omitted certain truths. A person's mind could only take so much before it collapsed under the weight of too much stress. And the fact was no one really knew exactly what was happening. He understood that Joanna Mercer had prepared for something like this, but that didn't mean she was right about everything.

Or maybe he just didn't want to believe she was right about everything. That wish was probably the latter too.

But it had been at least six miles since the last time that Gus had seen anyone, the road empty on its curving path toward the Army Reserve Depot. He hoped that his brother would be able to provide answers that would help fill in the blanks of what they didn't know, and he hoped those answers would ease his worried thoughts.

Gus had lived a happy life that hadn't brought him much hardship. But deep down he always believed that his good fortune would run out and he would be forced to pay the piper, because Gus held the firm belief that life was all about balance.

Bad things happened, and good things happened. Sometimes a bunch of bad things happened in a row, and sometimes a bunch of good things happened in a row. But eventually the streak ended.

Gus had been riding a good streak for the past twenty-five years. Looking back on his life, he couldn't remember a single instance that was unbearable. A little uncomfortable maybe, a few downbeats here and there, but the majority of his life had been nothing but happiness and sunshine.

From beneath the shadow of his cowboy hat, Gus peeked up at the sky and saw clouds starting to gather, and he hoped that his good streak would hold out for a little bit longer.

Because in the end, that's all anybody was trying to do. Just make those good days last as long as they could, and then hope that when they ended, they had the strength to survive the bad days as the scales balanced back to zero.

The last sign for the Army Depot was up ahead, and Gus knew that he was getting close. But as he got closer to the sign, he pulled back on the reins. "Whoa, boy. Whoa."

Black scorch marks ran up the front of the sign, and a few

bullet holes dented the metal. Gus glanced around, the road and woods empty.

"Keep your eyes open," Gus said, whispering to the horse, and then clucked his tongue and nudged the animal forward with his heels.

Gus drew his weapon when he saw the charred remains of a van and the smashed remnants of the gate that it had collided with. The wreckage made it difficult to pass, but Gus steered the horse around the worst of it.

Two soldiers lay on the pavement, as well as three other men whose attire looked more at home in the Middle East.

Gus dismounted the horse and then tied off the animal by the gate. He didn't want to become a sitting target should there be more of those extremists still lingering around.

Signs of the fight between the pair of forces were present all over the compound, and judging from the number of shell casings that Gus was forced to step around, it looked as though the fighting was heavily concentrated at the gate.

The Army Depot was a small facility. It wasn't a base or an armory, merely a training ground for soldiers who came up for the weekend that were part of the reserves. The place was nothing but a few administrative buildings, a live fire range with a warehouse for building clearing exercises, a mess hall, and some barracks for soldiers to sleep on the weekends.

But the further Gus penetrated the small base, the more he was convinced that it had been abandoned. It was the motor pool that gave it away. Half of the vehicles were gone, which probably meant they were either stolen or taken by the terrorists who had attacked the place.

Unless the enemy that ambushed them had some heavy artillery or just a massive fighting force, there was no way they could have gotten past the compound's defenses. And that led Gus to believe that most of the fighting force had already left, which would explain the reason why only half the vehicles were still inside the depot.

But all the cars and trucks that Gus had passed on his way down the road were broken down and not working. How could some of the vehicles here start up? And why hadn't he seen them on the way down?

Maybe the military had prepared for something like this. Perhaps their Humvees and armored cars were able to survive the EMP blast, and perhaps they took the bypass around the base of the mountain. It was the fastest route to the city. Maybe they were already helping people.

Gus had hoped that he would find his brother down here, and while Gus knew that he was more than capable of handling himself, after seeing the bodies at the gates, he saw the armor of that hope crack.

Nothing was more powerful of a reminder of mortality than the sight of death. And those fallen soldiers at the gate meant that they were not invincible. And neither was Gus's brother.

But with no one home, Gus decided to scrounge for supplies. He knew that The Village and the rest of the communities on the mountain would still need food, water, and medicine, and he bet that the mess hall had more than a few MREs lying around.

Gus made it one step toward the building when he felt the cold steel press into the back of his neck, and he froze.

He slowly raised his hands, and when the gunman behind him instructed him to throw the pistol on the ground in his broken English, he did so.

And then, around him, Gus saw others emerge from buildings, dressed like the foreign men near the gate. The kind of men who would strap a bomb to their chests and kill anyone that didn't agree with their way of thinking. Killing people who did nothing wrong.

Gus stared at the murderers as they surrounded him, knowing full well that his good streak had finally come to an end.

o held onto Stacy for a long time, the pair on their knees together in the darkness. She couldn't believe she had found her daughter. She couldn't believe she was alive. And she couldn't believe how close they had come to losing one another.

Jo finally loosened her tight hold on Stacy and then leaned back to get a better look at her daughter, which was tricky in such darkness. "Are you all right?"

"Yeah," Stacy answered, her voice breathless. "How did you find me?"

"I went to your dorm room, but you weren't there," Jo answered, brushing her daughter's hair back behind her ear. "Some people in your building said that you had left with your roommate and headed into the city. That's where I was heading when I saw you running from those men."

Stacy glanced at the dead terrorists, and then to the tall, lanky girl that had followed her mother into the theater. She recognized her from the dorm, but she couldn't remember her name.

"You're sure you're okay?" Jo asked, repeating the question with the authoritative tone that Stacy was more familiar with.

"Yes." Stacy removed Jo's arms from her shoulders and then stood, picking up the knife as she did. "I don't know how many more of those people are on the campus, but we should leave before they show up again."

Jo lingered on her knees a moment longer, realizing that their tender moment was over. Her tone had been harsher than she intended. She stood and then saw the girl behind her daughter.

"My roommate," Stacy said. "Melissa."

"Hi," Melissa said, raising a hesitant hand to wave.

Jo looked at her daughter. "Can she keep up?"

Stacy tilted her head to the side and then gestured to the girl behind Jo. "Can she?"

Jo knew that it was no use arguing with her daughter, and the only thing that mattered now was getting off the campus and out of the city alive. But Jo hadn't anticipated the additional bodies that were now attached to their group.

They were all just kids. Even Stacy, with all of the survival knowledge she had learned, she was still just a girl. She wasn't acting scared, but Jo knew that fear liked to root itself deep, only exposing itself out of absolute necessity.

"We're going to leave the city," Jo said. "There are more of these gunmen out there, and they will shoot on sight if they find us. We need to move quickly, and we cannot stop. We stop, and we die. Does everyone understand?"

Nods answered back, but Jo saw the concerned stares and the eyes that continually glanced down at the dead terrorists. She wasn't sure if all of them would survive, but she hoped that they would. She hoped that they would be able to make it because Jo didn't want the added weight of slaughtered innocence on her conscience.

"All right," Jo said. "Let's go." She let the girls leave the stage first, but grabbed Stacy's arm and held her back, shoving a pistol into her daughter's hand. "It's better than the knife. You still remember how to use it?"

Stacy stared at the weapon for a moment, and just when Jo thought that she would need to give her daughter a quick recap lesson, she watched Stacy flick the safety off, pull the slide back, examine the bullet in the chamber, and then disengage the magazine, inspect it, and then reload it into the weapon. "I remember."

Jo raised an eyebrow. "Let's hope your aim is still as good as your confidence."

The kids clustered by the exit of the building, all of them waiting nervously for Jo's instructions. Jo suspected that she would have to instruct them on several things on their way out of the city, but she took the time to tell them what she could.

"Anyone know how to handle a weapon?" Jo asked, but no one raised their hands. "Okay then. Stacy, you'll watch the rear of the group while I handle the front. Anyone that doesn't have a gun in their hands will stay between myself and Stacy the entire way. You don't go faster than me, and you don't go slower than her. Got it?"

Both girls nodded nervously, the muscles along their faces and necks twitching with a wild anxiousness that was plastered on each of their faces. She was glad to see that they were scared. Fear was a sign that you were smart enough to recognize your own mortality. And if you didn't want to die, then you tended to make decisions that prevented that outcome. It made Jo think that they might be able to make it through the city after all.

Jo hesitated before she spoke again, unsure of how the others were going to handle the next bit of news she was going to tell them, but she knew that she couldn't give them any false hope, and she wanted them to understand that their survival was her only concern.

"We don't have time to help people," Jo said. "You might see someone who's hurt or in trouble, but none of you have the training or the skills to assist." She paused to see if anyone would speak up. "So no matter how awful things get in those streets, you stay between Stacy and me. I will not chase after you if you leave the group. I will not linger behind to carry you if you fall. You stand and move on your own two feet, or you don't move at all. Do I make myself clear?"

Two quiet yes ma'ams answered back, and Jo took that as a good sign that all of them would do as she said. But when she looked to Stacy and saw the hardened stare of her daughter, she knew that Stacy didn't agree with the philosophy. But she understood what was happening now, and the reality of the way the world was heading, so she kept quiet.

"Let's move." Jo positioned herself by the door, the rest of the group huddling close behind her, and she pushed the door open and then stepped outside, moving swiftly with the caravan of college students on her tail. She fought the urge to check behind her and keep an eye on Stacy. She had to follow her own advice. She had to trust that her daughter knew what to do.

Outside of the walls of the college, Jo decided to keep north of the city, remembering that the last time she had seen the enemy combing the streets, they had been working in a grid-like fashion heading south. She thought that heading through a part of town that they had already hit would be a safe bet to keep them alive.

The terrorists had left the northern section of the city in

ruins, having torched some of the buildings that was still smoldering with fires.

Bodies, glass, and bullet casings lined the black pavement. But it was the bright clothes of the dead along the pavement that were out of place.

Jo weaved around the bodies, the city transformed into a graveyard after the terrorists had laid waste to its citizens. She kept a good, steady pace, staying north and moving due west toward the city's perimeter. She would feel better when they were off the streets and would be far more comfortable under the cover of trees.

It was hard to pinpoint the location of an ambush within the city because there were too many buildings and structures to manipulate the sound. It was easy to sneak up on someone on concrete, harder to do that in the untamed woods.

The stink of the dead was already starting to rise from the streets. Every new wave of hot rot that graced Jo's nostrils made her gag.

Jo was no stranger to death and no stranger to killing. But what she saw amongst the broken glass and bullet casings on the streets was a slaughter.

The deaths of all of these people served no purpose other than to conflate the whims of the madmen who had ordered his soldiers to carry out his dark deeds.

Every single body that Jo passed on the street had friends and family that would never see them again. Fathers lost daughters and sons. Mothers lost the same. Children lost parents. And wives lost husbands.

Jo couldn't hide the tremble of her arms at the last thought as Danny flooded into her mind. She could see him as clear as day as if he had never disappeared. It was strange at how often he would come to her when she least expected him to arrive.

And he was always smiling, that grin of his so full and exposing the overbite that the braces from his childhood never entirely fixed. "Hey, Jo."

Sometimes Jo would answer back, sometimes their conversations would last for hours out in the woods where they could be alone together, and sometimes she would just sit there and look at him, remembering the touch of his hand, the taste of his kiss, and the weight of his body when he lay on top of her in their bed.

Jo would do anything to get back all the moments that she lost with Danny. All of the stupid little things that most people take for granted every day. She wanted to yell at him for leaving the dirty dishes in the sink; to laugh at him when he rolled off the couch after falling asleep. She wanted to stay embraced in his arms after a long day when the only thing that could make her feel better was his touch.

But Jo wasn't in the woods now, and Danny's distraction blinded her from the moment, and her present reality was suddenly upended by the sound of gunfire.

By the time Jo finally saw the terrorists up ahead, they were less than fifty yards from Jo's position. Out of instinct, she ducked behind the cover of a nearby car, and without looking back, she screamed an order for everyone else to do the same. "Get down!"

The vibrations from bullets striking the front of the car traveled all the way to the rear bumper and into her right shoulder that lay pressed up against the rusted metal. Jo remained crouched and worked her way around the back corner of the vehicle, then quickly lined up her shot and squeezed the trigger.

The terrorist dropped, but it was the only person that Jo

was able to bring down before retaliatory gunfire tucked her back behind the car. And it was here that she saw what her distraction had cost her.

The tall girl that Jo had pulled from the dorm room, the one that followed her thinking that she would be safe, was on her back with Stacy trying to stop the bleeding from the bullet she took in the gut.

Jo watched her daughter's concentrated effort, but she knew that the girl was a goner. A gunshot wound to the gut, out here, in the middle of this, almost meant certain death. No one here was equipped enough to handle such an injury. It was all Jo could do to make sure that the rest of them didn't receive a similar wound.

She paused, waiting for a lull in gunfire, and then emerged from the other side of the sedan's trunk, catching the terrorists off guard and killing one of them, which was enough to stop their advance forward. Jo seized the opportunity when they stopped moving.

The nearest building was some restaurant on the right side of the street. A pair of bodies lay near the front door, but there was adequate cover in the form of other vehicles for them to make it to the restaurant unscathed.

Jo turned back to her daughter, Stacy's hands still over the wound on the tall girl, who was now motionless on the asphalt. "Stacy!"

Stacy whipped her head to her mother, glancing over her shoulder so Jo could only see her dark eyes and the blood that speckled her cheek like crimson freckles, her black hair matted to her forehead with sweat. For one brief flash, Jo thought she was looking at Danny.

Jo said nothing else as she pointed toward the restaurant, but when her daughter didn't move, Jo maneuvered to the opposite side of the car.

"Stacy, you have to go," Jo said, her voice panicked and hurried like the sound of gunfire ejecting from the rifles.

"I'm not leaving her," Stacy said, her hands slick with blood.

Jo picked up the girl's wrist from the ground and checked for a pulse, and felt nothing. "She's dead." She dropped the wrist and then grabbed her daughter's jaw, forcing those dark brown eyes that were now red with tears. "She's dead, Stacy. You can't save her. But you can keep her alive." She gestured to Melissa, and Stacy slowly turned away from her mother.

Bullets ricocheted off the side of a truck, skipping onto the ground before finding a nearby tire, and the close proximity of death helped pull Stacy from the throes of confusion and disillusion. She removed her hands from the dead girl's stomach and picked up the pistol that she had dropped on the ground.

"I'll give you cover in three-round spurts!" Jo returned to her position back behind the sedan and then looked back to her daughter and her friend, both of them poised to run, looking down at the dead girl they were leaving behind. "Go!"

Jo emerged from the cover of the sedan, her crosshairs quickly locating the tops of the heads of the enemy, and she pulled the trigger. The recoil of the weapon matched the terrorists ducking back behind cover before emerging again like a game of deadly whack-a-mole.

But Jo kept her focus on the deadly enemy ahead and didn't turn to look to see if her daughter had made it to the building. It was all about commitment now, and Jo knew that if that commitment wavered, then she might lose her line of sight on the enemy that meant to gun them all down.

"Mom!"

Jo turned, the shrill scream breaking through the ringing in her ears. She saw Stacy at the door. They had made it.

With her daughter now in a safe position, Jo returned her attention back to the enemy. She volleyed a few more shots, but was cut short on her retreat by one of the terrorists who had snuck past undetected.

Because the terrorist had the drop on her, Jo could only charge forward, throwing all of her weight into knocking the terrorist on his back before he had a chance to fire his weapon.

The pavement came at them fast, Jo crying out when her elbow struck the hard surface. But despite the pain, she managed to keep her wits and drove her knee into the terrorist's groin, disabling him on the ground.

She retrieved her weapon, put a round in his chest, and then hurried toward the restaurant door, a realization dawning on her when she looked back at the terrorists chasing them. The door and glass of the restaurant weren't going to stop the enemy from chasing them down. They would just follow, giving themselves more opportunities to kill Stacy and the other girl.

Jo knew that the best chance for her daughter's survival was to make sure that those bastards never made it through the door. And to do that, she would have to stand and face the enemy that threatened to tear her family apart.

Jo turned to stand her ground. She raised the rifle to shoot the remaining three terrorists that were chasing them down and squeezed the trigger, but the fatigue from the fight and the heat of the moment cost Jo her aim, and the bullet missed wide left.

She lined up again, this time the terrorists shooting back, but because of their hastened pace on the run, they missed her as well. But the gap was closing. Jo knew that she couldn't take them all out before one of them managed to shoot her. She only hoped that it would give Stacy and her friend time to run. She hoped that Stacy would understand and that she would tell Amelia that her mother had tried to keep her promise of coming home, but circumstances wouldn't allow it.

And then when Jo squeezed the trigger on her rifle once more, another roar of gunfire erupted, louder than anything that her weapon could have produced, and she watched as the remaining three terrorists were torn apart by bullets.

13

When the terrorists dropped to the ground, the threat neutralized, Jo remained paralyzed from the shock that she was still standing. But she slowly lowered the rifle's scope from her eye and saw more guns aimed at her, the soldiers who carried them barking orders for her to drop her weapon. And she did. Because they were American troops.

"On the ground! On the ground now!" The lead soldier kept a steady hand on the rifle, dressed from head to toe in his battle fatigues and body armor, a unit of at least fifty men behind him to ensure that his orders were followed.

Jo raised her arms and dropped to her knees. They were not the enemy, but she needed to convince them that neither was she.

"Stay put, ma'am," the soldier said, his voice calmer now that she was on the ground and unarmed. "Are you alone?"

"My daughter and her friend are in the restaurant behind me," Jo answered. "My daughter is armed with a pistol."

"Two inside, Corporal, only one armed," the soldier said, relaying orders to one of his men. "Bring them out."

Boots hurried by, and Jo felt the gloved hands of the soldier pat her down.

"Do you have any other weapons on you, ma'am?" the soldier asked, his Southern drawl and tone oddly cordial considering the circumstances.

"A hunting knife on my left hip."

Seemingly satisfied with the pat down, the soldier grunted and then lifted Jo off the pavement and stood her up against one of the cars. "You hurt?"

"Just some scrapes and bruises," Jo answered. "Nothing substantial."

The soldiers sent in to retrieve Stacy and Melissa returned, one of the soldiers now holding Stacy's gun.

"Two civilians and a pistol," the soldier said. "Just like she said, Lieutenant."

The lieutenant turned the weapon over in his hand while the rest of his unit continued a sweep down the road. The dark lenses of his glasses concealed his eyes from Jo, and she couldn't tell what he was looking at. "Lot of firepower for one woman." He repositioned his head to where Jo thought he was looking right at her. "Where you from?"

"Rebel Mountain," Jo answered. "I have property up there. When I realized what happened, I came to get my daughter."

The lieutenant drew in a big breath and sighed. "All right. I'm going to have a platoon get you over into the safe zone, and we'll collect your weapons." He nodded to one of his men and then turned away.

Jo stepped forward quickly, knowing that if they were to be stuck in some camp in the city, it would most certainly mean their suffering. "Lieutenant, wait—"

Jo's bold step forward was met with resistance as the two soldiers reached for her and pulled her back. But it caught the lieutenant's attention.

"I need to get back home," Jo said, trying to sound reasonable and calm. "I have another daughter up there with a friend."

"It's not safe out in the wild right now, ma'am. I have scouts telling me that there are more of these terrorists roaming the countryside, picking people off one by one. You'll be safer in camp."

"I don't care about safe," Jo said. "I care about bringing my family back together."

The lieutenant studied Jo, his sunglasses and stoic gaze preventing her from reading him. "I can't spare any men to escort you back to your property. If you go, you'll go alone."

"I can handle myself," Jo said.

The lieutenant cracked a slight smile and then nodded. "I suspect you can." He nodded to the men holding her. "Let her go, and give her weapons back to her. She'll need them."

"Do you have any men left at the Army Reserve depot?" Jo asked.

"A few to keep the place manned, but with our communications down, I don't have any way to check back with them," the lieutenant answered, and then paused. "I know you think it might be safer up on the mountain, but if things get hairy for you, we'll have a command post set up on the city's west entrance by the river. That's where we'll be if you run into trouble."

"Thanks," Jo said.

"Stay safe out there." They stepped back and waved his men forward. "Let's move!"

The rest of the soldiers passed by, weaving through the broken-down vehicles and cars, while Jo gathered the gear that she dropped on her sprint. She watched as the soldiers turned south on the next cross street continuing their sweep of the city. Once they were out of sight, she turned back to Stacy and Melissa. "Everyone ready?"

Stacy stepped forward. "What about the girl?"

"Who?" Jo asked.

Stacy pointed to the street where the dead college student lay.

"We can't do anything for her," Jo said, and then made it three more steps before Stacy bellowed her dissent.

"We have to at least bury her!"

Jo whirled around, her blood still heated from the fire-fight. "We have to get home to your sister! I'm not wasting time burying some girl I don't know."

It was a rant filled with all of the hate and fear and aggression that Jo had bottled up inside of her, releasing it at the most inopportune time against a daughter whose relationship with her was spotty at best.

"I'm sorry," Jo said, shutting her eyes and shaking her head, a sudden spat of vertigo causing her to take a step sideways. "I didn't mean—"

"I know you've always been a cold, hard bitch," Stacy said. "Guess time only made it worse."

Stacy marched ahead, leaving Jo alone with Melissa, who lingered behind for a moment and then followed Stacy, leaving Jo alone.

The journey back through the city was uneventful save for the occasional echo of gunfire somewhere to the south, and it made Jo remember the lieutenant's words about the terrorist units moving through the countryside, which confirmed her fear of a nationwide attack.

Once they were amongst the cover of the forest, Jo grew more at ease, but Stacy remained distant and cold.

Jo looked to her daughter moving forward with the ease

of a person who had spent her time in the wild, though she was struggling a little bit.

There was so much that Jo wanted to ask her about her experiences at school, but she didn't know when would be the right time. Probably never.

Halfway back to The Village they had to stop to rest, Melissa practically collapsing from exhaustion. And while they rested, Jo watched the edge of their perimeter, scanning the woods and rocky bluff of the mountainside, which were become steeper the higher they climbed.

"I can't keep going like this," Melissa said, gasping between sips of water. "I mean this is ridiculous. This can't be what people actually do in their spare time for fun."

"Survival isn't supposed to be fun," Jo said, shooting back the retort before she returned to her guard post.

"What hurts?" Stacy asked, ignoring Jo's comment.

Jo kept watch while Stacy coddled the girl, and the longer the girl kept them idle, the longer it would take for them to get back to Amelia. And Jo wasn't about to let some stranger put her daughter in danger.

Jo walked over to the girls, Stacy examining Melissa's foot, which was red and starting to show signs of blisters. Melissa grimaced when Stacy touched it.

"The sweat in your socks are causing your feet to rub against your shoe," Stacy said. "Grab a fresh pair out of your pack, and we'll bandage the blisters that are forming. It'll still hurt, but it might prevent them from getting worse."

Jo tapped her foot impatiently. "Your sister is waiting on us."

Stacy glanced up at her mother. "And?"

"And we need to keep moving," Jo answered.

"We're almost done." Stacy applied the bandages, and then

Melissa put on a fresh pair of dry socks. With the friend distracted, Jo pulled Stacy aside.

"She's slowing us down," Jo said.

"What do you want me to do?" Stacy asked, keeping her voice hushed. "She's moving as fast as she can. And I'm not going to leave her behind."

Jo glanced from Melissa back to her daughter, then leaned closer. "What you're doing is nice, but when push comes to shove, you might have to make a choice. And that choice might involve saving family over friends. I need to know that you'll make the right choice. Because I will choose you and your sister every time. No matter what."

"It doesn't have to be that black and white," Stacy said. "It never has."

Jo watched Stacy return to her friend, wishing that she could make her daughter understand. She hoped that her daughter would never be forced into that kind of a choice, but they were now in a world where those choices would have to be made. And Jo only hoped that when Stacy was put in that position that she would remember that family mattered most.

Jo gave the girl five more minutes before she forced them to press forward, and while there was still heavy breathing coming from everyone hiking up the mountain, Melissa no longer complained save for the few grunts of concentration that Jo recognized. They were the familiar sounds of someone pushing themselves beyond the limits of their capacity. It was the sounds of someone reaching for something greater than themselves.

Maybe the girl would make it after all.

Because they didn't have to stop anymore for breaks, they maintained a good pace the rest of the trip and returned to The Village before sundown.

Seeing the town, Jo broke out into a jog, Stacy running alongside her as the pair of Mercer women emerged from the forest and stepped out onto The Village streets.

Jo didn't break stride until she reached Mags' store and then stepped inside, finding Mags in her natural position at the register and then saw Amelia step through the back door, her face a little sunburnt and sweaty, but completely unharmed.

"Mom!" Amelia smiled brightly and then sprinted toward her mother. Jo met the girl halfway, scooping her off the floor and into her arms. "You made it back!"

Jo squeezed Amelia tight, thankful to feel the warmth of her daughter in her arms again, then kissed her cheeks. "Yes. I made it back."

"Hey, Em."

Amelia squealed and then wiggled free from her mother. "Stacy!" She sprinted toward her sister, the elation genuine from the sisterly reunion.

It was the first time that Jo had seen them together since Stacy left for college last fall. She had forgotten what they looked like together, and it was a feeling she was thankful to experience once more, despite the circumstances.

"Hey, Stacy," Mags said, stepping around the corner and giving the girl a hug and a kiss. "Look at you. The city agreed with you."

"Not as much as I thought it would," Stacy said.

"I'm so glad that you're back!" Amelia said, then turned to her mother. "Do you think that we can go home now?"

"Yes," Jo said. "But I need to go and speak with the sheriff before I do." She looked at Stacy. "I'll be back in a minute."

Jo left her daughters to catch up and then hurried down the street and toward the sheriff's station. She needed to tell Mike what she saw, and she needed to make sure that her advice was followed. Because people were coming to destroy all of them.

There was no one on guard outside of the sheriff's station, and Jo let herself in, hearing Mike's voice coming from his office in the back.

With the sun starting to set, the only source of light inside the building came from a lantern in Mike's office, and she found him speaking to Deputy Furst, the pair's discussion hushed even though they were the only two in the building.

Jo stood in the doorway, keeping her presence unknown until Mike saw her.

It was his reaction that brought a smile to her face, and despite what she had seen and experienced in the city, she was happy to see him.

"Are you all right?" Mike asked. "Where's Stacy?"

"With Amelia and Mags," Jo answered.

Mike nodded. The smile was gone entirely from his face now. "How bad was it?"

Jo took a breath before she told him the whole story. By the time that she finished, she thought that his face would be permanently set in that disgusted scowl. It was an ugly look. And he wasn't an ugly man.

Mike turned away and walked back to his desk. His chair groaned as he sat down, but Deputy Furst was the one to break the silence.

"Do you think they'll come to The Village?" Furst asked. He was a middle-aged man, only a few years younger than Mike.

"The military I ran into said they had reports of more groups in the countryside, going from town to town, killing people," Jo said. "I imagine it's only a matter of time before they come here." She looked from Furst back to Mike. "I've seen what these guys can do. They definitely have some kind of military training. And military grade weapons. I don't think most of our folks will do well against a well-skilled militant group. Not with their hunting rifles."

Mike nodded. "We'll grab some of our assault weapons out of storage." He gestured to Furst. "I'll leave that to you."

"Yes, sir," Furst said, then left.

After the deputy was gone, Jo stepped farther into the office, arms crossed as she stared at Mike, who rubbed his forehead in the way folks did whenever they were burdened with a weight more significant than their ability to carry. But Mike was stronger than he thought. At least Jo hoped he was.

"You all right?" Jo asked.

Mike lowered his hand, his forehead a light pink from where he rubbed. He was quiet for a minute, and Jo wasn't sure he heard her.

"Mike, you—"

"I'm fine," Mike said. "Just a little tired is all."

Jo nodded. "It's been one of those days."

Mike smiled. "Yeah." He took a breath and then leaned his hip against his desk. "What are you going to do now?"

"Take my girls back to the cabin," Jo said.

Mike raised his eyebrows. "And then what?"

Jo frowned. "What do you mean?"

Mike pushed off his desk. "We could use your help around here. You've been living off grid for the past four years, and I'm sure you have a few pointers you could show us."

Jo hesitated. "I don't want to get involved."

"Why not?"

"Because it's not my responsibility," Jo answered, become more defensive. "My only priority is to take care of my family."

116

"And what about all the families here, Jo?" Mike stepped closer. "They never expected something like this to happen."

"Part of preparation is anticipating what will go wrong," Jo said. "It's not my fault that people didn't see this coming. Not everyone will survive this."

Mike slammed his fists on the table, rattling the dense wood as if it were nothing more than flimsy balsa wood. "Christ, Jo, I know this isn't some theoretical game, all right? I can see what's happening. I'm not fucking blind." He quickly spun around and moved toward the window.

In all the time that Jo had known Mike, he had never been the kind to lose his head. He had never been someone who couldn't be trusted with a hard truth. But she had never seen him like this.

"My bedside manner has never been my strong suit," Jo said. "I'm sorry."

Mike shook his head and then turned back to face her. "No. I'm sorry. It's not your fault." He planted both fists on his desk and hunched forward. "Gus never came back from the Reserve Depot at the mountain's base. I don't know if he's alive, and I don't know if I have reinforcements coming."

"Your reinforcements are already in the city," Jo said. "I ran into the reserve soldiers after I pulled Stacy from the school."

Mike nodded, staring at the oak desk.

Jo studied Mike's face and saw that all of the angst that he'd been experiencing was from the potential loss of a friend and a deputy. "Some of the roads might have been blocked. He might have stayed to help people. You don't know what happened for sure."

Mike looked at her but only nodded. After a moment of silence, he pushed himself off the desk and moved closer to Jo. "You're right that the people in this town aren't your responsibility. They're mine. And I'd be a fool if I didn't try and get the best help for them that I could." He smiled and then took a breath. "Just think about it, okay?"

Jo nodded, but still guarded her feelings carefully. "Thanks for looking out for Amelia."

"Of course," Mike replied.

She smiled, and he smiled, and when she turned to leave, he called out to her one last time.

"Jo," Mike said. "Was it really as bad as you said down there?"

"No," Jo answered. "It was worse."

*M*uhammed was patient. While his men had wanted to attack the town the moment that they arrived, he forced them to wait.

"It's dark," Zahid said, unable to sit still as he fidgeted with his rifle. "You said we would attack at nightfall."

Muhammed kept his eyes on the town, watching, waiting for anything that might surprise him once they made their way down the road. "I also said that we would wait until my command to attack." He peeled his eyes away from the town only for a moment, staring at his brother with the tenacity of a man with a divine purpose and the strength to bring that purpose to fruition. "And I have not given my command."

Zahid bowed his head and remained silent while Muhammed returned to his study of the town. He was no fool. He knew that the people of this country wouldn't go quietly. He knew that most of them were armed, and he knew that most of them were competent with a weapon.

This was a different mission than what the cells were assigned in the cities, filled with people who had grown lazy from the modern conveniences. They weren't fighters. But out here there were outcasts, rebels looking for a fight.

It was why Muhammed had gone to the reserve depot first. He had anticipated a more substantial fight, but when he arrived and saw that most of their forces were gone, he assumed that they had left to go and help the city at the base of the mountain. He turned their absence into his good fortune.

"Send him down," Muhammed said.

Zahid barked the orders down the line, and then Muhammed turned toward the town and waited. He and his men had been outside the town for the past three hours studying the town's movements, getting a feel for their defenses, their people, the layout of the community.

From what Muhammed saw, it was a small mountain village. Less than five hundred people. But even though the town wasn't highly populated for its size, the people were still spread out, making its eradication difficult. So he needed to consolidate the people in the area, bring them out of their homes and their hovels, lead them into an open space where it would be easier for his men to kill them. And he hoped that his bait would lure them out.

Muhammed watched as the deputy they captured from the Army Depot stepped onto the main street. They kept his mouth gagged and his hands tied behind his back. Blood-stains marked his cheeks from the beating he took after Muhammed had questioned him.

It wasn't difficult to break a man. All you needed to do was push the right buttons. And there was one universal button. Pain.

A few cuts in the right places and the deputy had told Muhammed every town from the base to the top of the mountain. Muhammed and his men would go to each city, setting their villages to the flame and bringing an end to their meaningless lives, which they didn't hold sacred. These people held nothing sacred. It was the reason they would die. And it would be Muhammed that swung the sword to pass the sentence and end their suffering.

* * *

THE ROPES MADE it challenging to move, not that Gus would have been able to move quickly without them. Every step forward was agonizing, sending a wave of pain up his right side. The pain was like a thousand needles being stabbed into his flesh.

Every breath he drew in through his nose triggered a very quiet whistling. He figured it was because his nose was broken. The only good thing about the pain was that he couldn't smell the blood and piss anymore. He had wet himself after the third round of beatings by the terrorists that had captured him at the Army Depot.

When Gus saw those men and the rifles bearing down on him, he was convinced that he was a dead man. But he never would have guessed that his enemy would have kept him alive to question him.

And every answer that Gus offered, every truth that left his lips, filled him with a shame that made him long for death.

Because when they ordered him to throw down his weapon, he had done so, and he knew that was his first mistake. He should have fired his gun and forced them to kill him, just like he had seen in the movies when a hero was faced with an impossible situation.

It was a romantic thought, but the reality of being

surrounded by men who wanted to kill you and were trained to do it sucked the wind out of those sails fast.

Gus knew the people in town. They were good, honest folks. And no matter how loud he screamed or jumped or cried out, he knew that they wouldn't be able to understand him until it was too late. The gag prevented him from giving any type of warning.

And when the first few people stepped out, guns aimed at him, he jumped and trembled and tried to point to the woods where he had last seen the terrorists grouped together before he was pushed down the road.

Because maybe there was a chance, the slightest, minuscule opportunity for him to warn them. But looking at their confused expressions as they walked toward him, Gus knew that they weren't going to live. He had brought the shadow of death with him.

The terrorists came from all sides, the small unit using the element of surprise and their automatic weapons to mow everyone down, including the pair of men that had come to Gus's aid.

Gus dropped to the ground, and he lay there on his back next to the corpse of the man who had tried to help him. The bullet that killed him had sliced the top of his scalp off, blood spilling from the open wound.

And while the fight raged on above him, the soundtrack of death played by rifles and screams, Gus remained on the pavement next to a man who had been his friend. A man whom he had gone to school with and played on the baseball team in high school. Gus had attended the man's wedding, had seen how happy he looked when his bride walked down the aisle.

Gus remembered that the man's wife had a baby a few

months ago. A little girl. Healthy and happy the last he'd heard.

But now the man was dead. He wouldn't hold his little girl again. He wouldn't be able to hear her laugh. He wouldn't be able to do anything because he was dead. That's all that there was now. Just death and the sounds of horror coming from the town.

But Gus never looked away from his friend's eyes, because as much pain as his body was giving him, as much distress that all of this was causing, there was no greater torture than staring at the lifeless eyes of a man whom he considered a friend. And listening to the horrors of the hell descending upon the people that he had been charged with protecting, Gus deserved every bit of torture that he received.

15

The darkness made it difficult to see down the road. The light from the lantern in Mike's hand only penetrated the dark for a few feet before the night swallowed it up. Mike didn't like that the darkness was winning.

The longer he stood there on the road, the more convinced Mike became that something had happened to Gus. The man knew his way around the mountain. He'd grown up here his whole life, just as Mike had. It was impossible for the man to get lost.

Jo's words echoed in the back of his mind, triggering his imagination and the horrors that came with the possibilities of what might have happened to the man he had trusted with a task vital to the survival of the mountain communities.

But if Jo had seen the military in the city, it was possible that when Gus arrived at the depot, there wasn't anything left for him to find. It could be that maybe the only thing that was out there now were the terrorists coming for them in the night.

"Too many what-ifs," Mike said, then turned away from the path down the mountain.

If the terrorists were really on the mountainside, then The Village's saving grace was that it was at the top of the mountain. The enemy would have to climb from the bottom and work their way up if they wanted to take the territory, and that gave him at least a little bit of time to prepare and even warn the others that might be in danger from the terrorists that had come to destroy everything and everyone that they knew. But before he could help the other towns, Mike knew that he would need to secure this one first.

Most of the folks had turned in for the night, save for the volunteers that Mike had corralled to help keep watch. He had deputized them to help appease their egos, but he made sure to let them know that it was merely only for the ceremony. Should they actually see anything dangerous or encounter it, then they should report it unless a threat to their own lives was imminent.

A hot breeze blew at Mike's back on his walk toward the station, but when he stepped inside and saw the worried expressions from his remaining deputies, he knew what had to be done.

"If those people are in the woods, then what's preventing them from sneaking up here and killing every single one of us?" Deputy Furst had the wide-eyed expression of a man who wanted action. "If they got Gus, then that means he might have told them about us."

Mike grimaced, not liking where this conversation was headed. "Don't be ridiculous. He's a good man. He wouldn't do anything that would put us in harm's way."

"No?" Furst asked. "Not even if it means saving his own life?"

"Deputy—"

"Sheriff, I heard you talking to Joanna Mercer," Furst said, refusing to relinquish his time. "And I think she's right. I think that people are going to do whatever is necessary to survive, no matter what that might do to their friends or community."

Mike knew that out of all of his deputies, it was Furst who had always been the hothead. He was always of the mentality of doing things now and sorting out the consequences later. While Mike and Furst were only a few years apart in age, it was Mike who had always been the more seasoned thinker, and it was the main reason why Mike was the sheriff and Furst was not.

"And what would you like to do?" Mike asked. "Have us put together a raiding party and go out and hunt these people down?"

Furst pounded his fist on the desk and then straightened up. "That's exactly what I think we should do. Strike at them before they have the chance to strike at us. Hell, they already struck first. This is retaliation."

Mike stared at Furst and then looked to Jan, who had her arms crossed beneath her chest.

"Jan?" Mike asked.

"We could go after them," Janet answered.

"Thank you," Furst said.

"But that would be stupid."

Furst turned toward Janet, his cheeks reddening from the scolding. "How is it stupid? We'll be able to get them before—"

"How many soldiers do we have?" Jan asked. "How many trained trackers do we have? How many machine guns?" She unfolded her arms and moved toward him.

Furst worked his mouth, following Janet's logic, but unable to get the point. "We have the assault rifles in the vault—"

"Us three are the only trained SWAT members in the

THE LAST CABIN: EMP SURVIVAL

town," Jan said. "Other than a handful of recreational hunters who have never shot at anything that can shoot back, we're all we've got. You're the Marine. So you tell me how you'd think the average civilian would fare against an enemy that has been trained to kill?"

Furst lowered his gaze.

"Yeah," Jan said, then looked to the sheriff. "Our best chance is to fortify our position here, keep guards on duty, and brace ourselves for trouble that might come our way. We don't need to go looking for a fight until the fight finds us, which might never even come."

Mike remained standing and weighed his options. "If the military is gone in the city, then that means the rest of the communities on the mountain are unprotected. If I can warn them in time, then that could save lives. While I'm gone, Jan's in charge."

"You can't go out there alone, Sheriff," Jan said, unable to hide her worried tone. "What happened to Gus could happen to you."

"But we don't know what happened to Gus," Mike said. "And I'm not just the sheriff of this town. I'm responsible for the whole county. I need to check on the neighboring communities, see how folks are getting on. We've done what we can from a supply standpoint here, and I need to make sure everyone else is prepared too."

Mike instructed to have one guard on each end of the road into the main street, and then two guards watching the south slope to look for anything that might be coming uphill. One guard was placed on the north side facing the top of the mountain in case the bastards were smart enough to snake their way topside and take the high ground.

"We can put whoever is watching the north side in the old church bell tower," Mike said. "That should provide a good vantage point and good cover for anything that comes our way."

"We can use the stables on the south side as a guard station too," Jan said.

"Good idea." The stables were owned by the Behr brothers, who provided scenic horse rides through the mountains for tourists looking to reconnect with nature after their busy city lives brought them up north. Donny Behr had already loaned them a horse for Gus to use, and he suspected that the man wouldn't object to having more guards on his property.

The other two guards would be placed by the well at the east side of town, and the west guard would be posted up by the sheriff's office. It was as good a start as any.

"Furst, you go ahead and talk to the Behr family," Mike said. "Jan, you're with me."

Both deputies nodded, and Furst was out the door first, leaving Mike alone with Jan as he collected a few spare magazines from his desk, along with the keys to the gun vault.

"Mike, you know I think this is a bad idea." Jan followed him out of the office and around the back of the station toward the cellar doors. "Why not have someone go with you? You sent Gus alone, and he didn't come back. If you go alone, and something happens to you—"

"If something happens to me, I don't want anyone coming after me." Mike opened the cellar doors, then flicked on his flashlight and descended the old staircase, boots smacking against the wood in irregular clicks.

"And why wouldn't we send someone after you?" Janet asked.

Mike put his key into the vault lock and turned it, listening to the heavy thud of steel as the lock was disengaged. "Because if I don't come back, you'll already know that the mountain is overrun with the enemy." Mike opened the door, the hinges groaning, and he shone his light on the assault rifles that rested inside. He plucked one of the rifles from the rack and held the weapon in his hands. It was lighter than he remembered. It had been nearly a year since he'd fired it at their annual weapons retraining.

The assault rifles had been the state's effort to effectively arm the police against the growing threat of drug violence that had been sweeping across the state. But aside from a few meth heads cooking up Sudafed in the woods, Mike hadn't experienced much of a drug epidemic in his area.

But the world had gone a long way since the days of policing when his grandfather was sheriff. Back then he remembered the old timer carrying nothing but a shotgun everywhere he went. It was a staple, a part of the old man's image. And the sight of that old pump-action twelve-gauge seemed to be enough to cause people to pause whenever they thought about doing something that they shouldn't.

People had numbed to the violence that they saw all around them, compounded by the disconnect of watching the world through a digital lens.

And now they were now paying the price for their apathy, for their lack of care of how they treated others and themselves. The digital world was gone. All that remained was the composite and steel in Mike's hands. A deadly weapon with only a single purpose. To kill. And he was in desperate need of people who knew how to use it.

16

*J*o watched her girls from the kitchen. It had been a long time since both of them were home, and she forgot how much she enjoyed seeing them together. Because for all of the teenage angst and raging hatred that Stacy had felt for her mother, Jo knew that Stacy loved her sister.

Despite the large age gap of ten years, the pair had a unique relationship. To Amelia, Stacy represented the knowledge and beauty and independence that she would one day seek out. To strike out against the world and make her mark. She was the girl who knew about boys and kissing and putting on make-up and bras. She was the closest thing to a woman beside her mother that she could get.

For Stacy, her younger sister represented the pure intentions that had greyed like the water of dying flowers. She was bright and kind and saw the world through rose-colored glasses. She was still in the world of make-believe that so many adults missed after they grow old. Amelia was a link to a past that Stacy wanted to remember, and through her younger sister, she could still relive it.

Stacy's friend, Melissa, seemed like a nice girl, though based off of her interactions with Amelia, Stacy figured she didn't have many younger siblings.

There wasn't anything that could wipe away the smile on Jo's face, nothing that could turn sour the rare good mood. At least that's what she thought until she heard the knock on her door, startling both her and the girls.

It had been a long time since someone came along the path without being detected by her preps. But she knew that it could only be one of two people that were currently outside of this cabin: Mags, or the sheriff. And she desperately wanted it to be Mags.

But when Jo opened the door and saw Turner's big body standing in the doorway with the rifle over his shoulder and Jan standing behind him, that good mood finally spoiled.

"Jo," Mike said, his voice deep and grave in the way that men always spoke whenever they had hard news that they didn't want to deliver. "Do you have a minute?"

"Hey, Mike!" Amelia said, waving from the living room. "Do you want to come inside and play checkers? I've gotten better since the last time we played."

Mike smiled, a genuine look of hurt in his eyes. "I wish I could, Em. Truly. But I need to talk to your mother for a second. Hey, Stacy."

"Sheriff," Stacy said, the tone cold enough to frost the room.

Jo shut the door behind her, and the three spoke on the porch.

"I hate to come out here after dark," Mike said, then smiled. "I suppose I should just be glad that you didn't shoot me."

Jo didn't reciprocate the smile, still worried about the gun that Mike carried and why he had brought it to her front door. "What's going on?"

Mike exhaled, knowing that the small talk was over. "I'm going to look for Gus."

Jo had always prided herself on a good poker face, but she couldn't conceal the worry as she stepped closer to Mike. "The town needs you here."

"That's what I told him," Jan said.

With both women boxing him in, Mike raised his hands. "I'm leaving the town in good hands, and we're as prepared as we're going to get. But I wanted to make one last plea for you to get involved. I was hoping you could give us a few tips on defense. I know you've got this place wired like Fort Knox."

Jo retreated a step. "Mike, I don't think—"

"I'm not trying to deputize you," Mike sad. "I just need you to show some of my folks how to set up the traps that you have around your cabin. If there is a threat out there, then it'd be nice to have a bit of a heads up if it was coming through the woods or down the road. You know?"

Jo looked from Mike to Jan. She had always liked the woman.

"We already have guard locations picked out," Jan said. "But if we could give our undertrained recruits the advantage of a heads up when someone was coming through the woods, then it would help save lives. And that's all we're trying to do."

Jo snickered, and she knew the laugh sounded heartless, but after all the death that she saw in the city, after the bodies that had dropped and were now rotting in the streets, she couldn't help but be a little skeptical that they would be able to save any lives.

"The people who are doing this won't stop," Jo said. "I saw

them gun down women, children, the elderly, anyone that was breathing. You really think that stationing a few guards around the area is going to deter them from hunting every last person down?"

"I don't know," Mike said. "But right now it's the best we have. Please, Jo. We need help."

Jo had known that it would come to this, that when the world started to fall apart that she would be pulled into the bullshit of everyone that wasn't prepared. But if those gunmen came up the mountain, Jo thought that her family would have a better chance at survival if The Village was prepared to face them.

"All right," Jo said. "I'll come by in the morning. It's too dark to try something tonight."

"Thank you," Mike said.

Both parties separated, but when Jo placed her hand on the doorknob to enter her house, she stopped. She was compelled to speak to the man she had come to care for deeply. She never had a chance to say goodbye to Danny, and she had always regretted that.

"Mike," Jo said, turning, and her tone more worried that she would have liked to express.

"Yeah?" Mike turned, taking one step up toward her, but not coming any closer.

"Be careful?"

Mike smirked. "Yes, ma'am."

Jan offered one last wave, and Mike turned around. Jo watched them fade into the darkness, and once they were out of sight, a sudden rush of cold fear gripped her stomach. It had been a long time since she wanted something more than the peace and quiet that the mountain provided. And while those desires had been buried, she could feel them reaching for the surface, wanting to breathe free air once more. And that made her vulnerable.

Jo entered the cabin, finding Stacy and Amelia still playing checkers, Amelia agonizing over her next move while Stacy flicked a pair of accusing eyes at her mother before returning them back to the board.

Stacy had never been fond of Mike, and Jo knew why. Despite the prickly nature between herself and her eldest daughter, Jo knew that Stacy was still very protective of her family, and any man that came into their lives was disrespecting the man that had come before. At least that's how Jo thought Stacy saw it.

Jo returned to the kitchen to finish prepping dinner with her back turned to the girls when she felt a presence behind her. She turned to find Stacy with her hip leaning against the counter and her arms crossed.

Jo pressed the knife through the onion, the smell irritating her sinuses. When her daughter remained silent, Jo set the knife down. "Have I done something to offend you?"

Stacy pushed her hip off the counter and took one step closer to her mother. "Does the sheriff come here often to make sure the Mercer girls are safe?"

"Stacy, it's not—"

"It's not what?" Stacy frowned, shaking her head. "It's not what it looks like? It's not that you're sleeping with the sheriff so you can... what? Gain some kind of competitive advantage with authority?"

"Watch your tone." Jo stepped forward as well, the pair of women only inches from each other's faces. Neither was the kind to back down. It was the reason why they always butted heads, even before Danny's passing. They were too much alike.

"My tone?" Stacy asked. "I think you should watch who you spread your legs open for—"

Jo slapped Stacy's cheek.

Stacy quickly brought her hand up to cover the red mark that was appearing on her cheek. Jo's breath quickened, and she knew that she had stepped over the line, just as Stacy had.

The pair lingered in silence, and Jo looked past Stacy to Amelia, whose face had grown pallid, a frightened look in her eyes. Melissa remained stoic.

Jo turned back to Stacy and stepped toward her daughter, but Stacy retreated the same distance. She stared at her mother as if the woman was one of the terrorists that had killed her friend.

"Stacy, I—"

"No." Stacy trembled, the anger in her growing so hot that it simmered into tears, and her eyes grew wet and red. "After everything you did to us when Dad died, after dragging us out here, you don't deserve any kind of happiness. You hear me? You deserve to die alone on this fucking mountain." Stacy spun around and headed toward her old room, and Melissa followed, and then came the slamming of the bedroom door.

Jo lingered in the kitchen, staring at the hand that she used to strike her daughter. It was pink and still stung. She wiggled her fingers, hating herself for what she'd done, and hurt by her daughter's words. Because while they might have been spoken in anger, Jo knew there were shreds of truth in it.

It might have been an exaggerated truth compounded from the heat of the moment, but it was a truth nonetheless. And Jo didn't blame her daughter for saying what she did, because deep down, she had never wanted anything more than to be alone. But those feelings were starting to fade, and that frightened her.

"Mom?" Amelia said, suddenly standing in the kitchen. "Are you okay?"

It was the pure innocence of her question that triggered Jo's tears, tears that she hadn't let fall since the day that Danny's killer was sentenced to prison. But in the kitchen, she let her guard down for a moment and hugged Amelia. Because the truth was that she wasn't okay. She wasn't sure if she'd ever be okay again.

*M*orning came quickly, but Jo had slept hard. She was sluggish when she woke, and she stumbled to the shower, hoping the cold water would wake her up.

Jo lingered under the water, taking her time as she showered, knowing that she would have to face her daughter eventually and knowing that the longer she put it off, the more awkward it was going to become. She would apologize, even if Stacy wouldn't.

Jo reached for the towel and dried herself after she stepped from the small rectangular box that acted as their shower and dressed. She only had a handful of outfits, eight copies of each, which she rotated throughout the week. She had more clothes for winter, but they were stored away, ready to be used when she needed them. With temperatures climbing into the nineties, she only wore what would keep her cool.

Once she was dressed, Jo armed herself with blade and pistol. She was never caught in a position where she would be defenseless.

Jo stepped out into the hallway, and her eyes found Stacy's closed door. She moved toward the door so quietly and softly that even the old boards of the cabin didn't protest her presence. She leaned her ear against the door, listening for any movement inside. But she heard none. She walked to the kitchen, all the girls still asleep, and grabbed the tin for coffee.

Outside, the first light of dawn had crept through the windows. Jo had been getting up before the crack of dawn since she moved out here. She had learned that it was always best to have things ready to go whenever the day started up on the mountain.

Jo tossed some wood in the pot belly stove to warm the top when she heard movement behind her, and she turned to find Amelia up and dressed.

"You should apologize."

It was rare that anyone snuck up on Jo, and the fact that her nine-year-old daughter had done so caused her cheeks to blush. "I will."

"Promise?" Amelia asked, looking at her mother with a gaze that was far too grown up for a nine-year-old to possess but seemed perfectly suitable on Amelia's features.

"I promise," Jo answered. "Now, go and finish your chores. When your sister wakes up, tell her to help. Her friend too." She turned to leave.

"Where are you going?" Amelia asked, following her mother into the kitchen.

Jo picked up the boiling water and then poured it over the coffee grounds and into the glass carafe that she had bought shortly after coming up here. "I'm going into The Village to help the deputies secure the perimeter." Steam rose from the plain white mug, the bottom stained from its many years of use. "Hopefully it won't take long."

"Did the sheriff really leave?" Amelia asked.

Jo set the carafe down, keeping one hand on the mug. She knew that Amelia had a special relationship with Mike. As much as she had tried to avoid it, the man had become a bit of a father figure to her over the past three years. And while Jo had denied her true feelings for the lawman, she didn't let her own fears dissuade her youngest from starting a new relationship. "He needed to check on the other communities. He's not just a sheriff of The Village." She sipped the coffee, savoring the slightly bitter taste and reveling in the rush that the caffeine provided.

Amelia nodded, then kept her head down as she turned around and away from her mother to tend to her chores.

"Em," Jo said, and her daughter turned. "He'll be back before you know it."

And for once, Jo saw her own skepticism appear on Amelia's face. "Do you really think so?"

Jo walked to her daughter and dropped to her knee to stay at eye level. "I do. He enjoys playing checkers with you too much not to want to come back for a rematch."

Amelia's smile returned. "I think I can beat him now."

Jo kissed Amelia's forehead and then pushed her daughter toward the back door. "Those chickens still need to be fed."

Amelia skipped toward the back door, and Jo finished her coffee, grabbed some jerky for breakfast out of the jar in the kitchen, grabbed a pack which she loaded up with spare trip wire and a daily rations bag as she did whenever she left the cabin, and then walked through the forest and toward the town to help the people ready themselves for the coming threat.

It wasn't the first time Jo had tried something like this. Shortly after the construction of the cabin, she had tried to build a community of like-minded folks to join the type of lifestyle that she had. But it didn't take Jo long to discover that most folks enjoyed the idea of being prepared more than the action itself. It was time-consuming, and every person that she tried to bring to her way of life eventually drifted back to their old habits.

Jo was familiar enough with the town to know a few places where they could start setting trip wires. Any supplies they needed could be borrowed from Mark Plafter, who owned the hardware store. Her mind lost in the logistics of the preparations, she made it all the way to the town's west entrance without noticing the growing murmur of dissent that was growing in the streets.

But when Jo saw the mob standing outside of Mags' store, Jo instinctively placed her hand on the butt of her pistol, praying that she wouldn't need to use it.

The crowd had formed a half circle around the general store's entrance, the mob convulsing with angry pulses.

"We're hungry!"

"Just let us in!"

"Are we supposed to starve?"

Jo kept her distance from the crowd, trying to get a feel for how far they were going to go with this, but from what she could tell, they were all bark and no bite. They could have swarmed the store by now if they really wanted to, but they hadn't.

Jo saw Jan at the front along with Deputy Furst and the Behr brothers, all of them armed with the assault rifles that she had seen Mike carrying last night. But there was no sign of the sheriff. He must have left last night or before the sun came up. Jo was betting that his absence had something to do with the sudden demand for food.

"I understand everyone's concern," Jan said, shouting

above the dissent. "But this is about more than our individual problems. We all understand the risk of—"

"Some of us have kids to feed!" The angry voice was somewhere in the middle of the crowd, and the words triggered another convulsion.

Again Jan raised her hands to quiet the dissent, but it wasn't until she started shouting that anyone would actually listen.

Jo knew it was a natural instinct to want to hoard, to gather what resources you had left and face the coming storm, damn the consequences.

It made Jo sick.

The whistle was loud and forced, and every head in the mob turned, looking back to find Jo removing her pinched fingers from her mouth.

The crowd parted for Jo, and she walked right through the middle of it, every pair of eyes attached to those distrusting minds thinking about what she would do, but she would address Jan before she addressed any of them.

With her back still turned to the crowd, Jo kept her voice low so only the deputy could hear her speak. "What happened?"

Janet looked over Jo's shoulder to the crowd, but only once, the rest of the time her eyes were locked onto Jo. "Mags opened up the store this morning and saw that the lock on the dry food storage had been cut with bolt cutters. She came and found me, and then a few folks came over to check on some stuff, and then word spread like wildfire and everyone came running to collect."

"So now you're trying to ration?" Jo asked.

Jan nodded.

"Good," Jo said. "Mike's gone?"

"Headed out before dawn," Jan answered.

Jo spun around and looked at the crowd. The silence was only broken up by the occasional cough or shoe scuffed against the pavement. They were the wolves at the door, and it was hard for Jo to set aside the times that she had tried to help and realized that they needed to reassurance.

"None of you have seen what's out there," Jo said, raising her voice and aggressively stepping forward. That brought the entire mob one step back. "I've seen the enemy that's killing people in the streets." She swept her intense gaze across the crowd, causing a few to lower their eyes. "No one is coming to help you. There isn't anyone that you can call down below. You are on your own. And the easiest way for the enemy to win is for you to tear yourselves apart!"

More heads lowered, and Jo sensed the collective anger dissolving from them. If they couldn't band together now, if they squabbled amongst themselves without any regard to what was waiting for them in the wild, then they were already dead.

"The only way for everyone here to survive the storm that's coming in is to learn from what other people know," Jo said. "And to have the humility to know that you can't survive without what they know. It's a tough pill to swallow. But what is necessary is hardly ever pleasant."

The fight was entirely out of the crowd now, everyone's tense posture deflating with rounded shoulders and lowly hung heads.

Jan stepped next to Jo. "The best way to make our food stores last is to ration. Everyone will get the food they need, but we will do so in an orderly fashion."

Most folks kept their eyes down. The fight had run out of them. For now.

"Now, Jo is here to help us create a good defensive perimeter around the town," Jan said. "The folks we spoke with earlier who will be on guard duty throughout the day, I want you to go with Deputy Furst to discuss some general firearm training and safety with the new weapons."

The handful of folks that had been chosen for the duty all disappeared from the group and followed Furst over to the station, but no one else moved.

Jan lowered her voice and leaned into Jo's ear. "How many will we need for what you want to do?"

"A dozen should be enough," Jo said.

It took some coaxing before Jan collected the needed twelve. Jo knew that she didn't have a good reputation in town. Even though she visited The Village more frequently than after she moved away, she hadn't been able to shake the stigma of the crazy widow woman who lived in the woods with her children. But Jo would have to put that behind them because if they didn't band together, then they wouldn't survive.

*M*ike swayed from side to side in the same lazy trot as the horse he rode. He kept a keen eye on the woods on either side of the road, but he saw no movement, nothing that gave away he was being followed or watched.

Most of the road that he traveled was barren save for the few broken-down cars that had been left behind after the EMP was detonated. He remembered Jo mentioning that one of the detonation methods could be a nuke in the sky.

Mike glanced up, the brim of his cowboy hat no longer protecting him from the sunlight, and he still squinted from behind his sunglasses. It was like something out of a science fiction movie. But it wasn't science fiction anymore. It was real. Real as the blood that he saw on Joanna's shirt when she returned from the city. He lowered his head, blinking until the black spots from the sun's brightness faded.

The road down the mountain was a curving one with quick, sharp turns that blinded his line of sight. And every time that Mike neared one of these sharp turns, he slowed and tightened his grip on the reins, praying that there wasn't anything around the bend that could kill him, or wanted to kill him.

But while the threat of violence and discovering the enemy marching up the road was frightening, what scared Mike even more than the prospect of meeting his own end was finding Gus. Because as wild as his imagination could go about his own demise, it could become even more feral when it came to the people that he cared about.

A deputy hadn't died in the line of duty in Rebel County under a sheriff's authority in over thirty years, and it was a trend that Mike had vowed to continue.

The men and women that he appointed as deputies were good people. Smart, strong, skilled, and loyal to a fault. He couldn't imagine having to bury one of them. And up until yesterday, that was the farthest worry from his mind. But there were lots of concerns that were far from his mind since yesterday.

Yesterday he didn't have to worry if the people in his county had enough food to eat. He didn't know what was going to happen when people's medications ran out, or when the gas in the generators dried up. There was no backup coming, no one he could call, even if he could reach someone.

Everyone was in some kind of trouble. Everyone needed aid. The whole country had practically shut down, and now it was time for people to band together. No one person could do it alone.

It was why people formed communities and societies, so the burden of knowledge could be shared and passed around to the others.

Mike had always heard the theory that technology was what was wrong with people, but he had always shrugged that off. The technology wasn't the problem. It was the people who used it.

No law forced someone to spend all of their time in front of a computer screen. People had just become too dependent on their screens to take care of things for them instead of people. But it was people that still did all the work behind the scenes, regardless of how many clicks you had to go through to order your food and have it delivered to your door.

People were still behind all of it, the only difference now was that most folks didn't know or understand how to react to those people. No one knew how to hold a conversation, at least not an engaging one that held any depth. And now that all of that technology had disappeared, chaos had taken hold.

Confusion spread fear and fear helped spread the shadow of death. Mike hoped that the sun would shine on for a little while longer because he knew that people could turn it around. They just needed a short time to adjust, to fix what was broken.

People were resilient. There had been more than enough opportunities throughout history for their race to be completely wiped off the face of the planet. But they were still alive. They were still here. And they could survive the fight that was on the horizon, so long as they didn't tear apart each other's throats before that happened.

Mike hadn't lost his faith in people. He knew it was a hard road ahead, but he also knew that the people on the mountain were harder. They'd survived through tough times before. And they'd get through tough times again.

Mike passed the small sign for the Boulder Community, which was two more sharp bends around the side of the mountain, and Mike would be in the next town. It was named for the massive rocks that retained a place of honor among the buildings of the community's main street.

The town had been initially designed around the boulders to save money on construction and blasting costs, but over time they had become a tourist attraction and the town's claim to fame. Outside several of the windows in the streets, the view was nothing but rocks.

It was a novelty experience, but it was one that helped sustain the local economy after the mines closed so many years ago.

The closer Mike moved toward the town, the more he hurried the horse. But the closer he got, the more his heart raced, because he heard only silence.

No voices, no clamoring of people who were concerned or frightened. The silence was more terrifying than Mike could have imagined.

Finally, Mike made the final turn around the mountain, and he had no need to pull back on the reins to stop the horse. The animal did it for him, sensing the same stench of death that Mike saw before his very eyes.

Bodies lay in the streets, dozens of them, more bodies than he cared to see or look at. The horse lifted its front right leg, then took two steps back, shaking its head back and forth, a distressed bray spit from between the bit in its mouth.

Mike's own mouth hung open, shock keeping his jaw slack. The sun beat down on the bodies, roasting the dead flesh and slowly turning them the same black as the asphalt on where they laid.

Splashes of blood were still slick against the pavement, the heat from the sun keeping it fresh. Mike counted at least forty dead in the streets, and that was just from what he could see from the town's entrance.

There were probably more in the buildings and between the alleyways, and there could be others that had fled toward the woods, leaving their bodies to be picked over by the animals and crows.

Mike looked above and saw the carrion circling, their black, winged silhouettes easy to spot against the bright blue of the sky. He suspected that some of the bodies had already begun to act as fodder for the mountain.

The steady buzz of flies created a haunting soundtrack that contrasted against the peaceful sound of the wind passing through the trees and the chirp of birds in the sky. The sound of the flies was painful to listen to, the thick black clouds moving jerkily above the bodies, hastening the decomposition of the dead. The worms would be at them now, food for the soil as his father would put it.

Unsure of how long he stared at the dead before Mike finally kicked the horse to trot forward, he moved through the town slowly and the shock of the scene slowly waned, and his instincts as a law enforcement officer started to kick in.

He saw the shell casings spread amongst the dead. They were .225 shells, most likely fired from an assault weapon like an AK-47 or M-16. Judging by the number of shell casings he saw glittering on the pavement, Mike suspected that they were all automatic weapons.

The horse weaved around the dead on its own accord, so it provided Mike the opportunity to keep an eye out for any survivors, though he suspected that anyone that had survived this would be long gone by now.

No reason to stick around, not unless they were a glutton for punishment.

The bodies of the dead were splayed out in various prone positions. Some of them lay on their side, others on their backs, some on their stomachs. Some eyes were open, some closed, and more than once Mike caught the stare of the dead, and it sent a chill down the back of his spine so cold that it froze sweat to his skin.

Mike had always hated looking into the eyes of the dead. It always felt so hopeless, so empty. The light was gone, the one that told you that someone was home.

From what he could see, the bulk of the casings were located on the town's north slope, which had good cover from the woods. It was where the enemy came out and ambushed the community after taking the higher ground.

Mike searched the town for survivors, but he found no one. And he found no sign of Gus, and that brought the slightest breath of relief from him. Because while it didn't guarantee that the deputy was alive, it meant that he had missed this gruesome slaughter.

A door opened to the right, and Mike was quick to draw his weapon, but he lowered it just as fast when he saw the old man and young woman step out from the restaurant.

"Sheriff." The old man was covered with sweat, and the dark circles under his eyes told the story of a sleepless night. He was bald, liver spots on his head, and white scraggly beard that ran along his jawline. He held his hat in his hands, but didn't stare down at the dead.

"Are you two all right?" Mike didn't know the two on a first-name basis. They could have been tourists who had come up for the summer. But no matter where they had come from, Mike could see that they wanted to leave here quick as they could.

"We hid during the fight." The old man cast his eyes down, almost as if he were ashamed of it, but the young girl put his arm around him. "They killed so many."

The girl couldn't have been older than twenty. She was

pretty, with thick red curls that fell down to her shoulders. "There are more of us." She swallowed. "My grandfather managed to get some people in the cellar."

"Any wounded?" Mike asked.

"Not anymore." The grandfather looked up from one of the fallen in the streets and met Mike's gaze. "They've moved on now."

Mike nodded in understanding. "Have everyone start gathering supplies. Food, water, medicine, anything that's left."

The old man nodded and turned to leave with his granddaughter, but as Mike stared at the bodies in the streets, he called out to the old man one more time.

"Do you have any guns?" Mike asked.

"A few," the old man answered.

"Bring those too."

19

It had been a long time since Stacy had slept at the cabin, and she had forgotten how quiet the night was. Her dorm building was loud at every single part of the night, with girls coming back during the week from parties, drunk and stumbling down the hall, giggling to each other and whispering for the other to be quiet before the TA woke up down the hall.

But the TA didn't care. In fact, the TA was usually with the students stumbling home in the early hours of the morning.

Stacy had always been a light sleeper, but the earplugs helped drown out the noise, and she had been lucky to have a roommate in Melissa who rarely went out, and when she did, it was usually on the weekend and with Stacy.

And while the forest had its own noises, there was something harmonic about the melodies it played. The wind rustling through the trees, the snap of branches from animals roaming through the woods, the hoot of an owl nearby and the buzz of insects.

Beyond the walls of Stacy's room was the real core of life.

It was the quiet and steady heartbeat of the mountain that she remembered lulling her to sleep those first few months when her mother had moved both her and Amelia out here, tearing them away from the only home they'd ever known. Something was soothing about the noise of the forest at night. But last night, the mountain had failed to lull her to sleep.

Stacy lay in bed, knowing that her mother was up. She had expected a knock on her door to tell her to wake up, but the shadows from the sunlight grew shorter in her room, and Stacy heard the front door open and shut. She was gone.

Stacy brought her hand to the cheek her mother had struck. It had long since lost the tenderness from the slap, but Stacy hoped there was still a mark left behind to remind her mother what she had done.

Joanna Mercer was a different woman than the mother that Stacy remembered growing up. She was now a woman who lived in a cabin in the woods and off the grid. A woman who knew how to hunt and kill and fight against a threat that no one else was prepared to face. A woman who tried to rid her daughters of the weakness and dependency on the rest of the world.

But what else had you rid us of, Mother? What else had you rid of yourself? What parts did you rip out and burn and bury, never to be found or used again?

Stacy had never wanted to rip anything out of her past. She had never wanted to kill what was inside of her. She had never wanted to forget about her father, leave their home, leave their life. Because while she missed her father and of course wished that he hadn't died, she hated that her mother had tried to erase him.

And to some extent, she knew that it had worked. The more time that Stacy spent at this cabin in the middle of

THE LAST CABIN: EMP SURVIVAL

nowhere, the harder it was to remember the man that had raised her. Her mother had almost burned all of the pictures of him, but Stacy had managed to save a few, keeping them hidden.

The only person she told about the photographs was Amelia because Stacy knew that while she got more time with the man, Amelia had barely known him since she was so little. And Stacy refused to let her father's memory fade. She kept it alive, even if her mother didn't want to do it.

Head pounding with that thick glaze that always lingered after a sleepless night, Stacy rolled out of bed, pressing her bare feet against the weathered wooden floors.

Bits of dirt and wood pressed against the soles of her feet, but the wood was warm against her skin. She had always worn slippers when they lived in their old house because the tile in the kitchen was cold, even in the summertime.

But she didn't need slippers out here, not even in the winter. Because the wood was always warm, made so by either the sun or by the fires in the small heaters installed in each room.

Melissa was still sleeping, sprawled out in the sleeping bag and pillows that Stacy had lent her the night before. Stacy walked over and nudged her friend awake. "Melissa, c'mon. You need to get up."

"Why?" Melissa rolled from her side and onto her back. "It's not like we have class."

"No, but we have other stuff to do. So get up."

Still dressed in the clothes from the day before, Stacy walked to her small pine closet and opened the door. She had left most of her "off grid" clothes at the cabin because she never anticipated needing them again. And it wasn't as though they would make her blend in with the other students at the university. But now that she was back, she needed to protect herself against exposure.

Stacy dressed and then stepped out of her room, letting Melissa dress, and found the cabin empty. She walked toward the back door and saw her sister in the small clearing of their backyard. She saw the garden that she had tended for three years and saw that they had already rotated the summer seeds into the fold. She had enjoyed gardening. A small part of her missed living up here and the fulfillment it brought her.

Stacy knew that they were well-provisioned at the cabin. It was strange to think that they had everything that they needed out here, but what was even more bizarre was how at ease Stacy felt at being back, and for the first time since she left to rejoin civilization and find herself, it was returning here that she finally caught her breath.

Melissa walked up from behind her, dressed in long sleeves and jeans, running a brush through her hair and smacking her lips like she tasted something sour. "God, my breath smells like something died in it." She grew frustrated with the brush and gave up with the tangled mess of her hair. "Where's the bathroom?" She opened her eyes. "You do have a bathroom out here, right?"

Stacy smirked and then pointed toward the outhouse.

"You have got to be kidding me." Melissa flung her head back.

"Make sure you wear your shoes."

Melissa stomped off and Stacy couldn't help but chuckle to herself, knowing that she had been the same way when her mother had brought her out here, which felt like a life-time ago.

Stacy followed Melissa outside and joined her sister by the coop.

Amelia was collecting the eggs from the hens, pushing the birds aside, who fluttered their flightless wings in protest.

"I thought you'd sleep all day," Amelia said, her back still turned to her sister as she closed the coop's cage doors.

Stacy kept her distance. She knew that her sister had a tendency to side with their mother when it came to issues within the family. It wasn't something that Stacy got upset about. She had been alone with their mother for nearly a year. It was only natural for her to side with their mom.

"You know I can't sleep in," Stacy said, crossing her arms and glancing up to the sky, which was blocked by trees. "You still have to clean out the cages?"

"Yup," Amelia answered, picking up the basket and carrying it past Stacy. "But Mom said that I'm in charge of assigning chores, so you can go ahead and get started."

Stacy watched Amelia return to the cabin with the basket of eggs, leaving Stacy to her work.

The hens never liked the intrusion, making their distaste known with every peck and cluck from their beaks. But the gloves that Stacy wore helped protect herself. After she was done, she brought the feed bag over and all was forgiven by the birds as they ate to their heart's content.

"Simple life for you guys," Stacy said, placing the bag of feed against her right hip as she squeezed the top closed. "I don't suppose you have room for one more in that coop, do you?" She sighed, knowing that being back with her mother was its own kind of cage. "I guess not."

A gunshot fired in the woods. Stacy froze. It was a single shot, at least one hundred yards out. She turned toward the north, thinking that's where the bullet had originated, but the echo made it challenging to pinpoint the exact location of the warning shot.

But Stacy knew what it meant. Her mother had set up trip

wires all around the cabin in ten-yard increments. There was only one path to and from the cabin that was clear, and there were less than a handful of people who knew the route.

Stacy dropped the feed, moving quickly to the outhouse, and then banged on the door. "Melissa! Melissa, you need to get out of there now!"

"I'm a little busy!" Melissa barked through the door. "And what the hell was that? It sounded like a gunshot. I'm not target practice, am I?"

Stacy pounded on the door again. "Melissa, this isn't a joke!" She searched the woods for any movement, waiting for more shots to be fired. She hoped that it was just an animal, but if it was someone who was looking for trouble, well, Stacy had a shotgun waiting for them if they wanted to try anything.

In the four years that their family had lived in the cabin, they had never had an instance of violence on their property. Sure, there was the random case of some hunters getting lost, wandering onto the property, but they were always kind enough to apologize for the mistake and leave without incident.

"Melissa, c' mon." Stacy kept her voice hushed, unsure of how close the intruder could be. "I don't know who—"

Another gunshot, this one closer than before. Stacy couldn't wait, she needed to be with Amelia, she needed to keep her sister safe.

"Just stay in there and don't move!" Stacy sprinted toward the cabin, bounded up the steps, and found Amelia in the living room, her face white as a ghost.

"Stacy, who is out there?" Amelia asked.

Stacy grabbed Amelia's hand on the run to the hallway where the bedrooms were placed. She dropped to her knees and forced Amelia down with her. "Keep low." Stacy ran her palms over the wood, feeling for the divot that had been placed for her to grab hold of and pull the boards up. She took a breath and then slowed everything down.

Panic was deadlier than bullets, something her mother used to tell her. She found the familiar ridges of the grooves of the boards then lifted them up, revealing the safe room that her mother had installed a few years ago.

Stacy ushered Amelia down below first, lifting her eyes to the window to see a body move through the woods before she dropped below as well, closing the lid door behind her.

It was dark beneath the floors, but there was some sunlight leaking through the cracks. Both Stacy and Amelia remained hunched low, and Stacy reached for the pistol attached to the floor above and heard the first footsteps walk up the porch steps to the front door.

The gun was a revolver, something her mother had been adamant about because she never wanted the weapon to jam after not being used for a long time. She knew that if they were in a hurry to escape that they might not be able to take any weapons with them and that they would need to have some stored below. Stacy was thankful for that moment now.

Quietly, Stacy pushed Amelia behind her, aiming the weapon at the sounds of the boot heels that had just entered the cabin after the door opened.

The revolver was a Magnum, and Stacy gripped the handle with both hands. The weapon was powerful enough to blow a hole through the floorboards above and tear away anything else in its path. It was their one and only defense aside from staying hidden.

From what she could see through the cracks and what she heard, Stacy counted two people that had entered the cabin. They walked through the kitchen, checked the cellar door, checked the living room, and then finally made their way to the hallway and the bedrooms, searching all three of them before either of them spoke in hushed and hurried tones.

It was a language that Stacy didn't know, and the heavy accent made it sound like they were chewing large bowls of cream of wheat.

The wood panels groaned. The intruders were right above them, separated by less than two inches of wood.

Stacy's knuckles were white from squeezing the handle of the revolver so tightly. She kept her arms rigid and tried to control the heavy thump of her heart. Her pulse raced, and the speed put stress on her heart and caused her left shoulder to ache.

Stacy hoped that the two men standing above them couldn't hear the thumping of her heart against her chest or the quivering of her muscles as she struggled to keep the weapon steady in her hands.

The tip of the revolver's barrel blurred as Stacy concentrated all of her focus on keeping the weapon aimed at the feet of the men. If they stayed close together, then she might be able to wipe them out with one quick strike. That would be the best-case scenario. The worst-case scenario was she would miss her target, and both she and her sister would be captured and tortured.

Stacy imagined a few other horrors for herself, and then that one thought of escaping such a horrible fate entered her mind. But she wouldn't let them hurt Amelia. No matter what.

Stacy pressed her thumb against the hammer and the heavy metal dug into her skin as she attempted to cock the hammer back without making too much noise, which she didn't want as it would give away her position beneath the floor.

The fighters above didn't move, and Stacy was convinced

that this would end in blood. And she had already made the promise that the blood that would be spilled would not be hers or her sister's.

Stacy wished that she could understand what they were saying. She hoped that she could speak whatever language that passed between them. Maybe they were talking about how they were going to kill the girls beneath the boards. Perhaps they were talking about how no one was here, and they were upset that they wouldn't get to kill anyone.

It drove her mad not knowing, because it was uncertainty that was the real enemy. If you knew that you weren't going to die, then there wouldn't be any reason to be fearful. But she didn't know. No one did. And Stacy had always suspected that it was that uncertainty that caused her mother to come out here in the first place. She alleged that it was that uncertainty that made her want to be as prepared as possible and eliminate whatever chances of death that she could. Because that was all that mattered. Survival.

The pair of terrorists continued to talk as Stacy worked the hammer backward with her thumb, the movement slow and arduous. The Magnum had a heavy firing pin that required her to pull down with both thumbs. The pair of men were deep in conversation and just before Stacy was about to cock the hammer back and the rest of the world would fade away, she heard shouts from outside as the hammer clicked into place.

"Stacy?"

Stacy's blood went cold at the sound of Melissa's voice, and the moment the girl spoke up, the two men in the cabin hurried outside, shouting. Melissa screamed, but it was cut short by more shouting from the men.

"Stacy! Please!" Melissa moaned, and her voice and whimpers became louder, along with the terrorists' voices, until all three of them returned inside the cabin. "Stacy, help!"

Stacy made it one step toward the floor board when she stopped and turned back to Amelia. There was no way for Stacy to reveal herself without exposing Amelia.

The terrorists shouted more angry words, Stacy still unable to understand what they were saying. Maybe they were threatening to kill Melissa if whoever she was calling for didn't come out? Maybe they were deciding what to do with her? Stacy couldn't be sure.

But Stacy was sure of what Melissa was screaming. Her friend was begging for mercy, for help. But no matter how loud Melissa screamed, she couldn't drown out the sound of Jo Mercer's voice in Stacy's head.

You might have to choose between friends and family. I just want to make sure you know the right choice.

"Stacy, please! Help! Please, help—"

The gunshot silenced Melissa and a heavy thud hit the floor, causing Stacy to jump. She stared up at the wooden boards, numb with shock.

The pair of terrorists said a few more words, but then their footsteps echoed toward the door and outside.

But even after they were gone, Stacy remained quiet and still, staring up at the floorboards where Melissa now lay, dead.

Stacy dropped the pistol, shaking, and then fell to her knees. A pain filled her chest, and she became short of breath. It wasn't until Amelia was at her side, hugging her, that she was able to process everything that had just happened, and as those thoughts trickled in, the tears began to fall.

20

*M*uhammed stood back and watched the deputy with his gag in his mouth. The men had been working him for the past hour after they made camp outside of the entrance to the old mine. It was Muhammed who had chosen the location. He liked to have something at his back that he didn't have to watch.

The inside of the open mouth of the mine was dark. Muhammed saw some of the old crossbeams that held up the structure and the exposed, rocky earth that had been torn open as miners cut railway tracks down the middle of its throat, like some kind of life support system.

The sight was an open sore on an otherwise beautiful mountain range. Muhammed enjoyed the mountains, it reminded him of his home back in Afghanistan when he and his brother and father would roam the countryside with their flock, tending to the lands that his family had owned for generations. But that was before their world had been destroyed by the Americans and their war.

Muhammed had made a promise to himself all of those years ago. He might not have been to blame for the attacks

161

that had befallen the people of this country before, but he had made up for that fact with the attack yesterday. And he was just getting started.

The deputy gagged and kicked his legs during the waterboarding. He hadn't been a strong man, and he had given them most of what he wanted to know, but he wanted to make sure the deputy was truly whipped.

Muhammed held up his hand, and his men stopped. The deputy gasped for breath, then retched some water over the front of his uniform.

The deputy's gaze wandered aimlessly between his torturers until they landed on Muhammed, and that's where they stayed. "I told you everything I know."

"And I believe you." Muhammed waved his hand dismissively, keeping his posture casual as he tilted his head to the side. "But this isn't about learning more information."

The deputy scrunched his face up as if he were about to cry, but the only water that dripped from his face was the lingering droplets from his torture. "Then... w-why? Why are you doing this?" His voice grew more petulant as he spoke.

"Because I'm not here to conquer people or learn your secrets." Muhammed stood and dusted the dirt and leaves from his legs.

"Just let me go!" the deputy yelled, and then turned to the woods, screaming at the top of his lungs, the veins and muscles along his neck pulsating with every scream. "Help! Someone help me! Help me!" But his cries for help only ended with more tears.

Muhammed walked to the deputy and then bent forward, resting his palms just above his knees. "You can scream until your throat is raw. No one will come. And even if someone did hear you and they came looking for you, my scouts would see them coming a mile away and kill them before they got close enough to see your broken body."

The deputy sobbed harder, bowing his head in defeat. "I don't understand why you're doing this. I just want to go home. Please, let me go home."

Muhammed could hear the sincerity in the man's voice. "I know you do." Muhammed reached for the deputy's chin and then lifted the man's face to look him in the eyes. "But you will never see home again."

The deputy hardened, the last of his fighting spirit emerging. "You won't win."

Muhammed smiled. "No. But this isn't about winning. There is no land to conquer here. Only blood to spill. And I will spill more of it than anything you have ever seen in your life. I will spill more blood on this soil than it has ever seen before. I will make so there are no more crops for you to grow. I will kill the land along with its people. It's revenge I want. Nothing else."

Muhammed leaned closer, close enough to catch the stench of fear and blood and sweat radiating off the deputy's body. It was that pungent stench of defeat and rot and death, which was hanging over the deputy like a cloud. It wouldn't be long before the mercy of death claimed the man, but Muhammed would make sure the last bits of his life was nothing but wretched, torturous moments.

"My people were innocent," Muhammed said, whispering. "My mother, my father, my sisters. All of them were innocent. They had nothing to do with war, with the people who took over our religion. But innocence plays no part in the negotiations of the world beyond our lands. The only thing that counts in this life is striking down the enemy that threatens you, the entirety of that enemy. And I will slaughter every man, woman, and child I come into contact here that breathes the air on this land. Because that is my justice. That is the penance for balance in the world."

"But the people in that town had nothing to do what happened to your family," the deputy said, his voice growing more petulantly grotesque the more he spoke. "They are just people. Innocent people."

"No one is innocent anymore," Muhammed said.

The deputy shivered, and Muhammed held his gaze a moment longer before breaking away and moving to the edge of the camp.

It had been hours since his brother left, more than enough time to scout the next town to see what they were dealing with. But his brother had always lacked patience, and that had always gotten him into more trouble than he was prepared to handle.

Muhammed scanned the green and rocky terrain. The snap of branches to his left caught his attention, and he turned to find his brother emerging from behind a small rocky alcove.

Zahid shrugged his shoulder, readjusting the rifle strap that had started to cut the circulation off of his arm. The brothers embraced with muscular arms, and Muhammed held his brother's face before kissing his forehead.

"Did you have trouble?" Muhammed asked.

"No," Zahid answered. "But I found a cabin. There was only one girl there, but it was stocked with provisions. There was enough food to last our men for months."

Muhammed nodded. "Good. We could use the resources." He kept his hand on the back of his brother's neck and squeezed. "I'm glad you made it back."

Zahid smiled, shrugging off the compliment with his arrogance. "I'm the best scout you have."

Muhammed shook his head, but couldn't hold back the

smile and the laughter that rolled off his tongue. "What did you find?"

Muhammed listened intently to his brother, who told him that there were guards in the next town, people set up on the roads, and then in a bell tower. He didn't bother checking the south side because it wouldn't be advantageous for them to attack from the south. Muhammed didn't want to put his people in a position where he wouldn't have the high ground.

He knew that most people in the state had weapons, and what resistance that they had encountered so far had only been squashed because Muhammed had made sure that he and his men retained the tactical advantage of surprise and speed.

It was a well-worn tactic, but it was effective. He and his men would rush through the town like water from a broken dam, drowning everything and everyone in their path.

Men, women, children, it didn't matter, there was no discrimination. Death did not discriminate, and Muhammed and his men rode the steel-tipped wings of the beast with the commanding fury of a fighting force that knew what to do and how to do it.

"Tell me more about the cabin," Muhammed said.

"The place was well-provisioned," Zahid said. "There was a garden, chickens, and bees. Canned foods in the cellar, along with first aid kits and other boxes of supplies. I didn't go through all of them, but I'm sure it had things that we could use."

"Bees?" Muhammed asked.

"They make honey, brother," Zahid answered, making no effort to hide the condescending tone in his voice that caused Muhammed to punch his brother's arm.

Muhammed frowned while his brother continued to laugh. "Was the cabin close to the town?"

"No," Zahid answered. "It was closer to us."

Muhammed arched his eyebrows. "I thought that this town was the last on the mountain. There aren't any power lines that run out that far from the town. No utilities that I remember seeing from the schematics."

The utility information was how Muhammed had mapped out most of his targets. It was an easy way to see how many towns and houses were in rural areas. But Muhammed had picked this location because it was high above any of the other homes in the area. If this cabin wasn't hooked up to any of the standard utility structures, then it would make sense why he didn't see it.

"And you killed the person there?" Muhammed asked.

"Yes," Zahid answered.

"Take two men and some empty bags when we leave to attack the town at nightfall," Muhammed said. "Bring back as much as you can, and we'll meet you back at camp to celebrate our victory."

2 1

---

*I*t was mid-afternoon by the time that Jo had instructed everyone on how to handle stringing the line through the woods and how to hook it up to the shotgun shells that Janet provided from the sheriff's office.

The town was longer than Jo realized, but they managed to create enough barriers to entry to make sure that anyone that was coming from the north or south ends of the town would be heard with a loud gunshot.

And while Jo had been the brain behind the endeavor, there were no congratulatory slaps on the back as she left the others. She was there only on the orders of the sheriff, whose authority had granted her a brief glimpse into the town that didn't want anything to do with the widow in the woods.

It was incredible to think about it, but Jo believed that some of the townspeople felt that she considered herself superior to them. That she was somehow lording over the mountain like some vigilante protector out for justice against anyone that threatened to harm the mountain, including the people who called it their home.

For Jo, that couldn't have been farther from the truth. She did not think herself superior to the rest of the mountain, she didn't think herself superior to anyone. In fact, it was her own fear of inadequacy to handle life's surprises that drove her away. She left because she didn't know what else to do.

Jo returned to the cabin, following the hidden path from the road and into the woods that she owned and worked and lived for the past three years. Out here in the woods, she needn't concern herself with the opinions of others. They served nothing but as a distraction because in the end, there was only one person that could save herself from the wicked evils of fate and misfortune: herself.

The cabin came into view, and the moment that Jo had moved close enough to see the house, she knew that something was wrong.

It was too quiet, unusually too quiet now that Stacy was home. Amelia would be talking her ear off, and her youngest daughter had never been shy about wanting to express her opinion. She had always possessed a brutal honesty about her that never ceased to amaze Jo.

Jo drew her weapon and approached the cabin warily, her eyes scanning the forest for any signs of ambush. With the perimeter of the cabin seemingly okay, Jo moved back to the cabin itself, and she saw that the door was cracked open.

The girls wouldn't have left it open, not even Stacy, with all of her distaste for rules and authority. She would still have the presence of mind to shut the door. Unless they had to leave in a hurry, or unless someone who had come in unwanted had left, leaving a wake of destruction behind for Jo to walk in and find.

Jo entertained the thought in the way that a physician would welcome the prospect of treating a patient that they had no emotional attachment to. She considered her course of action should she walk into the cabin and find her two girls dead. She thought of how she would find the people who killed them and what she would do once she caught them. Because there was a certainty in her capture of the animals that tore apart her girls. There was a certainty in the way that they would be handled and the tremendous amount of pain that they would endure at her hands.

It would be slow, methodical, and she wouldn't stop until she was sure that she had squeezed out every remaining ounce of pain that she could bring them.

The door swung open, and the moment Jo saw the body on the floor in the living room, a hollow pit formed in her stomach.

But Jo only saw Melissa's body on the floor, and she forced herself to move through the rest of the cabin. She wanted to cry out for the girls, but she held back. She needed to ensure the threat was gone.

When Jo moved toward the hallway with the bedrooms, she kept the pistol aimed ahead of her, her hand gripping the handle firmly, making sure that she didn't have an over-bearing grip. It was a sign that she wasn't in control, and she needed to make sure that she was in control here. And she would not be the reason that her children died. She made herself a promise of that a long time ago.

Jo cleared each bedroom, the process quick since the rooms were so small, and now all that was left was the safe room that she'd built beneath the cabin. She stared down at the hidden wooden panels where the door rested, once again finding herself afraid that when she opened it, she would find the last of her family dead, and she saw the remaining threads of her sanity unravel.

If her girls were dead, then Jo had no other purpose in life than to hunt and kill the people who had done this. And while a part of her had hoped that she would be able to find love again, there was another part of her that wanted to embrace the isolation, that wanted to adopt the lone wolf mentality that would free her from any emotional connections with the world. Because that was the only way to truly live without fear of loss. To live without love.

Jo flipped the door open, keeping the pistol aimed in the darkness, and she saw Stacy with Amelia tucked behind her, her own gun aimed up at Jo, the pair exhaling a breath as they lowered the weapons and Amelia came screaming from around her sister and running up the stairs and into her mother's arms.

"Mom!" Amelia hit Jo's chest with a satisfying thud and squeezed tight. "We weren't sure if the bad guys came into town or not."

Jo shut her eyes, feeling the warmth of her daughter in her arms, and then lifted her off the ground. The girl's weight always felt good. She let Amelia slide down and then looked to Stacy, who climbed out of the hole. "Are you all right?"

Stacy nodded, but her face was white as a sheet. "I'm fine."

"What happened?" Jo asked.

"People came," Stacy said. "The same people as in the city. They found us out here, somehow."

"And Melissa?" Jo asked, looking at Stacy but still holding onto Amelia.

Stacy looked like the cold embrace of death as she looked Jo dead in the eye. "I had to make a choice."

Jo only nodded and then kissed the top of Amelia's head. "How long have they been gone?"

"I-I don't know," Stacy answered.

"Did you see where they went after they left?" Jo asked.

Stacy shook her head.

Jo nodded and then placed her palm against Amelia's cheek. If they were here recently, then she should be able to find some kind of trail. And if Jo could catch the scouts before they made it back to their camp, then the cabin would be safe.

Jo looked at bother her daughters, taking turns to examine each of them in the eye. "I want you both to stay below in the safe box, okay?"

"What? Why?" Stacy stepped forward, the gun still in her palm and at her side. "We need to leave, people know where we are."

"And pretty soon I'll know where they are," Jo said. "I'm going to look, see what kind of a threat that we're actually dealing with, and then I'll be back."

"You can't leave again!" Amelia whined and reached for her mother's hand, clutching it tightly as if she had the strength to keep her still.

"You'll be safe below," Jo said. "But if I don't come back before sundown, then I want both of you to head down to the base of the mountain, head to the outskirts of the city, and find those military folks that we spoke with."

"Mom, this isn't—"

"Stacy," Jo said, placing her hand on her daughter's shoulder, the fact that she had just called her mom for the first time in three years not lost on her. "I need you to stay here and watch her, but if I don't come back before sundown…"

"Then we go down to the base of the mountain and find the military camp," Stacy said.

"Good." Jo already had everything she needed on her

back, but she picked up the crossbow on her way out. If she needed to kill someone without making a lot of noise, then that thing would come in handy. She stopped when she passed the dead girl's body in the living room, her blood congealed in a puddle on the floor. She wouldn't let her daughters share that fate. No matter the cost.

2 2

---

*J*o picked up the trail quickly enough. The men who had come to the cabin had made no effort to hide their tracks. She moved stealthily, making sure that she didn't lose the trail, keeping her eyes peeled for any guards that they might keep posted.

If the terrorists were hiding in the mountains, she thought they might have someone keep watch, and after an hour's hike, she saw someone through the trees.

Jo crouched low, remaining hidden while the terrorist observed the woods. He was armed, and Jo scanned the nearby area until she saw a second lookout, this one much closer.

It wasn't hard keeping still. She had done it a thousand times before when she hunted. She was in tune with every single muscle in her body. She could stay motionless until the man's eyes bled and fell from their sockets.

But Jo didn't have to wait that long as the scout finally looked away from her position, and she quietly exhaled a breath.

Jo moved west, keeping low to the ground. Once she was

clear of the watchdogs, she was able to penetrate behind the lines for another fifty yards, and that's when she heard the voices from their camp carry on the breeze.

Jo staked out a spot in the woods and watched, hoping she could pass on the information to Mike when he returned. She counted twelve men, each of them with a mixture of weapons spread out amongst them, mostly AK-47s.

By all accounts it was a small group, but with the element of surprise against an unsuspecting group of civilians, they could do a lot of damage.

Jo wondered how many more of these cells were scattered through the mountains, and she realized that there could be dozens, even hundreds more. If these people were able to survive on their own in the woods like her, this could be a conflict that raged on for years.

But Jo couldn't take them all down without bring attention to herself. There were just too many. She had started a slow retreat from the edge of the camp, but stopped when she heard words yelled in broken English.

"Brave officer of the law!" The words were spoken mockingly. "Want to put me in cuffs, lawman?"

The words elicited laughter from the terrorists' comrades, and Jo moved to get a better look. And when she came around the base of a tree, she saw what remained of Deputy Gus Moynihan.

Beaten and bloodied, Gus was bound with his hands behind his back, defenseless against the barrage of assaults that the enemy gave him.

"Get up, Deputy!" The man that stood over him was dressed like the other terrorists that Jo had seen in the city. His face was thick with a black, coarse beard and the color matched his eyes, which glinted with pleasure from lording over Gus.

With Gus unable to do anything but groan with pain, the terrorist bent down and then spoke more softly, too quiet for Jo to hear from so far away. But she did hear the whimper that Gus made after the terrorist was done speaking.

The discovery of Gus made things more complicated for Jo. She had initially set out to find the group, then report back to the town so they could better prepare. But now that she saw that they had Gus, she found it more difficult to leave.

While she didn't know the man very well, his torture made it harder for Jo to just turn a blind eye. But the number of men in camp didn't tilt the odds in her favor, and even if she managed to get close enough to Gus to grab him and pull him out, he didn't look like he was in any kind of shape to move quickly through the woods, and they'd have to move fast if they were going to survive. The group was probably using Gus for information.

And if Gus was feeding the terrorists information, then it was possible that was how the pair of terrorists had found the cabin. It wasn't like it was easy to find, well off the beaten path and tucked away in some of the thicker portions of the woods. The thought of Gus selling her family out to those evil men made her blood boil.

The vengeful thoughts passed quickly, and they were replaced with the sudden onslaught of guilt. Guilt for thinking Gus deserved blame for wanting it to happen, and guilt for leaving him. Because that's what she needed to do.

The reality of the situation didn't allow for Jo to rescue Gus. She would die, or worse, and then he would die, or worse, and then she wouldn't be able to warn the people in the town, she wouldn't be able to save her children, and that was the only thing that mattered to her. That was the end game.

And so Jo retreated from the campsite with the information she could use to help The Village. Because if they couldn't stop the enemy, then every single man, woman, and child would share Gus's fate. Jo had spent her life preparing for that fight, making sure to stare down the face of death before it destroyed everything she knew and loved.

23

The sky twinkled twilight when Jo returned to the town, and she hurried quickly toward the sheriff's station, hoping that Mike had returned by now because she knew that he would be able to galvanize everyone behind him. He was that kind of man. He was a leader.

Jo shouldered open the station door, never breaking stride as she found Jan and Furst lighting some candles. Each of them turned with alarm, standing and reaching for the butts of their pistols.

"What's wrong?" Jan asked. "Are the girls—"

"The girls are safe for now," Jo answered. "I found a terrorist cell up in the mountain near my property. They have a dozen fighters, all of them armed with automatic weapons. And they have Gus."

Furst's eyes widened from the news. "He's alive? Was he okay? Where did—"

"He's alive, but he's hurt," Jo said. "But that's not what's important right now, what's important for us is—"

"What do you mean that's not important?" Furst asked, disgusted with Jo's response. "He's a deputy of the law, and an attack on a deputy is an attack on the law itself. We need to get him back."

"We don't have time!" Jo stomped her foot, refusing to back down. "You're not listening to me. They are out there, they are well armed, and they are going to come here. It's the only reason they're parked that high on the mountain. They have already sent scouts to my cabin. They might have been here watching us when we were setting the trip wires."

"Shit." Furst kicked the floor. "Fucking waste of time."

"Are you sure they saw us?" Jan asked, trying to sound like the voice of reason. "I mean, did you hear them say it?"

"No," Jo answered. "But we need to get everyone armed and ready. They'll be coming down from the northeast side. That's where the trip wires were the least prominent."

"And how do you know all of this, huh?" Furst asked. "I mean, did your daughters hear them talk about this? Did you hear them talk about this?"

"It's not important how—"

"Of course it's important!" Furst got in her face, his complexion reddening from anger. "If the information is bad, then we'll be getting ready for a threat that we don't know how to beat!"

"The information isn't wrong," Jo said, keeping herself eerily calm. "And the longer we argue, the less time that we have to prepare."

It was quiet for a moment, and Jo saw the little gears turning behind Furst's dark eyes. She had no reason to lie, and he knew that. What he was struggling with was taking orders from someone that didn't wear a badge. But she couldn't help that, and Furst finally stepped back and looked to Jan.

"Do you think this is the right play?" Furst asked.

Jan took her time before she answered, knowing that her

words would sway Furst one way or the other, and she didn't want to spook him too much. "I think it's what Mike would have done. He trusts her, and she has just as much to lose as we do if she's wrong."

Furst finally nodded, and then he went to round up the troops while she and Jan lingered in the station for a moment longer.

"The sheriff should have been back by now," Jo said.

Jan nodded, chewing her lower lip before letting it go to answer. "He told us not to go after him."

"What?" Jo asked, her eyebrows dropping down like daggers. "Why wouldn't he want us to go after him? He could be in trouble, he could be—"

"Dead? If that's the case, then we won't be able to help him." Jan sighed, and they looked out the window toward the street where Furst was gathering the people.

With Jan and Furst on board to round up the troops, she let them do what they did best, and Jo would need to do what she did best. Hunt.

Residents had gathered around both deputies, Furst relaying the information and pointing north up the mountainside. She heard him instruct the Behr brothers to position themselves in the woods toward the west, and that the line of fire would be directed toward the northeast since that's where the trip wires were the least prominent.

While Furst and Jan handled the reinforcements, Jo stopped by Mags' store to check on her friend and make sure that she got home safe.

Mags was closing up shop when Jo arrived, and while she was normally all smiles, Mags' face went stoic when she saw Jo. "What happened?"

"There's a fight coming," Jo answered. "I need to get you home."

Mags frowned. "Now? Here?"

Jo grabbed hold of Mags' shoulder, pulling her down the street. "Do you have your pistol on you?" She knew that Mags usually carried.

"Always, but—" Mags shook her head, which tasseled the white and grey curls that formed the perm on her head. "Jo, what is going on?"

Jo glanced toward the woods. It was pitch black now. "I don't know how much longer we have before—"

Gunfire followed a scream, and Jo pushed Mags into the nearest wall, trying to find the source of the shooting. She looked toward the northeast and saw the flashes from the muzzle fire in the forest as the enemy stormed down the side of the mountain, exactly where Jo said they would.

Jo looked back to Mags, who had already drawn her pistol, and Jo was glad to see that the old woman wasn't going to go down without a fight.

"What do we do?" Mags shouted, both she and Jo slammed up against the side of the accountant's office.

"You stay inside and stay low." Jo shook her head to accentuate the point, knowing that the old woman would be an easy target for any of the bastards that were looking to add another notch onto their belt. She opened the door for the building and pointed for Mags to enter.

"I won't help anyone in here!" Mags raised the pistol to show that she wasn't afraid to fight, but Jo wasn't concerned about that.

"I need someone to look after my daughters if something happens to me!" Jo said. "Stay put!"

Mags nodded and then disappeared into the building, allowing Jo to concentrate on the enemy bearing down on them.

With the terrorists having the advantage of the high

ground, Jo knew that the fight would be arduous and dirty. She needed to help even the odds.

Jo glanced up at the church tower near the fighting. It was unmanned, Furst having called down the man on duty for the meeting. She knew that she could get up there, but she needed to move quickly because judging by the number of bodies that were dropping in the streets, she knew that she didn't have much time. She hurried toward the fighting, keeping low and close to the buildings for cover.

She covered the distance quickly and then found Furst by the auto shop, reloading a magazine as bullets flew past the auto shop where the enemy had gathered for their infiltration point.

"We need someone in the tower!" Jo shouted, pointing toward the church.

Furst shook his head. "It's a suicide run. Rusty Behr tried to head there when the shooting started, but he didn't make it."

Jo looked past Furst and saw the stacks of bodies that were growing in the street. "Then let me go."

Furst looked at her with surprise. "You crazy?"

"If we can't retake the high ground, then they'll just keep pushing us back—"

A terrorist jumped from around the front corner of the building, and both Furst and Jo reacted in the same instant, putting two rounds into the bastard to bring him down.

The shock from the sudden brush with death stole Jo's breath, and she saw that it affected Furst as well. She cleared her throat and then punched Furst's arm. "You giving me some cover?"

With the dead terrorist at their feet and the roar of gunfire all around, Furst only nodded and then stepped aside to allow Jo the space to run. She was going to make it as far as she could, and she wasn't going to stop until she made it to the tower, consequences be damned.

"Now!" Furst shouted, and Jo bolted from the cover of the building, every ounce of her concentration focused on the church entrance.

It was forty yards of open space, and every thunder of a gunshot had the potential to spell the end of her life. Bullets zipped past, gunfire being exchanged in both directions, and while the heat of the moment wanted to turn Jo's head to the firefight raging around her, she knew that any loss in concentration would lead to her instant death.

The door to the church grew closer, and Jo's muscles burned as she provided one last spurt of speed to close out the last ten yards, then let out an audible groan as she gripped the sides of the doors and pulled herself inside as she caught her breath.

But Jo didn't dawdle for long. She rushed down the aisle between the two rows of the pew, momentarily glancing up at the cross that hung over the pulpit, and she saw where the bullets had torn through the wood from the side of the building. And while she only glanced up at the cross for a few moments, and while it was dark and hard to see, Jo could have sworn she saw blood oozing from the wood. But the image vanished as she entered the stairwell and hurried up the steps.

The staircase was narrow, the place built long before there were things such as building codes and fire regulations. The bell tower was off limits for most of the congregation, but it went unguarded and unchecked, and there was no lock on any of the doors. The town was too small for anyone to care about people sneaking up into the bell tower.

The structure was still sturdy despite its age, and Jo made it to the top without incident. The bell was almost too big for the small cage, and it took up most of the space, but it also provided good cover. The bell itself was six inches of solid copper. Unless the enemy started chucking grenades up at her, the bell was her bulletproof vest.

Jo positioned herself on the east side of the tower, bringing the rifle up to her shoulder and sticking her eye against the scope, which thrust her one hundred yards into the woods. It was harder to see in the dark, but because she had been outside the entire time as the sun was going down, her eyes were already adjusted to the low light. Even with the clouds blocking the moon and stars, her trained hunting eye was able to pick out the enemy in the forest.

Most of them had gathered around at the back of the stores along Main Street and were no longer protected by the cover of the trees.

Jo lined up her first shot and squeezed the trigger, knocking the terrorist to the ground where he lay still, blood oozing from the gunshot wound to his head. Because Jo wasn't sure if they were all wearing body armor or not, she started with headshots to make sure that whatever she brought down would stay down.

After the first kill, Jo lost the element of surprise, but she killed one more before the group scattered and retreated into the woods. Jo had tracked deer faster than those scrambling cowards below, and she pivoted her aim to bring down the next target that was scurrying up the side of the rocks before a bullet to his back flattened him to the ground as well.

Time passed slower for Jo when she hunted, and while it had only been maybe ten seconds since her first shot, she had already brought down three people. No, not people, she thought to herself. Animals. She was killing animals that had wandered into their home and started tearing things apart.

She was ridding the world of a pest that did nothing but destroy and murder and take the precious thoughts in your life away from you forever. Jo was enacting justice from the top of that bell tower.

Once Jo no longer saw the enemy through the foliage of the trees, she turned back to the street where some of the terrorists had snaked through between the other buildings. She saw Jan and Furst pinned down by the hardware store, where they fired from the cover of the building, shooting from now-busted windows as they tried to hold their ground and prevent the enemy from pressing forward even farther than they already had.

The terrorists were beneath the overhang of a row of shops, and Jo couldn't get a good bead on them because of the roof. If she was going to help them now, then she couldn't do it from the tower.

Jo picked up her weapon and hurried down the stairs, rushing back through the church and out into the night air.

Gun smoke hung heavy in the air, adding a layer of grime to the darkness, but Jo had a better line of sight on the enemy across from the hardware store now, and even with the night, even with the grime, she was still able to hit her mark and push the terrorists back.

With the enemy on their heels, Jo pressed forward into the middle of the street, taking the time to line up her shot, her muscles shaking from the exertion of the day and the miles that she had traveled. It had been a long time since she had pushed her body this far, and she felt the exhaustion rolling over her in thick waves.

The crosshairs wavered, and Jo tightened her grip on the weapon. When she finally lined up her shot again, there was another gunshot, this one that echoed behind her, and Jo

THE LAST CABIN: EMP SURVIVAL

spun around, aiming the gun at Mike, who had stood over the body of the dead terrorist who had nearly killed her.

Mike marched past her and started shooting at her initial targets that were beneath the overhang. The pair fought alongside one another, firing at the enemy, giving Jan and Furst the needed time to regroup.

With the enemy on their heels, Furst and Jan emerged from the stores, along with a few others, and together they chased the enemy back into the woods, firing at them, casting them back to the depths of hell from which they came.

Furst started to pursue them, but it was Mike who held everyone back.

"Let them run," Mike said.

Everyone caught their breath, a few folks coughing from the lingering smoke.

"Do you think they'll come back?" Jan asked, looking to the sheriff.

"I don't know," Mike said. "But we need to get a head count." He turned to Furst and Jan, instructing them to start sweeps and to collect the dead, both their own and the enemy.

Mike's words faded from Jo as she stared into the woods. She wanted to pursue the enemy, run them down until there wasn't any shred of them left, because she highly doubted that this was the end. But as much as she wanted to catch the enemy, she needed to get home.

Jo sprinted toward the cabin, deaf to the shouts that were following her because all that mattered now was getting back her girls and making sure that both of them were safe.

24

*E*ven after the sunset, the safe hole beneath the cabin was still hot, and neither Stacy or Amelia could get comfortable from the stuffy heat. Sweat collected in Stacy's eyes, and she continually adjusted her grip on the pistol in her hand. The shotgun rested up against the wall, and Stacy looked at it every now and then, hoping that she wouldn't have to use either weapon. Hoping that all of this would just end.

Neither of the girls talked, and while Stacy sulked in the corner, Amelia spent her time doodling with her finger in the dirt, not that she could see what she was making anymore.

Stacy stifled a laugh and then shook her head. Was this what her mother had planned for them? Was this the extent of their survival? All of that planning and all of those resources that had been used only to be stuck in a hole in the ground in the darkness, waiting for an enemy that would provide them no mercy and no quarter should they be found, and the best that they could hope for was a quick death?

This life had never made any sense to Stacy when her mother first started, and time hadn't provided her with any wisdom for her to change her opinion. Because she didn't understand the point of wasting so much time, only to die in the dirt.

"When is Mom coming back?" Amelia asked, her voice nothing but a whisper that was quickly swallowed up by the darkness.

"I don't know," Stacy answered.

"Why do we have to stay down here?"

"Because it's where Mom wanted us to be."

"I don't like it down here."

"No one does."

The silence lingered for a little while longer, and then Stacy saw her sister's shadow move toward her in the darkness until she sat down right next to her and continued doodling in the dirt. "I'm sorry about your friend."

Stacy looked away, hiding the tears from her sister. She had tried to push the thought of Melissa's dead body above them from her mind, but she couldn't stop her imagination from running wild.

"Do you remember when we used to play in the mines?" Amelia asked.

Stacy kept her looking in the other direction, unable to keep her voice steady. "Yeah. What about it?"

"I remember how scary the mines were," Amelia said. "So dark and cold, and it smelled bad too. I kept imagining so many monsters inside that would come and attack me." She touched Stacy's arm. "But you helped keep me safe. And you told me that there was nothing to be scared of."

Stacy looked back at her sister. "But I was wrong. Monsters are real."

Amelia moved closer to her sister. "Then I'll protect you." She pressed her head against Stacy's side. "Just like you protected me."

Tears fell down Stacy's cheeks, and she hugged Amelia, letting herself grieve for her friend, trying to set aside the guilt of what she had done. She knew that it would take time before she was even close to being healed from all of this. But it was nice to know that she didn't have to do it alone.

"I'm sorry that I didn't come to visit sooner. I'm sorry that I left you here with her all alone."

Amelia shrugged. "It wasn't so bad. I get to play outside a lot. And I like that. But it does get lonely." She looked up at Stacy, and even in the darkness, the whites of her eyes were visible. "I just wish you hadn't waited so long to come back."

Stacy wrapped her sister in a hug and then kissed the top of her head. "I'm sorry, Em. I really am." Her voice cracked. She sniffled and then Amelia squeezed back tighter. "I didn't know how to handle all of this. I still don't. But I'm sorry that I left you."

Amelia looked up at her sister again, her features cloaked in darkness. "Remember what Dad used to say?"

Stacy smiled, nodding along with Amelia. "You're never alone if you have family that's thinking of you." She cleared her throat. "I remember."

Amelia pressed her face into her sister's side again and then squeezed tight. "I miss him a lot."

"Yeah," Stacy said. "Me too."

The pair lingered in the quiet for a moment, but both of them perked up when they heard movement outside the cabin.

Stacy immediately reached for the shotgun and tucked it under her arm. It was already cocked and loaded, so all she had to do was squeeze the trigger. The barrel held four rounds, and she would pump them off as quick as she could to make sure that whoever entered was blown off the map.

Stacy moved herself and Amelia toward the back wall and watched through the crack in the boards as several shadows emerged from the forest. They moved quickly and stealthily, all of them armed.

Once the terrorist unit passed around to the front of the cabin, Stacy was forced to rely on her ears to follow them, and she heard their quiet footsteps as they passed through the front door.

Stacy kept Amelia behind her, following the enemy with the barrel of the shotgun. They slowed once they entered the cabin, moving through their home carefully and methodically, but with the same steady precision as their approach from the woods.

Stacy did her best to keep herself still, but the longer the enemy hovered above them, the faster her nerves unraveled, and the harder it became to keep the weapon steady in her hands. She thought of Melissa, remembered the blood that covered her body as she held her dead friend in her arms. She couldn't save her. Stacy didn't think that she could save anyone.

The voices continued to speak, continued to confer with one another, but she was convinced that there wasn't anything left for them to do but go. Except they didn't go. They moved back toward the bedroom hallway. They moved back toward where Stacy and Amelia were hiding, almost as if they knew they were below the floors.

Amelia pressed herself tighter against Stacy's back, her presence nothing more than that of a powerful heater.

Stacy tensed the closer they moved, and while she only

had a limited view of what she could see, she was able to fill in the blanks with her imagination. She saw them aim their weapons down at the cracks of the floorboard. She saw the wicked smile crease their faces.

Their fingers were on the trigger now, and they slowed their steps until they stopped altogether. They whispered back and forth, and Stacy imagined their conversation, and how excited they must have been to be so close to adding two more bodies to their cause.

But they didn't know that they were standing over the barrel of a pump-action twelve-gauge that would easily blow through the wood and then send all of those steel balls through their bodies, shredding their legs and their organs, dropping them to the floor.

Except when Stacy tried to pull the trigger, she froze.

Stacy shut her eyes, trying to break the paralysis, but instead she only saw Melissa and the blood, the memory was so vibrant and vile.

Stacy opened her eyes again and saw that one of the terrorists had crouched, feeling along the floor for a hidden trap door in the floor to check for anyone that might be hiding. She wasn't going to get a better chance to kill them, but as she applied the lightest pressure on the trigger, gunfire erupted from above.

Stacy dropped the shotgun and reached for her sister, unable to tell if she'd been shot or hurt. She knew that her adrenaline was running hot and that even if she had been hit she might not be able to feel it, but the moment after the noise of gunfire ended, she spun around to check on Amelia. She cupped her cheeks, staring into those big eyes that stared right back up at her, and waited for her voice to break through the high-pitched din in her ears.

"Are you okay?" Stacy heard herself ask, even though she wasn't sure if she was okay herself.

But Amelia only nodded, and both girls turned when the trap door opened and they saw their mother hovering above them in the darkness.

*M*ike lingered behind at the cabin longer than he should have, but he found it difficult to leave, especially with Amelia clinging to his leg. But he assured the little girl that he would come back and visit, so long as Stacy said that it was all right, which she did.

He also made sure to get the bodies out of the cabin before he left, but when he tried to bury them, Jo stopped him.

"I'll bury the girl and burn the others," she said. "Set them on fire in the road. If that's not a keep out sign, then I don't know what is."

Mike had wanted to tell her that it was a bad idea, but he didn't protest. Both Jan and Furst were still around, and it was Furst who changed the subject.

"We didn't get all of those bastards," Furst said. "I say we head out into the woods and finish the job." He spit, then crossed his arms to accentuate his stance.

"The fight's over," Mike said.

"No," Jo replied. "It's not."

Mike was surprised at Jo's response. "You want us to go after them now?"

"Not tonight," Jo answered. "But at first light. It's the only way we'll truly be safe. Because these people won't stop hunting us. We need to take the fight to them."

"She's right," Jan said. "I don't like it. But she's right."

Mike planted his fists on his hips, and then sighed. "All right. Tomorrow. I suppose we should get to bed and rest."

Furst and Jan departed, but Mike lingered, not wanting to leave Jo by herself. But he knew that he couldn't stay.

"Goodnight, Jo," Mike said.

"Goodnight."

Mike made it a few paces before Jo's voice made him stop. "Mike?"

It was the way she spoke the name that gave him pause. Jo Mercer wasn't a woman who presented herself as vulnerable. And he had never held it against her. Strong women always got a bad rap with most folks. They saw them as prickly and unmotherly or too masculine. If they had been men, other people would have just said that they were tough. But they weren't men. That was their only crime.

"Yeah?" Mike asked.

Jo had never been one to beat around the bush, but the way that she danced around the subject made Mike nervous because he wasn't sure what she was going to ask.

"Thank you," Jo finally said, after twisting her lips for the last minute. "For what you did in town. I didn't even hear that guy creep up on me like that. I could have died if you hadn't shown up the way you did." She kept her eyes on the ground but finally looked up at him for the last few words. "I owe you my life."

The first thought that passed through Mike's mind was something he let go because his first instinct was to be

JAMES HUNT

playful and make a joke. It was his failsafe whenever he was nervous, but experience and age allowed him to keep it buried, and he thought hard about what came next, because he knew it was important.

"I'm glad I was there to do it," Mike said. "But you don't owe me anything." He walked closer, propelled to her by some magnetic force. It was a force that he'd felt for a long time, but he'd always stopped himself. But not this time. He had gone through too much hell to deny him this one little piece of happiness, even if it was nothing more than getting closer to her. "I'm always here to help, Jo." He took her hand, feeling the calluses on her palm from the rough life that she had chosen. But the top of her hands was smooth, and her grip was secure in his own. He liked that.

"I know." Jo opened her mouth like she wanted to say more, but then reclaimed her hands and retreated a step toward the cabin. "I should get back inside, be with the girls."

Mike nodded. "Of course." He stood there and watched her leave, staying until she was all the way inside, and lingered a little bit even after she was gone.

The pair had known each other for a long time, but in that time, Mike had never felt like he really knew Jo. And while he wanted to learn more about her, he knew that he couldn't wait forever. He couldn't wait for the girl on the mountain to finally let down her guard and be with someone who wanted to be with her.

He knew that tearing down those walls would only make things worse for both her and him. The only way he would ever get to know the truth about Joanna Mercer was if she told him. She had to be the one to let him in on her own accord. But Mike wasn't sure how much longer he could hold out. Or even survive, given what they were facing.

There was plenty to consider and think about on the

walk back to The Village, where he was immediately bombarded with questions from the villagers about the attack.

Mike held up his hands as the Behr brothers led the charge to chase the terrorists down in the woods, hunting them before they had a chance to attack the village again.

"We know these woods better than some foreigners," Donny Behr said, the eldest brother and arguably the best shooter aside from Joanna on the mountain. "We hunt them all down before they have a chance to come back and hurt us even more!"

A resounding cheer erupted from the small crowd, everyone but Mike's deputies joining the heated excitement that the bloodlust from the fight in town had provided. But Mike kept his cool, knowing that it was his responsibility to protect people, even if it meant protecting them from themselves.

"We won tonight," Mike said. "But we also got lucky. If Jo hadn't come to warn us that the enemy was on its way, then we would have been slaughtered where we stood." He turned around, addressing the entire crowd, but kept the majority of his attention on the Behr family, because it was their excitement that the townspeople were feeding off of. "We need to be smart about this. It's dark, they're on the run, they've more than likely already retreated deep into the woods and fortified their position. And if we stumble across them in the woods in the dark with no idea of where they are, it wouldn't take much for them to turn the odds back in their favor, and that's exactly what they want." Mike steadily raised his voice throughout the speech, hoping that his reason would break through their hysteria.

"They killed our people," Donny said, his voice dropping some of its excitement, but what remained was something more sinister. "Innocent people, good people, people that should have never been lost—"

"I know," Mike said, stepping closer to Donny. "But I'm not going to send what good men and women we have left into the woods in the middle of the night to track down an enemy this dangerous." He nearly growled the last few words, and it was enough to force Donny to back down, and the rest of the energy that had inflated the town died down.

Mike turned to the rest of the crowd now that Donny had been dealt with and raised his voice. "My number one priority is the protection of this mountain and the people who live on it. It's also to bring justice down upon those that seek to harm it, but I will not sacrifice our well-being for the vigilante kind of justice that we all want to take part in."

"So what now?" Donny asked. "What are we supposed to do? Just wait for them to come back like they did tonight? With bigger numbers? More guns?"

"The military that was at the depot made it into the city," Mike answered. "We'll have them come up here to help us secure The Village and bolster our defenses. In the meantime, we'll bury our dead, crew our stations, and reset our provisions. We still have a long road ahead of us, and I don't want us to lose sight of what we still have to do."

It was enough to at least appease the angry crowd, and after Mike was finished, Furst and Donny helped direct the others to clean up the streets and find graves for the dead, many of whom were still being mourned in the streets on which they fell.

It was hard to see the blood in the dark, which seemed to soak and blend into the black asphalt. Under the cloudy night sky, the pools of blood next to the bodies looked like nothing more than rain puddles after a storm.

It would be a long night of burying the dead.

26

*J*o kept the girls inside as she tucked the bodies
around back. She would deal with them in the
morning, but for now she would let them rot in
the plastic that would help keep the animals from getting at
them, at least for the night.

Before Jo sealed the bags, she patted down the bodies to
search for anything that might give her any insight into the
enemy. However, the only thing the fighters had in their
pockets were spare ammunition and a few rations.

However, she did find a gold medallion around the neck
of the younger-looking fighter. It was stained with blood,
and Jo thought it was peculiar that the man should wear it,
considering the rest of his clothes were little more than rags.

From what Jo could tell, the medallion looked like it was
solid gold, and by the weight of it, she thought it would sell
for tens of thousands of dollars now. Not that money was of
use to anyone anymore.

Jo examined the medallion more closely, unable to read
the marks that had been carved around the circle's outer
edge, which she assumed was Arabic. She stood again and

flung the tarp over the dead, not wanting to waste any more time on them. She would have plenty of time for that tomorrow.

Jo entered the cabin to a somber silence. Neither of the girls had said much since Mike pulled them out of the hole, but Amelia was handling it better than her sister.

In the cabin, Amelia hadn't left Stacy's side on the couch, her eldest daughter staring blankly into the wall across from her. It was like she had gone into shock, but she didn't display the healthy behaviors of someone who was in shock. She wasn't cold or clammy, her pulse and other vitals were fine. She was just… vacant.

Jo stepped in front of Stacy's field of vision, blocking the wall. But the girl still didn't look up. "Are you guys hungry?"

Amelia nodded, but Stacy only shrugged.

"Stacy," Jo said, kneeling, forcing her daughter to look her in the eyes. "You need to talk to me and tell me what's going on. I can't guess. I was never good at that."

"Dad was," Amelia said, smiling as she looked between her sister and her mother. "Dad could always tell what was wrong. It was like a superpower."

Jo nodded, and one of the rare sweet memories of Danny came flooding back to her. "It was like he could always get in my head, even when I didn't want him there."

"That's because he was a good person," Stacy said, keeping her tone flat and her expression stoic. "They know because good people are the only ones that can ever fix the things that are broken. It's in their DNA." She shook her head. "I'm not a good person." She frowned, then looked to her mother. "You're not a good person either."

It was the plain and simple nature of the statement that threw Jo off guard. And Jo remained in stunned silence as Stacy stood and walked to her room.

"She doesn't mean it," Amelia said. "She's still feeling guilty because of what happened to Melissa."

Jo nodded. "Looks like you have Dad's superpower too."

Amelia blushed, and then slid off the couch and hugged her mother. "I still love you, and she does too. She just needs a little help remembering."

Jo closed her eyes as she held her daughter, surprised by the words of wisdom provided by such a little girl. When Amelia let go, Jo didn't feel as bad as she did before. "Yeah. You definitely have your dad's superpower."

"Does that mean we can have breakfast for dinner?" Amelia asked.

Jo smiled. "Sure."

Amelia followed Jo into the kitchen, and the pair got some dinner ready. It wasn't until she smelled the bacon fat sizzling in the pan that she realized how hungry she had been. She hadn't really eaten since breakfast save for the few snacks that she brought along the way when she went into town. After directing the townspeople on defensive training, she didn't have enough time to eat a proper meal.

But that wouldn't happen tonight.

Amelia mixed up some waffle batter, and they made a breakfast feast for supper, something that had always been one of their family favorites when their family had been whole.

The pair worked silently but happily as they prepared the meal, and Jo hoped that the smell of dinner would coax Stacy out of her room, but when they were finished, it was only Jo and Amelia at the small cubby cutout table where they ate their meals together for breakfast, lunch, and dinner.

"Do you want me to go get her?" Amelia asked.

"I'll do it," Jo answered, staring at the hallway entrance.

Jo didn't know why she was so nervous. It wasn't like

there was anything worse than her daughter could say to her or even do to her for that matter than what had already passed between them. But still, Jo was surprised to find her hand trembling when she reached for the door handle to her daughter's room. It wasn't like her to be so afraid, and she didn't like that she was so scared, but here she was, trembling like a monster stood on the other side of that door.

What could Jo say to a daughter that no longer saw her as a mother, or a human being for that matter? Jo had never been the one that was good really connecting with them, and it had been a struggle for her even before Danny died. Like Amelia said, Daddy always knew what was wrong.

Jo didn't knock, choosing to enter first and ask forgiveness later. The hinges groaned as she pushed the door open, just a crack at first, but when she saw Stacy's back to her as she lay on the bed, she opened the door all the way.

"Stacy," Jo said, standing in the doorway. "Amelia and I made dinner. Well, breakfast really. You should come out and eat with us."

Stacy remained motionless and unresponsive on the bed.

Jo walked toward the bed, then sat on the edge like a ghost, the mattress barely moving from her weight. She folded her hands in her lap, twisting her fingers. If she still wore her wedding ring, then she would have fidgeted with that. But she hadn't worn that since Danny's funeral.

"Stacy…" Jo placed a hand on her daughter's shoulder and felt her shudder beneath her touch. "You need to talk to me about what's going on, because if you keep whatever it is bottled up inside of you like this, then… then you're going to become me." She emphasized the latter, hoping that her shift in tone would trigger a laugh. But when the jokes didn't work, Jo tried sincerity. "Please, Stacy." She gently squeezed Stacy's shoulder. "Talk to me."

"How do you do it?" Stacy asked, keeping her back to Jo. "How can you just forget everything that happened? Keep it from killing you? How do you bury it?" She turned, craning her neck around, peering at her mother like she was some kind of guilty party to everything that happened.

But Jo didn't wholly understand. "What do you mean, how do I bury it?"

Stacy positioned herself so she was flat on her back and then fiddled with her hands the same way that Jo would do when she was nervous. The pair were more alike than either wanted to admit. "What you saw in the city doesn't bother you? All of those dead people? The bodies in the streets, the blood, the screams, the—" She scrunched up her face and grimaced. "The smell?" She relaxed her face again, then shook her head. "I can't stop seeing it, and because I can't stop seeing it and thinking about it, I can't stop being afraid of it." She glanced down at her hands and shook her head. "I just don't know what else I can do."

Jo paused for a moment, considering the situation, and then spoke. "After your father died, I didn't want to live anymore. I know that's wrong for me to say because I still had two wonderful daughters that I didn't deserve, but all I could think about was wanting to kill myself and be done with it." She curled her fingers and covered her hand over her heart like she would claw her way inside her chest and rip it out. "It was like everything inside of me was poison. Like I was sick, and the only cure was death." She dropped her hand and then shook her head. "I thought I was weak because I couldn't handle it. And because I thought I was weak, I thought that I didn't deserve you and your sister." She looked at Stacy, both their eyes reddening with tears. "So I came out here to make myself stronger. So I could protect myself, and you, and we would never have to worry about death again. But because I spent so much time thinking about how to make myself stronger and tougher than I was before, I had to leave a lot of things behind. I know that I was hard on you, both of you, but you especially. And I'm sorry I had to become this to survive." Her lower lip quivered. "I'm sorry that I had to leave so much behind, but at the time, it was the only thing that I could do."

Stacy reached for her mother's hand and squeezed, and the gesture only triggered the tears to roll down her cheeks and dripped onto the bedsheets.

"I know that I didn't make it easy on you either," Stacy said. "And I'm sorry for that."

Jo wiped her nose and shook her head. "You don't have anything to apologize for. You reacted the only way you could in that moment and at that time. It's just the way it fell." She calmed down, collecting herself, and then looked her daughter in the eye. "Whatever you're feeling right now, it's not because you can't handle it, it's because you're trying to handle it and stay who you are." She tightened her grip on her daughter's hand. "That was something that I couldn't do. I thought that I could, but I had to let the old me go, just like I had to let your father go."

Stacy nodded. "I knew you took it hard. But I didn't know you took it that hard."

Jo smirked. "I thought your father and I were going to grow old together, in that house. But that's not how things worked out." She wiped away the rest of the tears, her eyes dry but still red now. "So you do whatever you need to do to stay alive, Stacy, and to keep that part of yourself. Because the last thing I would want you to become is someone like me. Someone who forgot who they were, someone who never understood their place in this world, someone who didn't know how to forget and forgive, someone who—" She bit her tongue and drew in a sharp breath. "Someone who should have done more for her daughters, and for her family."

Stacy shook her head. "You're not a bad person, Mom. You didn't make the wrong decision about moving out here. I mean, how could you? Look what happened. If you hadn't come out here in the first place, then we all would have died. You helped get us ready. We had a place to go to. We knew what to do." She shrugged. "Maybe... all of this happened so we could live. Maybe we had to go through all of that bad stuff to get us ready." She grinned. "What did Dad always use to say? Sometimes you get some lemon juice in your eye before the lemonade is made?"

Jo tittered. "It was his way of always looking at the bright side. He always thought that his best days were ahead of him." The smile faded, like the shadows of all those memories she had lost.

But maybe Stacy was right. Maybe all of those bad things happened so that they would be prepared. Maybe Jo had become the woman she did to eliminate the evil that threatened her family. She knew that they were still out there, hiding in the woods, and her family wouldn't be truly safe until they hunted the last of them down.

But that would wait until tomorrow. Now it was time to be with her girls, at least for one night, and return to the family that they had been.

"You know," Jo said. "I remember your father saying that there was nothing to make you feel better than breakfast for dinner."

Stacy smiled. "He said it was like getting a start over for a bad day before the day ended."

Jo gestured to the kitchen. "How about a restart for today?"

Stacy sat up in the bed and then nodded. "I think that's a good idea."

Jo led Stacy back to the dinner table, and Amelia smiled brightly when she saw her sister come to join them. And for the first time in nearly a year, all three of them sat down around the dinner table, feasting on bacon and eggs and Belgian waffles. The conversation was slow at first but then turned to giggles and laughter as Amelia made a smiley face out of her food.

Jo couldn't remember the last time that she heard her daughters laugh together. It had been well before Stacy had left for school. And while the world around them was starting to crumble, Jo found it ironic that it took the end of the world to finally bring her family back together. Now, all she had to do was make sure that they survived the world around them before it consumed the very family that she had just got back together.

27

*T*he retreat from the town had been unexpected and chaotic. Muhammed had made the mistake of underestimating The Village and had allowed the information given to him by the deputy to let himself grow confident.

The darkness made it difficult to find their way back to the mine opening, but they finally arrived. It was easy to get lost in the mountains, especially at night.

All of the men knew to meet back at the campsite, but the hasty retreat had left many of Muhammed's men scattered through the woods, and even after he arrived back at the mine, the only people that had returned with him were the three men that had been around him when he first ordered the retreat.

Uninjured, Muhammed helped dress the wounds of those that had been hurt, but while his attention was focused on his tasks, his mind couldn't help but wonder when his brother would return. And every time there was noise in the darkness, Muhammed would pray it would be Zahid. But every time that it wasn't him, that resolve of hope was slowly chipped away, and he wasn't sure what would happen after it was gone.

Muhammed distracted himself with tending to the wounded, but most of the men that had been shot had died in the streets. He vowed to return to collect them, give them a proper burial, and ensure the people who were responsible for their deaths would be held accountable for them when the time came. Because there was no doubt in his mind that he was going to return to that village. He might have lost the battle, but he would not lose the war.

Because Muhammed didn't know if the enemy would return, he instructed two of the few men who could still stand and fight to string the forest lines with trip wires, using some of the mines that they had stolen from the Army Depot at the base of the mountain.

They were too weak and vulnerable to fend off another attack, and if those villagers were foolish enough to follow them into the woods at night, then he would make sure that they paid for their arrogance.

Men trickled in through the night, and when morning came, there were only five men left. But when Muhammed looked for his brother, he could not find him.

Muhammed found Khalid, who had been charged with guarding the deputy. "Has Zahid not returned?"

"No," Khalid said. "He went to the cabin, didn't he?"

Muhammed nodded. "He told me there were supplies. He said there was enough food there to feed us for months."

All of the cells that had been activated across the mountain range had gone about their work knowing that they would go in without the possibility of backup. But between the loss of his men and the disappearance of his brother, Muhammed wanted to bolster his forces, and that meant breaking the other cells away from their primary targets.

If this mountain went unchecked, then it could provide the infidels with the opportunity to regroup, and after the strength he had just witnessed at that village, he knew that he couldn't let them continue to live.

Muhammed instructed one of his men to go and locate the other cells along the mountain, and bring them back to their camp at the mine. "I want them here by nightfall, so we can mount an attack in the morning."

"Yes, Commander." The soldier hurried off without question. That was the kind of respect that he garnered. He was never questioned, but his authority wouldn't help to ease the worry about his brother.

There wasn't any reason for Zahid to not have returned by now unless he was hurt.

"I'm going to find him," Muhammed said, but Khalid pulled him back.

"Sir—"

"He's my brother," Muhammed said. "I will find him. Dead or alive."

Khalid released Muhammed's arm. "You do not know the way."

"No," Muhammed said, turning his gaze to the deputy. "But he does."

Mike stood over his sink. He hadn't slept but a few hours. He just couldn't get his mind to stop racing. He was restless and tired, but wired like he'd just drank three cups of coffee on an empty stomach. He stared down at his hands, which were dirty and grimy from burying the bodies.

The burying hadn't been a problem, but listening to the cries of the townspeople who had lost their loved ones had been difficult to hear. One second everything had been fine, and then the next second everything was broken.

It was his job to keep law and order and to ensure the safety and survival of the citizens of his community. But he had failed.

The images of all that death he had seen in the other towns would haunt him until the end of his days. It was like something out of a war movie where enemy forces marched into a community and slaughtered everyone. But death had a certain texture in real life that couldn't be matched in the movies.

Even now, in the bathroom, Mike saw every single pair of

eyes that refused to close in the streets. All of the blank stares, all of the motionless bodies, and the silence. The silence was probably the worst of all.

Because death silenced everyone and everything. It was a cold blanket of fog, numbing all of your senses. None of that would have happened if he had been better prepared. None of that would have happened if he had done his job.

But Mike made a promise to himself, then and there, that he would never fail again. He would uphold the law, because without it, people were only savages.

Mike stared down at his palms, the first few rays of dawn peering in from the window at the wall. He squinted, not recognizing the grooves of his own skin. But somehow he knew they were his. Just like he knew that he would have to face today with the same conviction that everyone expected him to. Because he had asked people to wait for their justice, for the wrongs against their friends and family to be right based off of his word.

And now it was time to deliver. Now, it was time to finish the war that someone else started. A war that Mike never wanted to play any part of. He bowed his head again, shutting his eyes and thinking that maybe when he opened them, he would be in his bed, and this would have all been nothing but a dream. The villages on the mountain would still be safe and intact. There would be no power outage. Mike would turn to the clock on his nightstand and see the red numbers blinking back at him the same way they always did when his alarm went off.

But the longer that Mike stood there, clutching the sink, waiting to hear that deaf tone beep from his alarm, the more he knew that this wasn't a dream. He was wide awake.

Mike opened his eyes and found his reflection in the mirror. He drew in a breath, then exhaled slowly, making sure he was in the mindset needed to finish it. He left the bathroom and got dressed, still choosing to put on his uniform. He wanted the people they caught to understand that they couldn't outrun the law of the land here. And he would make sure that they remembered the uniform that brought them down.

Once he was dressed, Mike grabbed his rifle and his hat and glasses. From what he could see from his front porch, it looked like it would be a sunny, hot day. These were days that he grew up on, days frequently spent finding some shade and drinking something cold. Today would be hot and rough because today they were hunting killers.

29

*J*o hadn't wanted to leave the cabin when morning came. She hadn't wanted the night with her girls to end either. She just wanted to stay home with her girls and laugh and talk about things that had nothing to do with the end of the world, or EMPs or terrorists or prepping or what they would have to do to continue to survive. She had wanted to freeze time last night and linger there forever.

But maybe that was why the moment was so sweet, because Jo knew that it wouldn't last forever. It was why she wanted to hold on for so long. And it was why it hurt so bad when the moment was gone. Especially now, because Jo knew that there was no guarantee that it would come back.

Now, all three of them were walking toward The Village because Jo didn't want to leave the girls at the cabin unprotected again. It was clear that while Stacy was slowly returning to her usual self, she was in no frame of mind to try and protect her younger sister from any kind of a threat. And while Amelia was smart and capable, Jo didn't want to put her youngest daughter in a position where she would be forced to do something beyond her years, even though that's precisely what she had trained her to do. Sometimes what was theoretical didn't match up with what happened in real life.

Jo knew that they would be safe with Mags, and at the very least there were still guards stationed around the town, people more alert after the big fight from the night before.

Jo glanced up to the sky. There were quite a few clouds for it being as early in the morning as it was. Sometimes that meant rain, sometimes it didn't. The weather was as fickle as people. But it was summer, and they were due for rain.

Mags greeted Jo outside of her store, giving Stacy a big hug and Amelia a kiss on the top of her head. The old woman looked a little rough around the edges, but after last night, Jo suspected everyone was rattled.

"Glad to see you girls are safe. Not that I'm surprised." Mags turned to Jo. "Do you know who you're heading out with?"

"I need to check with Mike and confirm, but I assume the deputies and the Behr brothers," Jo said, and while she had never particularly cared for the Behr brothers, she knew that she needed good shots, and the Behr brothers were the best hunters on the mountain. Besides Jo, of course. "If all goes well, we'll be back before nightfall."

"Then let's hope it goes well," Mags said, then ushered Amelia into the shop.

Stacy lingered outside, rubbing her arms nervously. "Do you really think it's the smartest play going after them like this? I mean we pushed them back. Now that they know we can fight, they'd probably just move on to easier prey."

"Maybe," Jo said, conceding the point. "But easier prey just means more lives lost." Jo stared down at the rifle in her hands, the weapon more familiar to her than she thought it ever would be. "And I think I'm done sitting on the sidelines." She looked to her oldest daughter, who was timid and shy, a far cry from the girl that she had known before she left for school. "What about you?" She stepped closer. "Are you tired of sitting on the sidelines?"

Stacy looked away, hugging herself tighter, and then shook her head, her cheeks paler than they should have been.

Jo stepped closer to her daughter, dropping her voice to a harsher whisper, and squeezed Stacy's arm. "You need to step up here, Stace. Because if you don't and something happens while I'm not here, you won't be able to survive. So I need the old you back. Okay? I need the girl who had the fire in her belly." She waited for Stacy to respond, but when she didn't, Jo tightened her grip on Stacy's arm. "*Okay?*"

Stacy nodded, trying to pull her arm back. "Yeah."

Some of the anger had returned, but Jo wasn't sure it would stick. And she needed it to hold. "Do you still have your sidearm?"

Stacy nodded, once again hugging herself in that unassured, self-conscious way she had during her early teen years.

Knowing that she needed to clear her mind of all distractions, Jo did just that on her walk down to the sheriff's station, but she found it hard as she passed the stores riddled with broken windows and bullet holes, and the pavement that was dotted with the bloodstains from those that had fallen the night before.

Perhaps it was better if that rain came after all.

Jan was outside the station with the Behr brothers, but nobody was talking. Jo knew that the youngest Behr brother, Rusty, had died in the fighting last night, and from the looks on their faces, it didn't look like any of them got a wink of sleep.

"Where's Mike?" Jo asked.

"He's not here yet," Jan answered.

"We're wasting time." Donny Behr spat on the ground, and he cleared his throat, shifting his feet as though he were agitated. "Should have left before dawn."

"If we left before dawn, then we wouldn't have the benefit of the light." Mike came up from behind all of them, Furst in tow, each man carrying a duffel bag. "And we need light to make sure we can see what we're shooting."

"I always see what I'm shooting," Donny Behr said, his voice as gruff as the stubble that ran down his face and neck, connecting to his exposed chest hair. "We leaving or what?"

Mike dropped his duffel bag, and Furst mimicked the motion. "We'll need to make sure that we're on the same page out there. So let's make a few things clear right now." He pointed to the woods. "No matter how deep we go, I'm still in charge. I don't care if we end up crossing over to Union County, you do what I tell you or I will put you in cuffs myself. Number two." He pointed at Jo. "She leads the expedition." He held up a hand before Donny Behr could protest. "I don't care how good of a tracker anyone else is, she's seen the layout of their camp and knows where to look. End of discussion."

Donny opened his mouth as if to speak, but then quickly shut it, and Mike continued.

"The last is this," Mike took a breath, almost as if he was hesitant to say, but then blurted it out before he thought better of it. "We take them alive if we can."

Donny laughed, and even Jo gave him a funny look.

"You have to be kidding me," Donny said, shaking his head, then pointed to the street. "Look at what they did to our town! And you said that they hit the other village down the mountain? Why wouldn't we try and waste every last one of these suckers?"

"Because that's not what the law demands," Mike answered, keeping his tone firm, but sounding like a man who was at odds with himself and the conclusion that he'd reached. "If they shoot at us, and they more than likely will, then we shoot back, and it's open season." He kept his eyes on the Behr boys when he spoke. "But if they throw down their weapons, and if they surrender, then we're going to take them into custody and put them in a cell until we figure out what is going on."

"That's the wrong move, Sheriff," Donny said. "You think they would show us mercy? What do you think they're doing to your deputy right now? Jo said they were torturing him. That's all they know. They're animals. Rabid animals. And they need to be put down."

"It's because they have my deputy that I don't want to start a firefight unless I have to," Mike said. "If we can get the jump on them, then we have a chance at solving this peacefully. That's the end game I want, no one else dies." Mike waited for Donny to keep speaking, but the man kept quiet.

"What's in the bags?" Jo asked, wanting to break up the monotony of the silence.

Furst knelt down and unzipped the one that he brought. "Some insurance policies for everyone." He opened the bag so everyone could peer inside, and Jo saw the body armor.

"Pick one that fits," Mike said. "We leave in five."

The Behr brothers were the first to pick out their vests, and Mike walked back into the station. Jo figured there wasn't going to be a better time to try and speak to him alone, so she took her chance.

The door swung shut behind Jo when she entered, and

she saw Mike's backside. "It's not a good idea to try and bring them in alive."

"That's not your call," Mike said, keeping his back to her.

"Like hell it's not!" Jo's anger surprised her, but it forced Mike to turn around. "They came to my house. They were going to kill my girls."

"And they slaughtered two of my communities," Mike said, matching her intensity. "Last time I checked, I'm still the one with the badge, not you."

"And I'm the one that can find them," Jo said. "You need me more than I need you."

It was the first time that Jo had ever seen Mike's anger turn on her, and it was enough to force her to think about what she said next.

"The people who did this aren't going to negotiate," Jo said. "They're not going to talk, they're not here to do anything but kill as many people as they can. I'm going out on this expedition to make sure that they don't do that anymore."

"They can't kill people from inside a cell," Mike said.

Jo knew that he had a point, but like everyone else in the town, she wanted revenge. She wanted to send a message. "How many other terrorist cells do you think are out there right now? This was a coordinated attack, and they're going to keep coming at us until we don't have anything left. Can't you see that?"

Mike sighed, shaking his head, the anger replaced with the cruel apathy that remained when all other options had been exhausted. "I'm not changing my mind about this, and if you're going to come with us, I need to make sure that you're following my lead. Because anyone that disobeys me out there will be disobeying the law." He stepped closer to her. "I've let you skirt by with more warnings than I should have,

Joanna. But I will not be crossed on this. Do you understand me? I can't let law and order just crumble around me into nothing." He stiffened. "I won't let that happen."

It was the way his jaw was set and how his eyes were focused and clear that Jo knew Mike wasn't going to bend.

Jo finally nodded. "Your county, your rules."

"Good." Mike turned around and finished gathering his things. "Make sure you grab some Kevlar. If this turns into a gunfight, I want everyone protected. From what we saw off the bodies that were left behind from last night, the fighters didn't have any body armor, so that combined with the fact that this should be a surprise assault means that we'll have the upper hand."

Jo watched the muscles along Mike's back ripple beneath his shirt. He was a strong man. A good man. But he was doing what he thought was right, and Jo knew that line of thinking just didn't work in this new world. Because it wasn't about doing what was right. It was about doing what needed to be done. And Jo knew that what needed to be done was to make sure that whoever they found in the woods didn't make it out alive. She would make sure that happened.

30

The vest that Jo had worn made it more challenging to move, adding a layer of weight that she wasn't used to carrying when she hunted. But she knew that it was smart to wear one. She'd take whatever advantage she could get.

Much to Jo's surprise, the Behr brothers kept their opinions and grumblings to themselves, for the most part at least, as she led them through the forest. She wasn't sure how seriously they would take Mike's orders, but they had hung back, only tossing a few glares in her direction when she checked behind her.

It was going to be at least a two-hour hike from The Village until they reached the mine, and before they arrived, Jo wanted to make sure that everyone knew what they were dealing with. If they were smart, they would be able to corner them into the mine, and then bring it down and wait for them to choke and starve to death from the collapse. Of all the deaths that she imagined for the people who attacked her family and home, that was the one that she kept returning to in her mind. It was the perfect combination of slow and painful.

Smiling at the thought of the enemy's demise, Jo dropped the smirk when Donny Behr appeared by her side.

"How much longer until we get there?" Donny asked, keeping his voice quiet as he spoke.

"It's another hour," Jo answered, also keeping her voice down to a whisper. "I saw blood about one hundred yards back. Some of them are already injured."

"I saw," Donny said, keeping his eyes forward. "I know you and I haven't always gotten along, but I think that we're on the same page about what needs to be done once we find these bastards."

Jo fought the urge to turn around to see if Mike was close and listening. "What are you thinking?"

Donny shrugged, playing it off like he was adjusting his pack. "I thought that it'll be a little chaotic, and the moment that one bullet starts flying, all hell will break loose. When that happens, I don't think those bastards will even want to surrender anymore."

Jo nodded. "I think that sounds like something I can get behind."

"Good." Donny wiped his nose and then cleared his throat, and he raised his voice as he slowed to head toward the back of the pack with his brothers. "Let me know if you need any help."

"Thanks," Jo said, calling after him.

It was funny the people that you found and turned to when things went to shit. It didn't seem like it was possible for her to ever be friends with Donny Behr, but hatred and revenge were powerful bonding agents. It was easy to set aside differences once you realized that you had a common enemy and were aligned with how to deal with that enemy.

Not long after Donny faded to the back of the pack, Mike appeared by her side.

"Need something, Sheriff?" Jo asked, keeping her tone conversational.

"What were you and Donny talking about?" Mike asked.

"He wanted to know how much farther we had to go," Jo answered, keeping it honest, but not giving the sheriff more than the question demanded.

Mike crunched some rocks and twigs beneath his boot and then adjusted the assault rifle in his arms. "Jo, if you're planning something without telling me about it, I'm asking you to let it go."

"There isn't anything to let go of, Sheriff," Jo said, playing it cool. "You're the law. I'll follow the law." She cocked her head to the side. "Well, I guess, technically, the law is following me."

"I'm serious, Jo," Mike said, his tone foreboding. "I will not tolerate anything that will jeopardize the people on this mission."

"The people on this mission knew what they were getting into," Jo said. "Everyone knows the risk. Everyone but you."

"You don't think I want to kill them? Is that it?" Mike shook his head. "I was elected by the people of this county to uphold the law. I won't fail them again."

Jo looked up at him. It was rare to find a spot of pain on the man's face, but when it showed, it was always something that you wished you hadn't seen. It was like watching the death of innocence. "You failed those people no more than I failed to protect my husband from the drunk driver that killed him. It's not your fault, Mike. Even I didn't expect them to be so well-coordinated." She shook her head. "Whoever planned this was well-funded and motivated. I found a gold medallion on one of the dead terrorists that attacked the cabin. It has some words written on it, but I don't know the language. The gold was real though. The guy was walking around with close to ten grand around his neck. It meant something to him. Just like killing citizens meant something to his comrades."

Mike remained by her side but kept quiet, and his silence disturbed her.

"Hey." Jo nudged his arm, and he looked at her as they navigated the rocky terrain. "It wasn't your fault." She pointed ahead of them. "It's those people that are responsible. And we're going to make sure that they don't hurt anyone else again. We're doing something. We're trying to make it right."

Mike nodded. "I know." He turned to her. "But murder is never right. No matter which side of the law you're on. You get me?" He frowned. "I won't go down that road."

She nodded. "I understand."

Mike said nothing and then fell back with Deputy Furst, once again leaving Jo to navigate the forest alone. But that was the way she preferred it. She hadn't gone hunting with people in a long time, and she forgot how noisy everyone could be.

Along the way, both Mike and Donny's words bounced around in her head. The last thing she wanted to do was get on Mike's wrong side, but she was in agreement with Donny about the way it would go down.

Jo held up her hand and signaled the group to stop when they reached a patch of thick vegetation, and she crouched low, examining the green moss, grass, and bushes. There were plenty of places for them to hide a wire or a mine.

Footsteps sounded behind her, and Jo again quickly held up her hand, sending eyes like daggers into Donny Behr, who froze when she made the second motion. After he stopped, Jo looked ahead again, cupping her hands around the sides of her eyes so that she could narrow her field of vision. She scanned the ground in small sectors, making sure that she didn't miss anything that would have easily gotten lost in the shuffle if you had to look at nothing but the entire picture. It was why trip wires were so useful. People were always getting lost by looking ahead.

After a few minutes of studying the layout, Jo motioned for the others to stay put while she walked ahead alone.

"Are you sure that's a good idea?" Mike asked.

Jo didn't answer, concentrating on her steps. Every step forward that she took could mean certain death. She strode very carefully, covering only fifteen yards in the same amount of minutes.

Halfway through the foliage, Jo lifted her right boot, but then stopped when she felt the familiar tension of wire over the top of her foot. She paused, staring down at her feet until she was able to locate the clear wire that ran over the top.

Slowly, and very carefully, Jo set her foot down and slid it backward, then crouched down to unearth the wire.

It had been carefully placed, and well concealed, but Jo managed to find the source which was attached to a nearby tree, and she also saw the landmine that was attached to it. It wouldn't take much pressure to pull the pin, but in order for her to make sure that it didn't blow, she would have to keep pressure on the pin while she untangled the wire.

She drew in a breath and then gently started to work. Beads of sweat appeared on her forehead and gently cascaded down her face. A few rolled into her eyes, which stung, but she never diverted her gaze from the task at hand. One wrong move and the mine would blow her off the face of this earth and into the next world. If there was one.

One hand pressed the pin down tightly, while the other

removed the string from the lever, and then once it was clear, she dropped the pin back down on the mine and Jo let out that pent-up breath that she had been holding in. She looked back to the group and held the mine up high.

Jo turned the weapon over in her hands. It was practically brand new, and she wondered where they would have gotten something like this stateside, and then Jo remembered the old Army Depot where Gus had gone. It must have been where he was captured. And if the terrorist cell had managed to get these from the base, then there had to be more.

"Jesus," Mike said, walking up behind her and taking the device out of her hands. "Where the hell did they get these?"

"The Army Depot," Jo answered, staring ahead, and then as the rest of the group joined behind them, Jo saw another wire, and then another, and another, and by the time everyone had joined behind her, Jo counted over thirty of the devices planted over the next fifty yards.

And those were only the ones that she could see.

31

*M*ost folks in the town were quiet. Everyone knew what was happening out there, but no one wanted to talk about it. It was like people were afraid if they spoke too loud that the terrorists in the woods would hear them, even through the walls of their buildings.

Growing up, Stacy couldn't remember a time in The Village when the streets were empty, not even in the dead of winter after six inches of snow. There was always someone outside, there was always something going on, and there were always people.

But not today.

Stacy didn't blame them. She didn't want to be back in town either. But she knew that her mother was right. If something happened again, if those fighters came back to the cabin, she wouldn't be able to stop them.

Amelia was out back in Mags' old car. Stacy knew how much the girl loved that thing. Mags was probably going to leave it to Amelia when she died. Stacy wouldn't be surprised if it were already in her will. Her sister had always been lucky like that.

Stacy tapped her foot nervously against the hot tile of Mags' store, glancing anxiously back at her sister, who was playing outside. "Do you really think it's okay for her to be outside like that? I mean after what happened? What if those people come back? What if they start throwing bombs or grenades or something?"

Mags sat on her stool behind the register, as if the world hadn't changed, reading her magazine and fanning herself with a notepad. She flicked her eyes up from the magazine quickly before tossing them back down dismissively. "Amelia will be fine. And we have guards watching all around the town. We're as safe as safe can get."

Stacy rolled her eyes, but still couldn't help but look out at her sister. She finally stopped shaking her foot and headed out the front door. "I'll be back."

She squinted from the sunlight, and the moment she was out in the open, she grabbed the butt of her pistol at her hip. A hot breeze blew some of the stench of blood and guts that still lined the streets beneath her nostrils, and Stacy's stomach churned.

If it didn't rain soon, then all of that rot would get worse, not to mention the animals that it would attract down from the mountain. Mostly scavengers, they were the worst kind of animal to come down from the woods.

Scavenger animals always reminded Stacy of all those friends and family that she hardly knew that attended her father's funeral. All of them were just out there, nipping at the scraps, trying to get their grief fix and telling them how sorry they were for Stacy's loss.

But if they had been really sorry, they wouldn't have flown out there and forced Stacy and her sister to go through the dog and pony show. People should have just let her mourn, let her sister mourn, let her mother mourn. Maybe if that had happened, they wouldn't have had to move into the middle of fucking nowhere.

Stacy kept walking until she reached the end of town and saw the pair of guards keeping watch. They glanced back at her, but then quickly faced forward again. Both of them knew who she was, and both of them knew the reputation that her family had garnered in town.

It was the same social stigma that lingered after she was pulled from school and her friends stopped hanging out with her, which was worse than her friends calling her names. She would have preferred if they just told her that they thought she was weird, that they thought her mother losing her mind and moving them into the middle of the woods was cause for being put in the looney bin. She would have preferred anything than the cold shoulder.

Because Stacy held out hope all through her high school years that things would get better. It wasn't until her senior year that she finally wised up and she stopped trying to contact her old friends in the first place. Instead, she focused on just getting into college and getting the hell off the mountain, but she never really escaped its shadow.

Stacy turned away from the front of the town and walked down to the sheriff's station, hoping she could find out what else was going on since her mother didn't think her capable of handling anything.

But deep down, Stacy knew that her mother was right. Melissa's death was still on the forefront of her mind, and the blood was still on her hands.

Stacy had grappled with what happened, wondering if there was anything else that she could have done that wouldn't have resulted in all of them dying. She didn't think there was. If she had exposed herself, then she and Amelia would be dead. At least that's what she was telling herself.

Stacy spied Jan coming out of the station, and she quickly jogged to catch up to her before she spun back. "Hey!"

The deputy turned, and she offered a friendly smile when she saw Stacy. "Hey, what are you doing down here?" Jan was one of the deputies that was still on the force when her father had died. In fact, she had been one of the officers on scene during the accident.

"Looking for something to do," Stacy said. "I'm going stir crazy down at Mags' store."

Jan nodded, then pointed around the back of the station. "I was just about to check on some of our ammunition. Want to help?"

"I'd help clean out the latrines at this point," Stacy answered.

Jan laughed and then guided Stacy around the back corner of the building and to a locked cellar door, which Jan unlocked. "Be careful of spiders. We don't go down here much, and they've claimed the place as their own."

Stacy followed Jan down into the cellar, and they left the doors open so they could use the sunlight to see where they were going.

The cellar was small, and Stacy was surprised to find it so disorganized. Everything about the village always seemed so neat and perfect growing up, but that was only at the surface level. She suspected that everyone and everything had things buried that they would rather keep in the darkness.

"They're over here." Jan pointed to a stack of boxes in the corner, the cardboard cubes unlabeled and blank on all sides. She picked up one of them and then set it on a nearby table by the staircase so she could use the light. She removed a knife, opened the top box, and removed one of the ammunition cases. "Perfect." She set it down and then gestured for Stacy to pick one up. "Grab one over there."

Stacy bid as she was told, and when she came back, she saw that Jan had a box of magazines on the table as well. "Loading?"

"You got it."

The pair worked in silence for a while, and Stacy fell into the monotonous routine of pushing bullets into the magazines and then setting them aside, then repeating the process. It was a welcome distraction, but the happy silence of the work was interrupted by Jan.

"I heard about your friend," Jan said. "I'm sorry."

A lump caught in Stacy's throat when she tried to speak, so she only offered a half smile and then nodded politely, hoping that Jan wouldn't notice the slight tremor developing in her hand.

"I know how hard this time of year is for your family," Jan said. "Especially yesterday. I lost my father when I was young, and I just want you to know that if you ever—"

"I'm fine," Stacy snapped the words, and forced a smile when she looked at Jan. "Really. I'm fine." But even when she spoke, the words cracked in her throat and she dropped the bullet in her hand, biting her lower lip as she shook her head. "I'm sorry."

Jan set down her magazine and placed a warm hand on Stacy's shoulder. "It's okay. Really. You can talk about him."

"No," Stacy said. "It's not that. I mean, maybe it is, but… my friend." Tears filled her eyes, and when she turned to Jan, the sunlight made the tears dance like little crystals in her eyes. "I watched her die. I *let* her die. I could have done something, but I didn't." She trembled, her body thrumming with the same fear as before. "Maybe if I had—"

"Don't do that to yourself," Jan said.

Stacy wiped her upper lip free from snot and shook her

head. "You know, after my father died, I told myself that if I could help someone, then I would do it. No matter what. Because I used to wonder what would have happened if a friend would have stopped that drunk driver from getting into his car. I mean someone must have seen him."

Jan was quiet for a moment, but then removed her hand from Stacy's shoulder. "Life takes us in all kinds of directions. And as much as we might want to believe we control where we go, I've come to believe that we're all just along for the ride. But while we might not get to choose where we go all of the time, we always get to choose how we handle what happens to us." She moved into Stacy's line of sight. "And you need to make a choice, here and now, not to be a victim. Because you're not. You did not kill your friend. Your friend was murdered by some very bad people."

Stacy nodded.

"Say it," Jan said.

"My friend was murdered," Stacy said.

"That's right," Jan said. "And it wasn't your fault." She raised her eyebrows, waiting for Stacy to repeat that part too.

"And it wasn't my fault." Stacy stuttered over the words, but the moment she spoke them aloud, she felt the weight that she had been carrying around lighten.

Jan smiled. "That's right."

The pair returned to their work of loading the bullets into the magazines, and when they were finished, Stacy helped carry the spare ammunitions to the guard posts around the community.

Stacy thanked Jan again, offering the deputy a hug, and then walked back to Mags' store feeling better than she had all day. Because Jan was right. She needed the courage to face what was behind her.

The smile still hadn't faded by the time she returned to Mags' store, and she found the old woman in the same spot she left her.

"I see that no harm became of you during your stroll through town," Mags said, again not looking up from her magazine.

"No." Stacy laid her forearms on the counter and leaned over to get a peek at the magazine. It was one of those trashy magazines that folks read with all of the celebrity gossip, and Stacy shook her head in disbelief. "Why do you care about this stuff?"

Mags looked at Stacy, raising her eyes, and pressed her finger into the page of the article that she was reading. "This is some grade-A investigative journalism."

"It's gossip," Stacy said.

Mags shrugged, returning to the article. "Who can tell the difference anymore?"

Stacy smiled and then looked out the back door where she still had a clear line of sight on Mags' old Thunderbird. "Where's Amelia?" She pushed off the counter and walked toward the back door. "Em?" She stepped outside and found the back of the store empty, the Thunderbird unoccupied and Amelia nowhere to be found.

Mags walked out behind Stacy, an urgency to her voice. "She was just outside, I thought—"

Stacy reared around on Mags. "You weren't watching her?"

"She was playing," Mags said. "She knew that she was supposed to stay close."

Stacy walked around the back yard, looking for any sign of her sister, but found no trace at all. She turned back around to Mags. "Go and check with the watch guards on the south and west sides and see if they saw her. I'll do the same with the north and the east." The pair quickly separated, and Stacy removed the pistol from its holster, finally feeling as though she were ready to use it.

*A*melia sat in the Thunderbird's driver's seat, but she didn't try and play pretend. She was worried about her sister, worried about her mother, and wished that all of this would just end.

When Amelia had heard that her sister was coming home, she had been so excited. She thought that it was going to be the start of life returning to normal. But then the EMP happened and now things were wrong again.

Amelia hadn't seen Stacy this sad since their dad died. She desperately wanted to cheer her sister up, and she'd been sitting in the car trying to figure out what she could do. And then a thought struck her, and she perked up in the seat.

After their mother had moved them out to the cabin, Stacy had hated every second of it. But during those first few months, Amelia and Stacy would sit out on the porch and listen to the wind chimes that her father had made.

The pair would sit there and listen to the beautiful sounds, and they would talk about their father and happier times. It always cheered Stacy up. All Amelia had to do was head to the cabin, get the chimes, and then bring them back while they waited for their mother.

It wasn't hard to slip past the guards around the town. Amelia had been sneaking her way through the woods even before they moved to the cabin. She had always loved nature, which was probably why it was a little easier for her to adjust to life after the move.

Along the way, Amelia made sure to be mindful of her surroundings. She spotted a few bunnies and one deer. Amelia made sure not to spook it, moving quietly and carefully through the trees as the young buck munched on some grass. She always thought they were lovely and always felt guilty whenever her mother killed one.

A steady breeze followed Amelia all the way to the cabin, and she smiled when she heard the windchimes that rang on the front porch. She hastened her pace, suddenly glad to be home. She moved effortlessly over the rocky ground and bounded up the steps as fast as she could churn her little legs. She'd need to get the ladder to bring the windchimes down, and she went into the cabin to find it. She needed to hurry before Mags and Stacy found out she was gone.

Before Amelia grabbed the ladder, she packed up a few of her toys in a bag and was reaching for a board game when she heard voices outside. Amelia turned her head toward the noise with worrying speed. She had been in the woods long enough to know that whatever had stepped outside wasn't an animal, and the subsequent heavy stomps through the woods confirmed that it was a person.

But the trip wires hadn't been set off.

Amelia brightened and then hurried to the window, her feet padding against the solid wood floors. She peered out the glass and quickly ducked back below the window line. It was the bad men. She kept her back against the wall, listening to see where they would go.

Muffled voices came through the window, and while Amelia couldn't hear them through the cracks, she knew that they were heading toward the front door. Amelia hurried toward the bedroom hallway and opened the hidden door in the floor to the saferoom.

Footsteps were on the front porch now, and Amelia ducked inside, closing the lid behind her as the bad men entered the cabin.

33

---

*T*he field of trip wires that had been laid as a defensive structure for the enemy had cost them a lot of time. But Jo navigated the traps, and everyone survived. Once they moved closer to the camp, Mike took the lead.

"We'll attack in two groups," Mike said, leaning into the middle of the circle. "Myself and Furst will lead the groups. You follow the officer's lead. Donny and Billy, you're with Furst. Jo, you're with me."

"I think it might be better for me to go alone," Jo said. "We can cover more ground, and I'm more than capable of handling myself."

"If she gets to go alone, then so do I." Donny Behr pointed to himself. "I'm just as good as—"

"These are the rules," Mike said. "If you can't follow them, then you will stay behind, do you understand me?"

Everyone nodded.

"You're sure they're close?" Mike asked, looking to Jo.

"Fifty yards, maybe less," Jo answered.

"I don't hear anything," Furst said, frowning. "Shouldn't

they be making more noise or something?"

"They're probably laying low," Mike said. "And remember, no one shoots unless the officer you're with shoots first. I don't want any mistakes out there. No happy trigger fingers, got it?"

Again everyone nodded, but Jo could sense the trepidation.

"Stay safe," Mike said, looking at everyone in the eyes. "Stay smart. And for the love of God, don't get shot."

"I don't plan on it, Sheriff," Donny said, then spit the brown dip that puffed out his lower lip into the can that he was given. "Nothing out there can kill a Behr."

Except they already did kill a Behr, Jo thought. It was the reason why the other brothers were out here in the first place.

With everyone knowing their roles and where they were supposed to go, Mike broke the group apart and had everyone move toward their positions.

The two groups would attack in a standard L formation that would box the enemy back into the opening of the mine while also making sure that none of their people were hit by the crossfire of their own bullets.

Mike and Jo approached from the south of the camp, while the others approached from the east. Jo was able to keep the line of sight with the other for the first twenty yards, but then the forest became too thick, and she lost them.

Jo saw the mine before she saw the first terrorist, and she immediately knew something was wrong. She counted only three men, and Gus wasn't among them.

Jo tried to get Mike's attention, but he just kept staring forward at the camp, and when he finally turned around, the first gunshot popped from the east.

Before either of them could react to see who fired first, the camp of the terrorists was already shooting back, and the fight was underway.

"They're moving into the mine!" Mike shouted, his voice rising above the spatter of gunfire.

Mike and Jo penetrated the camp, and Mike and Jo were the first to reach the three men who had thrown down their weapons in surrender.

"You fucking sons of bitches." Donny appeared from the woods, his face twisted with rage that was only made more intense by the blood that spattered his face. "You think you deserve mercy after what you've done?" He raised his rifle and fired before Furst could get to him, dropping one of them dead.

With the death of their comrade, the remaining two terrorists quickly reached for their weapons, forcing everyone else to open fire lest they die before they killed.

The gunfire was loud and over as quickly as it started, leaving Jo and others to do nothing but catch their breath and count the bodies.

"Fucking rag heads," Donny yelled, stomping around, his cheeks even redder than before, but his anger was slowly slipping into the throes of grief. He spat, continuing to spew nonsense until Mike walked over and grabbed him by the scruff of his neck.

"I told you to hold your fire if they surrendered," Mike said. "Now we know nothing about what else they might have been planning."

"I can tell you what they were planning, Sheriff," Donny said, still seething anger. "They were planning on killing every single one of us and taking this land for their own!" He shoved Mike off him, but the sheriff wasn't having any of it and quickly subdued the big redneck and shoved him into the ground, cuffing his hands behind his back. "It was my right to kill them! My God-given right! No law was going to take that away from me! You hear me? It was my right!"

Billy, the other Behr brother, said nothing as he watched his oldest brother be cuffed by Mike, but Jo suspected that was because Furst had a bead on him, and he didn't want to cause more trouble than he'd already started.

Once Donny was finally subdued, the fight had gone out of him, and Mike sat him by a tree. His brother walked over and sat by him. A little while later, all of that anger was washed away by tears, the pair of brothers mourning their kin all over again through the process of revenge.

Jo walked over to Mike, who was examining the dead bodies, and then flashed a light into the mine, finding nothing but dirt and the rotting wood beams that held the excavation from caving in on itself.

"Gus isn't here." Mike flicked off the flashlight and looked to Jo. "You're sure you saw him?"

Jo nodded. "He was here. Along with a lot more terrorists than this."

Mike glanced around at the bodies. "We must have killed more than we thought back in town." He chewed the inside of his cheek and then grimaced as if he didn't like the taste. "You're sure Gus was alive when you saw him?"

"I know it," Jo said.

"Well, he's not here." Mike stepped away, instructing everyone else that they were going to move out, but not before storing the dead bodies in the mine. "Let them rot in there. I'm done burying those bastards."

Jo lingered at the mouth of the mine, wondering what they would have done with Gus. She knew that they wouldn't have buried him if they killed him. So where did they take him?

*K*halid knelt to the ground, running his hand over a lump of foliage. After he examined it, he stood and then came back to Muhammed. "There are many wires like this. We'll need to move carefully."

Muhammed nodded, keeping a tight hold of the deputy. "Make a sound, and I'll cut off your manhood and shove it down your throat." The deputy whimpered, but he didn't resist when Muhammed pushed him forward.

Muhammed followed Khalid step for step through the woods, and just when he thought that they were entering into the middle of nowhere, he saw the cleared land that surrounded the cabin.

Khalid and Muhammed waited on the edge of the wood, watching the house, trying to see if anyone was home.

"What do you see?" Muhammed asked.

Khalid remained still as lake water on a calm day. "Someone is inside."

"Just one?" Muhammed asked.

Khalid looked to Muhammed and nodded.

Muhammed squeezed his comrade's shoulder. "Any sign of my brother?"

Khalid shook his head, and dread filled Muhammed's stomach. He found a nearby tree and tied the deputy to it, then gagged him to ensure he couldn't scream. "If my brother is dead, then you will soon join him."

The pair moved in unison toward the front of the cabin, both aiming their weapons up at the front door and the window, ready to shoot anything that tried to fire back at them.

Khalid entered the cabin first, moving through space efficiently. They checked the stovetop, but it was cold. There was no sign that anyone had been here today.

"Maybe they left and joined the town?" Khalid said.

But Muhammed paced around the room and saw a picture of a family on the wall. It was a woman and two daughters. He grabbed it, shaking his head. "Where would he have gone?"

Khalid stepped toward his leader. "If they took him, we will get him back."

Muhammed tossed the picture to the floor, then nodded. "Let's go."

The pair headed out the door, and when Muhammed was walking down the front steps, he glanced at something from the corner of his eyes.

Muhammad reached for Khalid's shoulder, and the man immediately turned on a dime, acting as though the enemy was near. But this was no enemy.

Muhammed approached the object, Khalid covering him from behind. And the closer that Muhammed moved toward the object hidden around the backside of the cabin, the more it began to take shape, and he struggled to catch his breath.

A pair of bodies lay beneath a tarp, and before

Muhammed removed the plastic sheet, he knew who it was. He reached for the tarp's edge and flung it off, dropping to his knees when he saw Zahid's body.

While Muhammed knew the risks of war and the campaign that they were fighting, he had held onto the unthinkable hope that he and his brother would wipe the continent clean of their enemy and then return home to live out their final days in peace.

But Muhammed would never have peace again. Eyes red and watering, rage flooded his heart and pumped the hot hate through his veins until it boiled away all of the grief.

"Bring me the deputy," Muhammed growled the command through clenched teeth, and Khalid hurried away, leaving Muhammed alone with his brother. "I will avenge you, brother. The person who claimed your life will die. I will see to it that I choke the life from them with my own two hands." He brought two fingers to his lips, kissed them, and then placed it over his brother's still heart. "From flesh to dust that drifts to the heavens."

With his eyes closed, Muhammed heard the movement before he saw it, and he snapped his head around to the front of the cabin, listening to the sounds of churning feet. Weapon at the ready, he chased the sounds of the person fleeing through the brush.

Wanting to capture his enemy before he killed it, hoping to question the person, Muhammed was surprised to catch up so quickly, and even more so when he snatched the neck scruff of a little girl.

"Let me go—"

The girl thrashed, but Muhammed clamped his hand over her mouth and pinned her against his body with his arm. The girl still squirmed, but she could do little more than wiggle as she was too small and too weak to do anything else.

Muhammed examined the girl, and then looked back to the cabin. When he turned back to her, the girl's eyes were wide as saucers, and he understood who she was.

The girl wasn't the party guilty of his brother's murder, of course not. She was nothing but a child. But the girl probably had parents. The same parent as in the picture in the cabin.

Muhammed smiled as he watched the realization dawn on the girl's face as well. It was a mutual understanding of the sides that they had chosen, and the fact that their fates were now crossed. It was a gift from Allah.

Muhammed dragged the little girl back to the cabin, and by the time that Muhammed dropped her at the feet of his dead brother, she had worked herself into a frenzy.

"If you don't stay quiet," Muhammed said, pointing the gun at the little girl. "Then you will wish for a quick death that will not come."

The threat didn't have the desired effect that Muhammed had hoped for, and the girl only turned up her nose in a defiant gesture that was far beyond the girl's years. "I am not afraid of you."

"No?" Muhammed asked, amused by the little girl's antics.

Khalid emerged from the woods with the deputy and shoved the officer to the ground.

"Gus!" The little girl quickly stood and tried to rush to her friend, but Muhammed snatched her up and then held a knife to her throat. The sight was enough to cause the deputy to use what little strength remained to him to try and lunge and help the girl, but it was Khalid who kicked him down.

Muhammed laughed.

"Please," Gus gurgled, spitting blood the ground. "Just let her go. She's a child."

"And how many innocent children have your government killed?" Muhammed frowned. "Thousands? Tens of thousands? What is one more little girl in the wake of bodies that I have killed over the past two days?"

"You're just a bad person," the little girl said. "And my mommy will stop you. She's already done it before."

Muhammed stared down at the little girl. He had met warriors with less grit than this. "You're right." His answer surprised her, and the confident grin she sported faded. "I am a bad person. And do you know what bad people do?" Muhammed removed the blade from her throat and then pointed at Gus. "They kill."

3 5

---

*T*he return trip to The Village was shrouded by the unpleasant truth of what happened in the woods, but Jo was glad to be done with it. And now, with the enemy defeated, she and her family could return to the home that they had built and stay there to weather the rest of the storm.

Mike hadn't said anything to her since they left the mine. He was too busy speaking to Furst, but while Jo did her best not to let his cold shoulder bother her, it did.

Because Jo had seen the look of betrayal in Mike's eyes when he looked at her in the mouth of the mine, with all of those dead soldiers at his feet. It wasn't something that Jo thought the man could forgive. It wasn't something she was sure she wanted him to forgive.

It was always more comfortable to walk away from someone when they were angry with you because then you didn't feel guilty about leaving. They didn't want you in the first place, so why stick around? And while Mike's anger and disappointment provided the perfect scenario for her to leave, it was still hard. Hard because she had hurt and betrayed someone who had done nothing but help her since Danny's passing.

"You made the right call."

Distracted from her own thoughts, Jo didn't hear Furst approach her, and she jumped a little, which she hoped he didn't see. "What are you talking about?"

Furst rolled his eyes. "You know what I'm talking about." He glanced back to Mike, who was now walking alone with Donny. "The mine. Killing the terrorists. Donny told me about the plan."

Jo frowned. "You knew?"

"Look, it was them or us," Furst answered, and then set his face in a hard gaze. "I wasn't about to let our people die."

It wasn't surprising that Furst had sided with the Behr brothers when it came to their desires to crush the enemy, but even though she had disobeyed the sheriff, it was different with Furst. He worked for Mike. He was insubordinate.

"All I'm saying is, don't worry about any blowback," Furst said. "Deep down, I know that Mike is glad they're dead. They slaughtered nearly every other village on the mountain. We brought justice today."

But as Jo glanced back at Mike and saw Donny Behr still stumbling forward in his cuffs, she wasn't so sure it was justice. "Calling it justice doesn't denounce the fact that it was murder." Furst said nothing as he fell back with the others, and Jo walked the rest of the trip ahead of them in silence.

Jo glanced around to the trees and rocks to the moss and grass that covered the ground in patches. She felt the uneven ground beneath her feet and how steady her legs felt on it. Few people could survive up here, and she was glad that she was strong enough to do it.

However, the reprieve of silence ended when they returned to The Village, and the raised voices triggered alarm, causing Jo to sprint ahead, her complexion a pale white. Not because of the urgency in the people who were shouting, but because of the name that they screamed.

"Amelia!"

"Amelia!"

"Em! Em!"

The first person that Jo saw when she broke through the woods was Mags, and she was on the old woman before she even realized she was there, and the surprise was enough to make Mags jump.

"What happened?" Jo asked.

"She left," Mags answered. "She was playing out back and then she was gone. I don't know where she might have been, but Stacy went back to the cabin to check—Jo!"

Jo sped past everyone else in the woods, all of them searching for her youngest daughter, the same people who knew her growing up, the same people that Jo had wanted to turn her back on, now searching for the one thing that meant more to her than anything else in the world. She couldn't believe what was happening. She didn't want to consider it.

Once Jo turned off the road and into the foliage, she was able to move more quickly. The past four years of living off the grid had made her feet more nimble and powerful when they were in the forest.

"Amelia! Stacy!" Jo shouted. She was red-faced, covered in sweat, and panting by the time she reached the cleared plain of the cabin. But she stumbled to a stop when she saw Stacy standing motionless on the side of the cabin, staring up at something on the wall.

Ignoring whatever her daughter was looking at, Jo grabbed her daughter by the shoulders, whipping her around so quickly that Jo thought that she might have snapped her daughter's neck. "Stacy, where is your sister? What happened?"

But the face that stared back at Jo had regressed to the scared little girl that Jo remembered raising. The girl that couldn't go to bed without her nightlight, the girl that would sneak out of her own room and climb into her parents' bed in the middle of the night.

The only answer that Stacy gave was returning her eyes toward the side of the cabin, and this time Jo followed them, slowly peeling her hands off her daughter's shoulders as she did so, shaking her head in disbelief as she finally saw what Stacy was looking at.

Deputy Gus Moynihan was nailed to the side of the cabin, his body splayed like a crucifixion. His stomach had been sliced open, and his guts rested in a pile on the ground beneath his feet. Written in blood was a sentence just above the deputy's corpse that caused Jo to drop to her knees, the color running from her cheeks as her innards were carved out like Gus's had been.

You will watch her die. You will watch everyone die.

Jo wasn't sure how long she stared at the message before she finally opened her mouth to scream, but when the noise finally did come, it was harrowing.

36

*W*hen Jo searched the rest of the cabin, she found it picked clean. But she wasn't interested in the food and water that they took. She only cared about collecting every hidden weapon in the cabin that they had missed.

Jo didn't know where Stacy was, probably still outside staring up at Gus, who was still nailed to the side of the cabin.

With her back to the cabin's front door, Jo heard Mike enter, knowing that it was him before he even opened his mouth to speak.

"I'm sorry," Mike said.

When she didn't turn around or respond, Mike walked to her.

"Stacy told me what happened," Mike said. "You can't go out there alone."

"I can and I will," Jo said, keeping her focus on loading more ammunition. "There's not a damned thing you can do to stop me."

"Jo, listen to me, I—"

The ease in which she whirled around and pressed the end of the pistol's barrel under his chin was startling. She even had her finger on the trigger. That's how far she was willing to go to get Amelia back.

Mike gently raised his hands, saying nothing.

"I should have stayed here," Jo said. "My priority was to protect my family, not some fucking village. That was your job, not mine. And you failed." She spit the words out like venom, and every syllable that was uttered made Mike wince. But she wanted the words to sting. She was done pulling punches now.

Jo finally lowered the gun and Mike stepped back. He left the cabin without a word, but Jo heard the muffled voices of Furst and Jan outside.

With every spare magazine loaded and every weapon that she could get her hands on having been collected, Jo stepped back and examined the tools at her disposal.

The crossbow held a dozen bolts, the .223 Remington rifle with the mounted scope had five twelve-round magazines, and the two 9mm Glocks had four sixteen-round magazines apiece.

She wasn't sure if it was enough to kill all of them, but she thought it was enough to get her daughter out or at least die trying. Because if she couldn't get Amelia back, then she planned on killing as many of those bastards as she could before she died. And she had no intention of going quietly.

"Mom?"

Jo turned and saw Stacy standing there, shoulders sloped forward, dark circles under her eyes from crying after she found the deputy's body. The tears were long gone, but the remnants of streaked lines were on her cheeks.

Stacy had never been pale, but standing in the living

room with sunlight streaming through the window and reaching her face, she looked more ghost than a person.

"I want to help," Stacy said. Though it was a statement, she spoke it like she was asking permission. "I want to help get Amelia back."

That same anger that Jo felt when Mike walked into the cabin flooded back at her, but she kept enough restraint to keep the pistol at her side. "If you wanted to help, then you should have done what I asked you to in the first place." The muscles around her eyes and mouth twitched from the seething anger that coursed through her veins. "I put you in charge of her."

"I know." Stacy remained hunched over for a second, but it didn't take long before the girl was back and upright again, and when she locked eyes with her mother again, the hesitation that had existed earlier vanished. "That's why I'm coming with you." Stacy stepped around her mother and picked up one of the handguns, along with the magazines that were associated with it. "I'll meet you outside."

Jo watched her daughter leave, knowing that she had pushed Stacy too far. She had done to her daughter what she had done to herself all those years ago.

But things had changed. Jo's little girl had been taken by the savages who had unleashed their hell onto the world. But they weren't invincible. They were nothing but men, and all men could bleed. And Jo was going to make sure that all of them suffered before this was over.

* * *

MIKE WATCHED as both Stacy and Jo vanished into the woods. Deep down he knew that he should be doing more to stop them, but for another fifty acres, this was still Joanna Mercer's land.

"Shouldn't we go with her?" Jan asked. "I mean if they do run into the terrorist group, then what? She can't take on an entire army by herself."

"I'll let you tell her that," Mike answered, and then turned his attention to the tarp that covered Gus's body. "We have other things to worry about."

It had taken some time to get him down, and while Mike knew that it was the slice across the belly that delivered the final blow, it looked like his man had been tortured very thoroughly since his capture.

Gus's face was nothing more than a swollen purple and black lump between his shoulders. They'd stripped him of most of his clothes, but they did manage to pin his sheriff's badge through the skin on his chest.

"We should be going with her," Furst said, the words coming out like steam from a teapot that was boiling over. "For Christ's sake, just look at what they did to him!" He ripped the sheet off to expose the corpse. "They're goddamn animals!"

Mike stood there, hands on his hips, staring at Furst instead of looking at the body. "I know what they did, Furst. I pulled down his body before you got here."

Furst puffed his chest, taking the comment as a blow to his pride. "Are you saying that I wouldn't have gotten him down?" He walked within inches of the sheriff's face.

Mike didn't break his calm, wanting no further animosity between himself and his deputies. "All I'm saying is that I pulled him down, and I saw what they did to him."

Furst lingered in his aggressive stance, but he finally backed down, and Mike noticed that Jan took her hand off

JAMES HUNT

the butt of her service pistol, something that he was grateful that Furst hadn't seen. "So what do we do then?"

Mike looked to the portion of the woods where Jo and Stacy had entered, but they had already vanished from view. They would disappear, heading deeper into the woods. He couldn't track them now, not even if he wanted to. This was their land, and they were a part of it as much as the rocks and the trees and the sky that watched over all of it.

"We need help," Mike said.

"And where do you expect us to find that help?" Furst asked, refusing to drop his childlike tone. "You have a cell phone that's working? Thinking we can call over to the next county? Or do you have a direct line to the President?"

"Knock it off, Furst," Jan said.

Mike shook his head. "When Jo first came back up the mountain after she got her daughter from the city, she said that there was military trying to fight off the terrorist attack." He nodded. "They're our best chance."

"You don't know if they're still down there," Jan asked. "Or what condition they're in, or if they'll even help. It's too much of a risk."

"Everything is a risk now," Mike said. "It's a risk to wake up in the morning. It's a risk to walk outside. One twisted ankle and that could be the end of you. Got a cold? Who has any medicine for you to take that can help you get over it?" He shook his head. "I can't keep using risk as an excuse anymore." He looked down at Gus. "Not after what we've been through."

"Let me go down," Furst said, stepping forward. "I'm faster than you, and if they're not there, then I'll be able to make it back quickly so we can start making preparations to survive whatever comes next."

Mike scoffed. "And leave the negotiations to you? I don't think so."

Furst slunk back and turned around, kicking his shoe against the dirt.

"Mike, are you really sure this is the best idea?" Jan lowered her voice and made sure that Furst couldn't hear the next part. "If we lose you, then the town splits in half. Half of them following Furst, and the other half following themselves. We need you alive."

"You'll be fine without me for a little while," Mike said. "And you're not as smart as I thought you were if you think that the people in this town will follow him." He stared at her poignantly until she picked up on what he was trying to tell her, but she only rolled her eyes in disbelief. "Hey." He grabbed her arm, hoping that his seriousness would cause her to really listen to him, to see what he was trying to tell her. "I always thought that you'd take my seat one day after I was done, or if something ever happened to me. You're a leader. You just have to embrace it. And until I return, you're in charge."

Jan opened her eyes wide with surprise.

"I'll be back as soon as I can," Mike said. He took one last glance at Gus's body and the words written in his blood that promised more violence. "And hopefully I'll bring the cavalry with me."

37

Jo didn't pay much attention to Stacy, only tossing her looks when her daughter was too noisy. And while Jo knew the girl wanted to help, sometimes the best way to help was to stay out of the way of the people who were trying to get things done.

But the longer that the pair walked together in the woods, the more regret plagued Jo's thoughts. She had been too harsh on the girl.

"You remember how to use that?" Jo asked, pointing to the pistol that Stacy gripped with both hands as they walked. She hadn't let it go since they started their walk a few miles back.

"I remember how to use it," Stacy answered, keeping her eyes forward.

Jo nodded, and while her daughter's answer suggested that she was done speaking, Jo didn't want to drop the subject. Because silence only forced Jo to think about what came next.

The best-case scenario was that Amelia was still alive and that there might be a slim chance for Jo and Stacy to get her out without being seen. But that best-case scenario had about a one percent success rate. What was more likely to happen was that Amelia was dead, or some other terrible fate, and both Jo and Stacy would die trying to kill as many of the terrorists as they could before they fell.

In a perfect world, Jo wouldn't have chosen any of the scenarios. In an ideal world, she would still be married to the love of her life, living in town, and the end of the world would be the farthest worry from her mind.

But that wasn't the world that Jo lived in anymore. This was her new reality; hiking through the woods with as many weapons as she could carry in hopes of tracking down the terrorists that had abducted her daughter. It was a sick, twisted world.

And if Jo was going to meet her end, then she wasn't going to go to her grave leaving things the way they currently landed with Stacy. She needed to go into this with a clear conscience.

"I shouldn't have said what I did," Jo said. "It was wrong for me to put that blame on you. I was upset and angry, and... I've never been good at saying the right thing. Your father was good at it though. I suppose that's why you girls didn't really notice that I was so bad at it."

"We noticed," Stacy said, then after a pause, she turned to her mother and smirked.

The brief moment of levity gave Jo hope that she might be able to fix what she broke, or at the very least apologize for everything that had happened between them since Danny had passed.

"I mean it though," Jo said. "What I said... it should have never even been thought about, let alone said aloud." She frowned, shaking her head. "I know I haven't been a good mother. And I'd like to say that it was just after your father died, but the truth is I've always struggled with it. I don't know why, because everything people told me made it seem like nothing but sunshine and rainbows. But it's not like that."

"But you were right," Stacy said. "About everything."

Jo was quiet for a moment, not wanting to jump to quickly at her daughter's words, and after the crunch of their boots filled the silence, she cleared her throat. "I wasn't right about everything. I know I was hard on you. And I know how difficult it was for you to leave everything behind. I wish I had done things differently, but if I hadn't..." She looked at Stacy, her daughter listening with an attentive gaze. "Then you would have lost two parents."

Stacy nodded, and then looked around to the forest and trees and rocks. "I hated you for bringing me up here. And that hate festered for a long time. I shouldn't have treated you like that. I shouldn't have held onto that grudge for so long." She looked at her mother, and Jo saw the hardened gaze of a person who had truly outgrown their childhood. She wasn't the angst-filled teenager that had gone off for college, thinking that she had to leave her family behind to become the person that she wanted to be on her own.

The pair remained quiet for a while, and then Stacy spoke up.

"Do you regret it?" Stacy asked, her full attention now on her mother. "Having kids?"

"No," Jo answered, and it was the truth. "You and your sister made my life more complete than I anything I could have done on my own. No matter what happens to me, no matter where this ends up taking us, you should know that you're the best part of me, Stacy. You and your sister. You're better than me in every way." She wiped the tears away, hoping that it passed off as only sweat. "And I'm so glad that you are."

After Jo finished her piece, she didn't expect a thank you or any type of forgiveness or things like that. When Stacy finally spoke up, it took all of Jo's strength not to break down and cry.

"I know that you've always thought you were a bad mom," Stacy said, watching the ground now as she navigated a rocky stretch. "Ever since I was little. And I used that against you, and I'm sorry for that. I know that all you've ever done for me is trying to lift me up to be a better person, but maybe I'm not that better person. Maybe I'm just broken. I mean, my dad died on my birthday. How fucked up is that?"

Jo walked to her daughter and stepped in her path, holding her by both arms as she looked her dead in the eye. "You're not broken. You hear me? You've never been broken, and you're never going to be broken. You know why you're out here? You know why you're risking your life to save your sister?"

Tears in her eyes, Stacy shook her head.

"Because you love your sister," Jo said. "Just like I love you, and just how your father loved you too. Any person who's capable of love, real, selfless love, can't be broken. Because in the end, that's all that we have to hold onto. After everything else is gone, including the people that we loved, it's that feeling that lingers. And we can't be afraid to feel it again. We can't be afraid, because if we are, then we don't just lose ourselves, we lose the people we love." She caught her breath and tried not to let her daughter's fears prevent her from seeing the truth. "I almost let myself forget that. I almost let myself forget what I could feel, how I could feel, and how the relationships with the people that I cared so much I nearly lost." She pressed her hand against her heart and brought Stacy's hand over hers as well. "We are the same blood. Me, and you, and Amelia, and your father. And so long as blood keeps pumping in one of our hearts, we're not gone. Do you hear me? None of us are. And it's that thought that keeps me moving, it's the thought that keeps me going whenever I feel like I'm going to be afraid. And I'm deathly afraid right now. I'm afraid of what we're going to find when we walk into that camp. I'm afraid of what I'm going to see, what those animals have done to my little girl." She drew in a breath and clenched her jaw. "But so long as I'm breathing and my heart is beating, so is hers. And so is yours."

Stacy was crying now. The tears rolled down her cheeks and collected at her jawline where they rolled to her chin and dropped to the forest floor. She lunged forward and hugged her mother tightly. The pair held onto one another, and the silence that passed between them was an understanding of all that happened to each other.

And they would talk about it more. But first, they needed to find Amelia.

3 8

---

*M*uhammed returned to the mine and saw the men that he had left behind slaughtered. The bodies had been clustered around the tunnel, and the way that they were stacked over one another told the story of an execution. But he would avenge them, and he would be sure their sacrifice would not be for nothing.

Based off of what the deputy had told Muhammed before Khalid gutted him, he knew that it must have been the Mercer woman who had found their location. Apparently she was quite the hunter. But so was he.

Muhammed helped dig the mass grave, but made a special one for his brother that he placed on top of the mine. He collected rocks to build it, encasing his brother in a tomb of stone.

When Muhammed set the final rock into place, he whispered the last words, said the prayers, and did everything that he could to ensure that his brother's soul would rest in peace.

Muhammed removed his hand from the warm stone and

stood, the sun beating down on his back. "I will kill them, brother. Just as we promised. Every. Last. One."

The rocks remained still as the wind brushed against Muhammed's back from the north. He lingered for a few more seconds, but then turned, knowing that the dead couldn't answer him. It was only the living that concerned him.

With only himself and Khalid left alive, Muhammed walked back into the mouth of the mine where Khalid sat watch with the little girl.

The girl had stopped squirming and screaming once they were deeper in the woods. She knew that whoever might have been close wasn't coming, and the girl chose to preserve her strength. She was smart. Smarter than most children her age. And when Muhammed looked at her, he saw no hint of fear in her eyes. But then again, the young and stupid were often too ignorant to recognize fear, and he knew that the girl checked at least one of those boxes.

"Your mother was here," Muhammed said, pointing back to the mine. "She helped kill all of those people. Did you know that your mother was a murderer?"

The girl's forehead formed a subtle crease that ran perfectly horizontal above her eyebrows, where Muhammed suspected there would have been many wrinkle lines if the girl had been lucky enough to grow older. But she would not get that chance. Still, that defiant ignorance remained. "They were bad people. Just like you."

"And why am I a bad person?" Muhammed asked.

"Because you hurt people," the girl answered.

"So does your mother," Muhammed said, leaning into the girl. "She killed all of those men. And did you know that all of those men have children? They have little boys and little girls just like you." He pressed his finger into the center of that creased line on his forehead. "And now none of them have a daddy. Why is that right? Why is it okay for your mother to kill the fathers of other little girls, but that doesn't make her a bad person?"

The little girl's confidence wavered, and she worked her mouth trying to come up with an answer. But before she could speak, Muhammed cut in. "You are not as stupid as I thought you were, girl. But that doesn't make you smart." He stood to leave when the girl finally spat out a rebuttal.

"It's because she doesn't have hate in her heart!"

Muhammed froze, staring at that little girl who stared right back at him, all of that fear and doubt that Muhammed had planted just moments ago ripped out seed and stem.

"But you do," the little girl said. "It's why you're here. It's why all of these daddies left their children. Because they have hate in their hearts, and that hate forced them to leave, forcing them to leave behind the love. But my mommy still loves me, and that's why she'll come for me, and that's why you'll lose."

Muhammed remained silent for a moment. Then, very slowly, he walked to the little girl, never breaking eye contact with her. He stopped just short of her feet and then knelt. "Maybe you're right. Maybe we do have hate in our hearts. But that hate has kept me alive my entire life, and I will always take my hate over your love." He stood and then quickly ordered Khalid to keep the girl in the mine. "The only way she leaves this camp is in a body bag."

Khalid nodded, but kept his eyes on the woods. "Someone is coming." He raised his rifle in preparation to shoot, and Muhammed did the same.

The pair lingered in silence for a while. and then Muhammed saw the scout that he had sent through to the mountains return.

"Brother." Muhammed lowered his weapon and greeted his comrade with open arms. "What news?"

"I contacted the other cells," he answered, still catching his breath from the hike. He grabbed the canteen that Khalid offered to him and drank thirstily, the water spilling over the sides of his mouth and dampening his thick beard. "They will be here before dawn tomorrow.

Muhammed smiled, clapping his loyal comrade on the shoulder. "We will attack these people with our full force. And we will spare no one."

39

*M*ike moved quickly down the mountain and crossed the halfway point as the sun set. He hadn't wanted to travel so late and so far, because while he was familiar with the mountain as any other person who had lived here all their lives, he also knew what was out in the woods waiting for them. Based off of what Jo had seen, Mike knew the enemy was spread out. They could be anywhere.

At the base of the mountain, Mike followed the two-lane mountain road until it connected to the highway and then veered off on another back road into Knoxville, which was familiar territory.

It had been his main route up the mountain when he was still a deputy and he lived in the city. But the older he got, the less appealing city life became, and the more he wanted to live out his days away from the hustle and traffic. And if he thought that rush hour traffic was terrible when he had his commute, the current gridlock made what he experienced look like a cakewalk.

When Mike arrived in the first suburb outside the city, he

slowed the horse's trot, unsure of who had won the fight between the military and the insurgents.

The horse's hooves clacked in an eerie cadence in the dark. It was the only sound in the neighborhood, and with the sun going down, it was becoming harder and harder to see without any lights. There weren't even any candles burning. It was like the area of town had been abandoned.

The horse whinnied and shook its head, suddenly stopping in the middle of the road, which caused Mike's heartbeat to skip and jumpstart into a higher gear. He placed his hand on the service weapon and squinted ahead in the darkness, unable to make out anything, but the horse refused to go any further.

"Hands up." The voice was firm, direct, and came from directly behind him. "Up high, above your head, and dismount the horse on the left side. Keep those hands up."

Mike didn't bother turning around but did as he was told when he heard the shuffle of more footsteps surround him from his peripheral vision, and while he had at least a half dozen weapons trained on him, he felt calmer than he had on the entire ride down. These guys were military. American military.

"I'm Sheriff Mike Turner from Rebel County," he said after he dismounted, keeping his hand up as a soldier came to relieve him of his weapon. "I have a problem up on the mountain."

"Sheriff, we got problems all over the country." The man who had instructed him to dismount the horse stepped forward, and Mike got his first good look at him. He was dirty, stank to high heaven, and was dressed from head to toe in combat fatigues. The soldier gave him a look up and down, noticing the uniform. "You really Mike Turner? Or did you just steal that off his dead body?"

"Wallet is in my back pocket," Mike said.

The soldier laughed as another man grabbed the wallet from Mike's pants. "Wallet? Hate to tell you this, Sheriff, but your credit card won't work down here if you're looking for a fill-up."

"I have a village on the top of the mountain filled with people that are in danger of being slaughtered," Mike said, putting his hands down.

The soldier lifted his gun. "I didn't say you could do that, Sheriff. Keep those hands up."

Mike raised his hands again, but not as high this time. "There's a terrorist group that's been terrorizing my county and every small town on the mountain. Anyone that survived the first few fights made their way to the top, heading for higher ground. But they've threatened to retaliate, and I'm inclined to believe they'll make good on their promise."

The soldier looked up from the wallet. He paused for a moment, then folded the wallet back up and handed it to Mike. "So what do you want us to do about it?"

Mike frowned in confusion. "We need reinforcements."

"So do we," the soldier said, then raised his eyebrows. "Anything else?"

Mike lowered his head, and a slow, maddening chuckle rolled off of his tongue. "You've got to be kidding me."

"I've never been much of a comedian," the soldier said. "But Billy over there has one hell of a joke about a priest and a hooker that walk into a bar—"

"They're going to come back and slaughter us!" Mike flung his hands down, cutting a breeze through the air and clenching his hands into fists. "Do you understand me? They're going to come back and kill all of us!"

The soldier didn't move, but even in the darkness, Mike could see the square set of his jaw and the narrowed look in his eyes. He wasn't a man that took orders from anyone that didn't follow his chain of command, and Mike was nowhere in that line of succession.

The soldier was quiet for a long time, but he never broke eye contact with Mike. The soldiers that surrounded them shifted uneasily, and it wasn't until their commander spoke that they finally sat still.

"And what about the people down here?" the soldier asked. "What happens to the innocent people in this neighborhood when we leave? Do you think the terrorists that are still running around down here will honor a truce or a cease-fire?"

Mike knew that the man was only goading him, and he looked away, staring at the houses and the people that suddenly emerged from them. All of them were scared and shivering and most likely hungry. They were barely holding on down here. Everyone was barely holding on everywhere.

"We have orders to hold the city, Sheriff," the soldier said. "We leave, and those bastards march right back in here and take every inch of ground that we've gained. And I'm not having us give up a single inch. I don't care if you're telling me the fucking president is on the top of that mountain, you hear me?"

Mike turned away from the people that had collected outside of their homes, and he looked back to the soldier, lowering his eyes as he nodded in understanding. They would get no help down here, and he knew that facing a threat alone on that mountain meant near-certain death. But with his eyes lowered, he caught the name on the patch of the man's uniform. "Moynihan."

The soldier that stood in front of him frowned. "So you can read. That doesn't make a difference to me, Sheriff."

It was the sleep deprivation that had made him slow and

caused his memory to fracture. But that was why he had sent Gus down to the Army Depot in the first place. Gus had family down there. He had a brother. "You're Gus Moyni- han's brother."

The soldier's frown deepened, and he stepped forward. "Yeah?" A hint of worry graced the soldier's voice.

"There's something you should know," Mike said.

40

After night fell, it provided better cover for both Jo and Stacy in the woods. But it also made it harder to track the enemy. However, she knew that the night would provide a better atmosphere for sneaking up on the terrorists that she had tracked to the mine.

Jo heard the terrorist camp before she saw them, and she forced Stacy to hang back while she scouted the location. She wasn't sure if they had enough time to set more traps or trip wires, and she didn't want to risk Stacy setting one off. Jo knew that she could move more swiftly and securely if she went in by herself. Because while she knew that her daughter was capable, Jo had always hunted better alone.

She also wanted to spare Stacy the visual of finding her sister in danger, because there were some images that stayed with you forever.

Jo found no wires on her slow and arduous crawl through the woods, but she did spy one guard that they had on duty, keeping a lookout for people such as herself that might try and snake their way into the camp. But what was more concerning were the increase in the number of fighters that she saw. They had suddenly tripled.

Every single man was armed, and they clustered in the camp in tight groups. They had made it more challenging to get through and tightened their formations. It was smarter than being spread out. They didn't want to make the same mistakes as last time.

But Jo couldn't infiltrate the camp until she knew where they were keeping Amelia, lest she be caught and set off a chain reaction that killed them both. She couldn't risk that. Every move from this point forward needed to be precise and efficient and calculated. She wasn't going to leave her daughter's life to chance.

A rock cropping to the west provided a path deeper into the camp while still keeping herself hidden. She remained low, crawling on all fours twice during her approach. Her senses were heightened, and she felt the coolness from the ground blow up against her stomach. It was a welcome reprieve from the heat of the day.

At the rock formation, Jo slowly lifted her eyes above the hidden line. She was only ten yards from the nearest cluster of men. If they spotted her, she wouldn't be able to take them all out before one of them gunned her down.

Jo remained still as water, only her eyes moving as she scanned the rest of the camp. She saw the three other groups, along with the provisions that they had taken from the cabin, enjoying the spoils of their pillaging. She also spotted her own weapons in a few of the hands of the terrorists, and she snickered at the prospect of being killed by her own guns. She wasn't sure if that was some kind of irony, but she thought that the universe would enjoy the cruel joke.

Jo didn't see her daughter, but she saw three men standing at the mine's entrance, all of them armed, all of them watching. She frowned. They were guarding something.

Wanting to confirm before she got her hopes up, Jo snaked to the east, darting between trees and shrubs in the darkness, her feet padding against the earth like a ghost walking through a graveyard. She was as silent as the dead.

When she was finally in position to view the mine more clearly, Jo craned her neck from around the tree and then saw a small and hunched figure in the darkness of the mine. And while Jo couldn't physically see that it was her daughter, she knew that it was Amelia in the way that a mother always knew who her children were and how they were feeling. But what was more important than seeing her daughter was the fact that Amelia was alive.

Jo lingered longer than she should, watching her daughter, staring at her, fighting the urge to charge into that mine and pull her out by herself. But she knew what would happen the moment she revealed herself. She'd cut down four or five of them before she was gunned down herself. And then her little girl would scream in horror as her mother was torn apart in front of her or worse. But what was more, Amelia would still be a prisoner.

Slowly and carefully, Jo retreated to Stacy, who had remained where she was told to stay after Jo had chosen to move closer to the camp on her own.

Stacy's eyes were wide and attentive, waiting for the news, and Jo grabbed her hand, giving it a gentle squeeze.

"She's alive," Jo said. "She's being held in the mine. They have three guards watching it, and another thirty men stationed around the camp. All of them are armed."

Stacy reciprocated the squeeze and then exhaled a pent-up breath as she nodded. "Okay."

"We'll need a distraction," Jo said. "If I can draw enough of them away from the camp, or create enough confusion around them, then I think I can create an opening big enough for you to go through and get her. But I don't know if the guards will move once the fighting starts. They might have orders to stay and guard the mine no matter what." She raised her eyebrows, making sure that Stacy understood what that meant, and her daughter nodded.

"I understand," Stacy said.

Jo glanced at the weapon in Stacy's other hand. "Remember to aim before you shoot, line up the shot. You've done it enough times, so just let your instincts take over. It's like an extension of your arm, a part of you. You have to own it. You hear me?"

Stacy nodded.

"Good," Jo said, then glanced back to the camp, trying to think of the best way to cause a big enough distraction that would allow her daughter to slip through the forces undetected. She tried to think of a scenario that didn't involve her death, but if her life was required to save her daughters, then she would gladly pay the price.

"Wait," Stacy said, urgency in her voice.

Jo turned, thinking that her daughter had a sudden change of heart, but there was a smile on her face.

"You said she's in the mouth of the mine," Stacy said.

"Yeah?" Jo confirmed.

"Amelia and I used to play there," Stacy said. "It's not sealed."

Jo reciprocated the smile.

"I can sneak through the backside and try and pull her out. I think I remember where the second entrance is." Stacy frowned, biting her lower lip. "It might be a little harder to find it in the darkness, but I should be able to get to it with no problem."

271

Jo looked at her daughter, searching for any hesitation, but she was glad to find none. "If you do this, and they see you or hear you, then both of you will be trapped." She grimaced. "It should be me that goes."

"No," Stacy said. "You're a better shot at me, and if we do get caught, then it'll be important for you to cause a distraction to give Amelia and me a chance to get out." She reached for her mother's arm. "It's the best way for us to get through this, Mom. It's the best chance to get Amelia out of there alive."

Jo hadn't wanted to send her daughter in on a mission like this, but the more she thought about it, the more she realized that Stacy was right. They couldn't get to Amelia without risking killing her, and if there was a way for Stacy to sneak in through the back door, then Jo knew that it was the best possible scenario for the pair of them to come out of this alive. And that was the end game, making sure that her family survived.

*S*tacy moved quickly once she and her mother had worked out the plan as best as they could. But she knew that she didn't have much time. If they were going to get Amelia out before dawn, then Stacy would have to hurry.

The back entrance to the mine was at least an hour hike, and it would take twice as long to make it through the twisting and winding tunnels of the mine itself. She had only been through all the way once, and it was when she was much smaller than she was now, but this was their best chance.

Knowing that every second counted, Stacy never stopped to rest on her hike around to the west side of the mountain. And despite the darkness, she moved quickly, and the haste cost her solid footing more than once.

But every time Stacy slipped and smacked into the hard rock, she swallowed the pain and forced herself to remember that it was her sister that was trapped by the same animals that tried to slaughter them in their own home. She had failed her sister once. She would not fail her again.

Arms and legs covered with more scratches than she

could count by the time she reached the boarded-up entrance of the mine's back exit, Stacy finally paused for a moment to catch her breath.

The boards had been put up to deter anyone from trying to enter, but time and age had caused two of the boards to wither, and when she was little, she was skinny enough to squeeze through the bottom gap. She dropped to her knees and tried to slide under like she had done so many times before, only to stop herself. She was too big now.

Stacy slapped her hand against the dirt and then tried to dig her way under, but there was less than an inch of soil before the rock was exposed and she couldn't dig a trench any further than that. "Shit."

She stood and then tried prying one of the boards loose, but even when she heaved all of her weight behind it, they wouldn't budge, no matter how hard she pulled.

Frustration forced Stacy to punch and kick the boards, but despite the years that had weakened them, she wasn't strong enough to break through. Defeated and exhausted, Stacy slid to the ground with her back against the boards. She didn't cry. She didn't sob or pout, she felt nothing at all as she sat on the ground.

Ever since her father died four years ago, Stacy had thought that she wasn't enough. Not enough for her mother, or her sister, or even herself. It was like a piece went missing when her father died. She had always thought it was stupid when it came to mind, but sitting in the dirt with her sister trapped inside, she realized how right she had been.

"I'm sorry," Stacy said. "I'm so sorry."

The words left her lips and quickly dropped to the ground like pieces of lead. There was no one to hear her apology. No one to care about what she had to say. She was nothing in this world. Nothing but a stupid girl who was too weak to do anything.

Stacy repeated those words over and over in her head. Stupid. Weak. Failure. And every time she thought of them, she felt something stir inside of her. It was anger. She clenched her fists at her sides and forced herself to stand. She was not stupid. She had led her friend out of the college dorm before it was too late and the campus was overrun. She was not weak. She had made it all the way from the city and to the top of the mountain. She was not a failure, because she was still alive, and in a world that had devolved into a bit of chaos like the one she was currently living, sometimes staying alive was the best way to get back at the people that wanted to hurt you the most.

Stacy forced herself to stand and spun around, taking another look at the boards. She pushed against each of them, feeling along with the weathered and splintered wood for any weak points, any spot that she could take advantage of, and when she stretched for the top piece, she felt the board rattle.

Both ends of the plank were loosely attached to the side of the mountain, the nails nearly coming out of the rock. But she needed better leverage if she was going to get the board out of the stone. She found a few foot holes on the left side that provided the required height.

With half of her body pressed against the rock and the other half reaching for the board, Stacy pried her fingers over the top of the wood and held the firmest grip she could muster, then pulled.

The board groaned from her effort, but it didn't budge. She kept the pressure on it, her muscles already burning from fatigue even after only a few seconds. But she kept at it. Her cheeks reddened, and her thin, wiry muscles pulsated from the effort, and the nails on the board moved a quarter inch. It was working. She was doing it.

Stacy's bangs fell in her eyes. Her heart pumping and the sweat oozing from her skin was causing her to lose the grip on the board. But the nails were nearly out now.

Stacy pulled back with what remained of her strength, grunting between clenched teeth, and one final tug broke the nail's hold. She was catapulted from the rock and quickly dropped the two feet from the air and landed hard on her back, knocking the wind out of her.

Stacy gasped, quickly shoving the board that she removed off of her, and rolled to her side. Her back cracked from the motion, and everything was tender and bruised, and it took all of her strength not to cry out and give away her position in the night.

Instead, she looked up at the empty space where the board had been laid and smiled in triumph. "I'm coming, sis."

Stacy climbed back up and managed to sneak her way inside, ducking through the narrow entrance and into the mine. She landed hard on the heels of her feet, nearly twisting her ankle in the process, but she managed to stand.

It would be the last time that she would stand at full height again for the next two hours because the winding path of the mine would take her through narrow crevices and low ceilings.

Stacy remembered what Amelia had said about the mine, and how she thought monsters lived inside. But she would protect her sister. She would get her out before those monsters could hurt Amelia.

* * *

TIME PASSED SLOWLY FOR JO. Waiting had never been her

strong suit, but she had to trust that Stacy would make it through the mine. She had to trust the plan. But she didn't sit and do nothing.

Slowly, Jo moved closer toward the camp, better positioning herself for the ambush once her daughters were together.

Nothing more than a shadow in the darkness, Jo penetrated the camp another twenty yards, close enough so she could see the entrance of the mine and the outline of her daughter.

Amelia remained motionless, and that only caused Jo's imagination to run wild with worry. Was Amelia chained up? Was she hurt? Did they already kill her and her corpse was already rotting in that dark place like some sort of tomb?

Jo couldn't stop shaking.

But she shut her eyes, and after a few slow breaths, Jo calmed down, pushing the hysteria to the back of her mind. She couldn't let her fear win out over her reason.

Still, it was hard being so close to her daughter without being able to help her. A little girl who was wondering why her mother hadn't come to save her yet.

Jo remained hidden behind her cluster of rocks, staring at her daughter, when a band of another thirty men marched into camp through the woods.

The additional fighters were greeted with open arms. But amongst the celebrations and happy greetings, Jo watched two men separate from the main group to speak privately.

Assuming they really were the leaders, Jo was confident that she could get two shots off and kill both of them before either knew what had happened. And if she were to cut the head off the snake, then it was a safe bet that the people who followed them would be floundering at what to do next.

But if she were to shoot them now, if she were to expose

JAMES HUNT

herself, then she would be putting Amelia and Stacy in danger. The moment shots were fired, there would be a flock of terrorists storming through the woods and combing every square inch. And while Jo was confident she could evade them, security would be worse for Stacy and Amelia.

Jo knew she couldn't take the shot. Not now. But once her daughters were safe, all bets were off.

* * *

STACY HAD LOST track of how far she'd crawled into the mine, and after all of the twists and turns she took on the way through, it was easy to feel like she had lost her way. But when the tunnel narrowed to a crawl space which stretched for two hundred yards, she knew she was close.

It was here where Stacy and Amelia would always turn around because neither wanted to crawl through space on their belly and get covered in soot and God knows what else that might be lurking deep in the darkness.

And the darkness of the mine was unlike anything Stacy had seen before. It was darker than any blackness she'd ever seen. This place swallowed all light, and it could potentially swallow her too.

The ground was rough from the pickaxes that scarred the earth, carving out the veins of coal. She had heard stories of the cave-ins on the mountain that claimed the lives of hundreds of men. And with her belly flat against the earth and the top of her head scraping against the same rough ceiling, she understood the fear that had plagued those men that were trapped.

She imagined the crushing weight of all that rock, trapping her in place, the earth swallowing her whole and suffocating her to death. It sounded like a terrible way to go, and

278

she moved a little quicker from the sudden, inexplicable fear of being trapped, and the anxiety of not being able to stand, of being afraid that she would never rise again, all of it came pouring out of her in the form of frenzied panic.

Stacy lost all sense of rationality, her reason replaced by the animal instinct that told her that she needed to flee a danger that was all around, a danger that was tightening her chest.

The roof felt like it was coming down on her, ready to grind her into the same fine coal dust that was choking her now. She coughed, her lungs clotting with enough black silt that she didn't think she would ever breathe again.

Hot tears cut straight lines through the black soot on Stacy's cheeks, and the light bounced wildly from her fast pace. She wanted out, she wanted to stand, she wanted to be able to breathe, she didn't want to die underground, she didn't want this to be her final end. She wanted out of this fucking mine! She wanted out! Out! *Out!*

Stacy stretched her arm out and felt a ledge. She pulled herself forward and slid down hard onto the hill of loose gravel that she slid down on her stomach, rocks filling up the front of her shirt. When the small slope bottomed out to the level ground, Stacy used both shaky arms to push herself up and stood, the cuts on her legs stinging from the soot.

She turned around and shone the light through the small crack where she had crawled for two hundred yards. It looked even smaller standing on the other side of it. But she had made it, and the small measure of success provided a boost of confidence in herself and what she could accomplish. Because if she could make it through that kind of hell, then maybe she stood a chance at rescuing Amelia from people that wanted to harm her.

Covered in black coal dust, blood, and sweat, Stacy knew

that this was her opportunity for redemption. She couldn't waste her second chance now.

Stacy clicked off the light and put it back in her pocket. The darkness consumed her, and because she was covered from the black coal dust, she blended in seamlessly with the dark. It was the perfect camouflage for the hell that she was tasked to walk through.

She had walked through hell before. When her father died, when her mother left, when she and Amelia were forced to stay with their aunt, clinging onto one another in hopes that the days would become more bearable.

They had made promises to one another during those dark times. Promises to always be there for one another, promises that Stacy hadn't been able to keep after she left for college.

Stacy stepped forward, propelled by a new sense of purpose and a determination that she knew wouldn't fail her no matter what. She would get Amelia out of there and keep her safe. No matter the cost. No matter what it meant for her.

She continued to move quietly but quickly through the remaining section of the mine until she saw Amelia through the cracks in the back foundation wall that hadn't been thoroughly sealed. To the naked eye, the back wall made it look like there was no exit, but that was what the public works team that had been tasked with closing the mines down had wanted it to look like.

Stacy knew that there was a small cutout where kids could sneak through, because that was where she and Amelia used to hide when they would play in the woods.

The same three guards that her mother had spoken of still stood at the mine's front, their backs turned. The night was so quiet that she was afraid that even her breathing would cause the guards at the front to turn around and shoot her on sight.

Stacy gently picked up a small rock, small enough to fit through the cracks in the boarded-up section of the wall. She pinched the stone between her thumb and forefinger and carefully aimed it at her sister, who had her head down, shoulders slumped forward. Stacy wasn't sure if Amelia was asleep or not, but she needed to get her sister's attention without causing alarm to the guards.

Stacy flicked the rock, and the small piece of granite landed by Amelia's foot and made the slightest pop that caused both Amelia and one of the guards to stir. She ducked low and then heard the distant voices of the guards drift through the mine's cave.

Footsteps echoed inside the mine, and Stacy peeked through the crack in the boards and saw one of the guards towering over her sister, who still had her head bowed. She gripped the bottom of her shirt the way she always did whenever she was scared.

The man shouted, causing Amelia to shrink even smaller than she already was, but she didn't shake, she didn't cry. She'd always been tough.

Eventually, the guard returned to his post and turned his back on the unassuming little girl, who quickly turned and looked at her sister, the pair making eye contact with one another. Stacy pressed her finger to her lips, and Amelia nodded in understanding.

Stacy moved toward the compartment as silently as she could, gently resting her feet onto the rocky ground as Amelia moved silently toward the door as well from her side.

The guards had continued to talk, adding a needed background to the escape that the girls were hatching as Amelia neared the door.

Stacy held her breath as she pressed both hands against the small gate and pushed, shutting her eyes for only a second in anticipation of the groan that would follow and alert the guards behind her.

But there was no groan of the old hinges, and when Stacy opened her eyes, she saw her sister coming through the hole that she had made. Two seconds later and Amelia was by her side, a barrier of rock and wood now standing between them and the men with the guns.

Stacy grabbed Amelia by the hand and then led her back through the hole in which she came. While she knew she was accomplished for the first half of her mission, she knew that she couldn't celebrate until they were free from all of this, and when she heard the shouts of the terrorists back at the mine's mouth, she knew they needed to hurry.

THE LONGER THAT Jo stared at the mouth of the mine's entrance, the more her vision blurred. She had lost all track of time, and her restlessness had worsened.

Because it was getting late, half of the terrorist camp had turned in for the night, the rest keeping to small groups with the low conversation. Jo had lost the pair of leaders that had been talking in the darkness. She hoped that Stacy was close.

The tunnels were old, unsafe, and if Stacy had found her way into a passage that was crumbling or about to fall apart, then she might be trapped.

Jo's imagination picked up every single scenario that she could think of until she couldn't stop herself from shaking. And because of the fatigue, she found it harder and harder to keep everything straight in her mind, harder to not become overwhelmed by the truth that she had no idea whether or not this was going to work.

Living off the grid and providing for her own needs gave Jo complete control over her life and how she could deal with life, how it impacted her family. And while she understood that despite everything that happened she had still positioned herself to be in a better spot than most other families, she couldn't help but think of what she could have done differently.

But while Jo rehashed old choices that couldn't be undone, she became lost in her own thoughts, and it wasn't until the shouting in the camp that she was pulled from her memories. She glanced up and saw a swarm of fighters storming into the mine, their bodies blocking her line of sight to see if Amelia was still there.

Knowing that she didn't have much time, Jo quickly lined up her first shot and pulled the trigger. She watched one of the gunmen drop to the ground and then quickly moved onto the next before the others had a chance to pinpoint her location.

Three more dropped before any retaliatory gunfire came her way, and Jo was finally forced to retreat away from the camp, still unsure if Stacy had gotten Amelia out.

Wanting to give her girls as much time as possible, Jo moved east and west along the camp's perimeter, keeping close enough to continue to engage the enemy, but far enough away so the terrorists couldn't see how many of her there actually was.

The chaos and confusion that Jo could conjure would make her one weapon feel like a dozen so long as she kept on the move. She darted back and forth, muzzle flashes lighting up the night as the entire camp was awake and armed now that the fighting had started.

Even in the darkness, Jo moved effortlessly, her feet with minds of their own always finding the sure footing on the uneven ground. And while she moved quickly, she also moved efficiently. The night brought its own kind of confusion, and it only took a handful of steps in a different direction to completely disorient the enemy and send them reeling backward on their heels.

It was a dance that Jo could keep up for a little while, but she knew that the sheer number of terrorists that were flooding into the woods would eventually force her into a retreat, and after that, she would be forced to wait to see if her daughters survived the trip through the mine.

* * *

The shouts from the terrorists waxed and waned in the confines of the mine, but Stacy never stopped moving, and she never let go of Amelia's hand.

Stacy hadn't been sure how long it took the terrorists to figure out the hidden door that Amelia had snuck through, but it wasn't enough time to ensure their escape. But she was more concerned with their crawl through the narrow tunnel. If they didn't put enough space between themselves and the enemy, then they would be shot down like dogs.

"Sta—cy…" Amelia wheezed through the words. "I—can't —breathe."

Stacy didn't slow down even though Amelia tugged for her to stop. "It's all of the dust. I know it hurts, but we have to keep moving, okay? We can't stop until we make it out the other end."

Stacy's arm was pulled down, and she turned around to find her sister on the ground, gasping for air, convulsing like she was having a seizure.

"Amelia." Stacy knelt by her sister, shining the light in her eyes. Her sister's cheeks were turning blue. She wasn't going to last much longer. She set the light down, ignoring the shouts of the enemy that echoed from somewhere behind them, and concentrated on only helping her sister. "Just look at me, hey, look at me." She waited until Amelia's wandering eyes found hers, and then nodded. "Good. Now, breathe with me." She inhaled, and Amelia mimicked the motion with a wheeze. "And exhale." The girls were locked in with their breathing, and Stacy repeated it until Amelia fell into a rhythm. "That's it. Good, just keep doing that."

Amelia's breathing was still raspy, but she was breathing in regular intervals, so Stacy took that as a win.

"I'm going to sit you up, okay?"

Amelia nodded, and then Stacy helped prop her sister up and kept her hand against her back. "Very good, now just keep breathing like that." She scooped her arms around Amelia and lifted her off the ground. "Now we have to crawl through this space. If we don't, then we're going to die. So I just need you to crawl forward as fast as you can and keep breathing just like this. And keep moving. It doesn't matter if it's slow, just keep moving."

Stacy felt Amelia nod into her shoulder, and then she lifted the girl up and into the crevice of rock as she flattened to her stomach. "Now, go, Amelia, go!" She placed her hands on the back of Amelia's feet, so the girl had something to push off of, and then went back for the flashlight, pausing when she heard the terrorists.

They were closer now. Too close.

Stacy hurried back to the crack and then heaved herself up and inside, giving herself enough room to shimmy through the space. It wasn't as claustrophobic as she remembered from before, but she figured that was because of the enemy that was nipping at their heels.

Stacy made sure to keep her body between Amelia and the exit behind them. She didn't think the terrorists would be stupid enough to try and follow them through this, but she couldn't be sure. "Keep going, Amelia, you're doing great."

Five minutes into their crawl, Amelia still wheezing but managing to keep up the steady rhythm of her breathing that they had practiced just moments ago, and she saw the flicker of light coming from behind her.

Stacy stopped, craning her head back around, and saw two pairs of lights cut through the narrow crack of darkness that lay behind her, followed by the excited shouts of the men chasing her. She faced forward again and pushed Amelia ahead. "Keep going, Amelia! Don't stop! No matter what, don't—"

Gunfire thundered in the mine, and Amelia's wheezing turned to screams as the bullets ricocheted violently through the narrow space, which also happened to be their saving grace. Because space was so tight and the terrorists didn't have a clean shot from the uneven ground where they stood, the bullets scattered wildly against the rock, veering off in a thousand different directions, missing their intended targets.

"Keep going, Amelia," Stacy said, her voice high-pitched from the hysteria and excitement that was running through her veins. "Just keep going!" She wasn't even sure if her sister could hear her at the moment, because the gunfire was still echoing behind them. She couldn't even hear herself. It was only the vibrations in her throat that confirmed she was actually yelling.

But they still had a long road ahead. Stacy whispered a silent prayer to keep them alive just long enough for them to get home. Because Stacy had made a promise to her mother, and she wanted to prove that she could follow through.

* * *

THE VOICES of the terrorists faded once Jo moved west to meet up with her daughters. She had kept the camp on their toes for at least an hour and hoped it provided enough time for Stacy and Amelia to keep moving through the tunnel and escape to the other side.

Tired from the long day and what would continue to be a long night that would bleed into the early morning, Jo's brain and body were fried.

When she finally made it to the mine's entrance, she went inside, searching for any sign that her daughters had made it out the other side, but found nothing.

Jo knew how small those cracks and crevices were through the mine and the winding and curving nature of the beast. No, if they survived coming through the mine, then they would stay put because they would be out of danger. Jo had to wait.

Without the distraction of the terrorists to keep herself busy, she could not prevent her mind from wandering through the minefield of traps and stress that was sure to follow. She thought of all of the things that she should have done differently, all of the things that she should have said. And so she began to bargain with a God that she didn't even know existed or not.

"I know I should have been a better mother," Jo said, rocking back and forth as she stared at the mine's entrance. "I should have told them that I loved them more. I shouldn't have pushed so hard."

The tears came next as she continued to stare into that

empty void that had swallowed both of her girls, a void that she was unable to pull them out of by herself.

"They were only children when they lost their father," Jo said, whispering through the whimpers in her head. "I know that it was weak of me to leave them when I did, but I promise that I won't ever do that again. No matter what happens, no matter what comes my way, I will face it with them. I promise." She squeezed her hands tighter together, shutting her eyes. "Please."

And in the silence of the night, there was no answer to Jo's prayers, no sign from any God or higher beings that her daughters were going to be all right. There was only the mountain.

Jo bowed her head, suddenly exhausted from hanging on so tightly. She wiped her eyes and then wiped the snot collecting on her upper lip right beneath her nostrils and took a breath. There was nothing to do now but wait. But she would wait as long as it took.

Jo kept her ears peeled for any noise in the woods. She didn't think that the terrorists would be able to track her with any success in the darkness, but she wasn't going to make the mistake of underestimating them again.

She kept her weapon at the ready, poised to fire at anything she found suspicious. It was a way to focus her scattered thoughts and the worried grief that kept pulling her in different directions. The defensive stance was something she was familiar with, something that she understood.

And while Jo watched the darkness that surrounded the mine's second entrance, she caught a flicker of light in her peripheral. She nearly dropped the weapon in her hands, but she had the presence of mind to keep it up. It was still possible that the people coming through the mine were the enemy, and that she had somehow missed her daughters coming through.

But when she heard the muffled grunt of her youngest daughter, a grunt that she knew better than her own voice, Jo dropped the weapon and rushed to the entrance, colliding with Amelia and Stacy, all three of them falling to their knees in exhaustion.

"Oh my God," Jo said, the words escaping with exasperated breaths. "Oh my God." She kept a tight hold on each of them, pressing them firmly against her body. After a few minutes of silence, Jo leaned back to get a better look at them and saw that they were both covered in black dust from the mine. "Are you all right?"

Amelia nodded, but then she coughed, a phlegmy, rattling thing that sounded like her lungs were falling apart.

"It's the coal dust," Stacy said, her voice haggard and her eyes tired. "We both inhaled too much. She needs oxygen."

"They have some in town at the doctor's office," Jo said. "We'll head there and get some." She nodded and then hugged both of them tightly again, hoping that they couldn't see her tears. She sniffled and then whimpered, shutting her eyes, remembering the promises that she made. Promises that she intended to keep.

The longer that Stacy and Jo walked with Amelia resting on Stacy's shoulder, the more concerned that Jo became. Because while the girl was still breathing, she had passed out, and her breaths were so ragged and weak that Jo wasn't sure how much longer that she would survive.

"The doctor will be able to help her," Jo said, speaking aloud more to calm herself than anyone else. "She's just tired."

"It was dangerous to go in there," Stacy said. "Maybe there was another way to get her out. Maybe if we could have just—"

"There wasn't another way," Jo said, then looked at Stacy. "Amelia is alive because of you. And we'll make sure she stays that way."

Stacy nodded and then adjusted Amelia in her arms.

The sky slowly transitioned from black night to the dull grey and purple that appeared just before dawn when they arrived at The Village.

Jo was the first to the doctor's door, glad to find it

unlocked. "Doc!" Jo screamed, her voice more panicked than she intended. "Doc!"

A few seconds later and the old man emerged from the hallway, fixing the glasses that had gone crooked on his face. He patted his hands against the wall to keep himself steady as he met Jo in the waiting room when Stacy walked in with Amelia in her arms.

"She's inhaled a lot of coal dust," Jo said. "She needs oxygen."

The doctor nodded and then moved back down the hallway, gesturing for Stacy to follow. He led them into one of the patient rooms and pointed to the table. "Lay her down."

Once Stacy put Amelia down on the table, the girl wheezed even harder, and Jo feared that the girl was going to die right there on the table. But both Jo and Stacy stood on either side of Amelia, each of them holding one of Amelia's hands, and Jo used her one free hand to brush her fingers through Amelia's hair.

"You know that she had asthma when she was little," Jo said.

"I remember," Stacy said. "All the doctors thought that because the case was so bad that she was going to have it for the rest of her life."

"Yeah," Jo said. "That's what the doctors said." She brushed in a soothing, rhythmic gesture. "But they were all wrong. She was stronger than they gave her credit for."

Stacy smiled. "She was always the tough one. Even when she was little."

"She is tough," Jo said. "Both my daughters are tough."

Stacy and Jo locked eyes over Amelia. What small amount of strength remained to Stacy gave way, and she cried. Her knees buckled, and she let go of Amelia's hand as she collapsed in the chair next to the bed and buried her hands in her face. Jo didn't walk over to her daughter because she knew those tears were not from pain or anguish, they were the sweet tears of relief.

Jo had shed those tears long ago after Danny died when she realized what she had to do to survive. It had brought her to the next step in her journey, and it made her stronger. And she had no doubts that her daughter would grow just as strong.

They would all survive.

The doctor returned with a tank and oxygen mask, but first administered anesthesia to knock Amelia unconscious. He began to clean some of the muck from her lungs. "How long was she in the mine?"

"Four, maybe five hours," Jo answered. "But only two during the real bad portion."

"I can give her some oxygen," he said. "But that's about it."

Jo nodded. "Do what you can."

Both Jo and Stacy remained in the room while the doctor did his work, both holding Amelia's hands, hoping that they could pass on their own strength through a type of telepathy that only worked through touch.

The doctor placed the mask over Amelia's mouth and looked at both Jo and Stacy. "Do you girls need anything?"

"We're fine," they answered at the same time.

"Call if you need me." The doctor looked down at Amelia one final time, bowed his head, and then walked out of the room.

Jo gently ran her thumb over Amelia's hand, watching the steady rise and fall of her daughter's chest the same way she did during those first nights after she and Danny had brought her home from the hospital.

"She's not wheezing as much," Stacy said.

"No," Jo said.

Stacy rubbed her sister's hand and then gently placed it over Amelia's stomach. She pressed her fists into the side of the bed and leaned over. "Are they going to hit us again?"

Jo kept hold of Amelia's hand as she looked at her eldest daughter. She was already looking for the next fight. She had found her purpose, and it was the same purpose as her mother: to protect the family. "They called for more men. I counted over fifty fighters before you collected your sister."

The number didn't bring any shock or doubt to Stacy's expression. "So what do we do? We can't go back to the cabin, they already know about its location. So do we head down the mountain? Try and regroup at the base in the town?"

Jo gestured to Amelia. "She wouldn't make the trip. She barely made it here."

Stacy was quiet for a little while, and then after a few minutes, she nodded her head. "So we fight."

Jo nodded. "So we fight." She brought Amelia's hand to her lips and then kissed it firmly, her wet lips warming the skin they touched, then she brought it down and placed it over the hand that Stacy had set down. "You'll stay here and make sure she's safe."

"And what are you going to do?" Stacy asked, walking around to her mother's side as Jo picked up her gear from the corner of the room.

"I'm going to gather the deputies, see if the sheriff is back," Jo said, gripping the rifle with one hand and the crossbow in the other as she turned around. "I'll be of better use in the bell tower than I will in here. But you can keep her safe." She extended the rifle to Stacy, who took it with a bit of a surprise.

"You always told me never to touch your gun," Stacy said.

"And since when did you ever listen to me?" Jo smirked,

and then shouldered the crossbow along with her dozen bolts, pistol, and a hunting knife. "I've always been better with the bow." She glanced down to her own knife. "Though I suppose I'll be using this once I run out."

Stacy set the bow aside and then flung her arms around her mother, squeezing tight. "Don't die out there, okay?"

Jo smiled, returning the embrace. "I don't plan on it." When the pair separated, both returned back to business. "Brace the doors with what you can, but keep an exit open for yourself in case you have to move her. I wouldn't be surprised if they tried to burn us out, but they might just go for a complete slaughter of everyone and everything that we love."

"This is really happening, huh?" Stacy asked.

"Yeah," Jo answered, then looked back toward Amelia. "And we're going to win."

Jo left Stacy with Amelia and found the doctor again before she went, telling him to prepare as many beds and triage supplies as he could. "There's a fight coming, and I have a feeling there won't be many folks left by the time it's finished."

The doctor sighed and then removed his glasses to rub his eyes. "You think it'll be worse than the last time?"

"I do," Jo answered. "Much worse."

uhammed stared at the entrance to the mine. He'd worn the same scowl for the past hour, and the expression was starting to set permanently on his face. "She was a little girl."

"A little girl who had help."

Muhammed whirled around, setting his fiery gaze on the guard that had spoken up, and the man immediately stared at his boots. He took two large, quick strides toward the man and bore down on him like an alpha wolf to an inferior member of the pack that had tried to lash out at him. "There were three of you in this cave. Three of you to watch one little girl. And you let her escape right from beneath your noses."

The other two guards stood off on either side of the main guard, neither of them looking at Muhammed, both choosing silence over the alternative.

Muhammed tilted his chin up, still staring down at the man who had failed him. "On your knees."

The guard shook, quickly glancing up at Muhammed with pleading eyes. "Commander, I—"

Muhammed swept the legs out from beneath the guard, and the man hit the ground hard, then two more men moved to restrain him and keep him still.

"Please! I will find them, I swear it! I won't rest until I bring them back to you! I swear it on my life!"

Muhammed removed the pistol from his side holster from beneath his robes and aimed it at the man's head, right between the eyes. "You can't catch what you can't find." He fired the shot, and the bullet split through the skull, leaving an exit wound out of the back of his head the size of a walnut and a trail of brain, blood, and bone behind him as the body slumped from a lack of tension.

The men who held him started to drag the body away, but Muhammed stopped both of them. "You do not bury him. Set him in an open place on the rocks where the animals will be able to pick at him."

Both soldiers nodded, and once they were gone, Muhammed focused his attention on the other two guards that had failed him. He briefly considered executing them, but the impulse passed quickly. He knew that he needed men if he was going to continue his conquest, and these two looked too frightened to fail him again.

"You two will be responsible for finding the girl again," Muhammed said. "And you will bring her back to me alive, or you will join your brother in the forest where the wolves can pick at your bones."

"Yes, Commander."

"Yes, Commander."

Both men bowed their heads and then quickly fled the scene before Muhammed changed his mind, and as he watched them turn tail, he thought about sending a bullet through their skulls because he doubted that they would return with the girl. She was gone. It was the mother that had come for her. That Joanna Mercer the deputy had spoken about.

The same woman that owned the cabin, the same woman who had shot and killed half a dozen of his men last night while she was leading them all on a wild goose chase while her daughter escaped through the back of the mine.

Muhammed turned back to look at the darkened mouth of the cave. He should have known that these people would know their own land better than him. It was the same arrogance that the American forces had when they came to his country. He had become the one thing that he had hated, and now he was paying the price.

"Commander."

Muhammed turned away from the mouth of the cave and found Khalid with the other leaders of the men that had come in the night. "Thank you, Khalid."

Khalid bowed and then dismissed himself from the group, leaving Muhammed with the four other battalion commanders that had come with him from their homeland to kill the infidels.

"All of us are a long way from home," Muhammed said. "All of us chose to come here and bring justice to those that thought themselves above the laws of our God."

The hard faces that stared back at him nodded in agreement, but Deshah stepped forward. "We have all made sacrifices, Muhammed. But why have you called us here? Why have we stopped our missions to come and attack this village?"

The other commanders behind him agreed.

Muhammed knew it was a question that he would have to face, and while his men would follow him anywhere, he knew that they would be more willing to fight to the last man if there was a good reason behind their summons.

"There is a resistance here that cannot stand." Muhammed pointed to the ground. "Their stubborn will must be broken if we are to have free rein over every town, village, and city along the mountain ridge."

"Muhammed," Deshah said. "We knew that the best way for us to win these battles was to keep to our guerilla tactics. Combining our forces now is dangerous. We need to keep moving."

Muhammed tilted his chin up. "If you're afraid, then I will gladly take over your command." He gestured to the rocks and trees that surrounded them. "We might be on foreign soil, but this is terrain that we are familiar with." He walked around them and to the covered crates that had been stashed nearby the cave, something that the woman had missed last night no doubt, because if she had seen them, then she probably would have tried to burn them. "And if you're worried about the kind of weapons that they'll have against our rifles—" he ripped the tarp off the collection of boxes. "—then I believe you will enjoy our new armory."

All four of the commanders stepped forward, their jaws dropping with a sense of awe as they stepped forward to examine the weapons and the loot, and Muhammed stepped aside to let them open the boxes filled with grenades, heavy caliber weapons, and enough ammunition to fight a dozen American battalions.

Deshah lifted one of the heavy fifty-caliber weapons from the crate and all of the other commanders moved forward, marveling at the weapons that Muhammed provided, but again it was Deshah who remained skeptical as he placed the heavy caliber weapon on the ground.

"I didn't see your brother when I came in this morning," Deshah said, his tone hinting that he was already leaning toward a question that could prove problematic in regards to Muhammed's intentions. "Where is Zahid?"

The rest of the commanders stopped what they were doing and looked back at Muhammed, waiting for an answer. Muhammed knew that the moment the other commanders learned of his brother's death, they would question his true motives, but he chose not to lie about them. He leaned into the truth, toward the light and path of righteousness.

"Zahid was killed," Muhammed said. "By a woman who lives in The Village. I had abducted the woman's daughter, brought the little girl here to act as a bartering chip, but she escaped last night. I executed the guard that was charged with holding her."

Deshah nodded, the shadow of a smirk on his face because he knew that he had caught Muhammed red-handed. "So there is more to this attack than just wiping out the enemy. You want revenge. Isn't that right, Muhammed?"

The other commanders waited for Muhammed to speak, and he knew that what he said next could unite or divide them, and he needed all of their men to fight for him with the same passion that brought them on this crusade in the first place.

"That's right," Muhammed answered. "I want revenge for the death of my brother." He looked to the other commanders. "It's what we all want. It's why we're all here." He raised his voice so every man in the camp could hear. "We traveled across an ocean to get here, worked our way down half of a continent to fight the enemy in the heart of their country! We made a promise to the family that we lost in the fight for our home that we would drive a knife into the heart of the infidels that lived here!"

The rest of the camp slowly moved toward Muhammed

and the other commanders, all of them with eager ears, and a fire growing in their eyes.

"My brother was one of the greatest fighters that I have ever known," Muhammed said. "And he was shot in the back by cowards! By people who care nothing for our lives or our traditions or the one true God!"

A cheer of assent rippled through the crowd, and Muhammed felt the churn of momentum grow in his favor as he turned back to Deshah and the other commanders. He had them all in the palm of his hand now.

"I made a promise to avenge those that have fallen," Muhammed said. "For my brother, and all the brothers and sisters who have fallen for our cause. We have a chance to keep our good work alive! We have a chance to turn the tide in this great war! Because this is the only war that matters! And if we band together now, if we truly believe in ourselves and our God, then we will never know defeat!"

The crowd erupted in cheers now, the chanting growing louder and louder until all the commanders joined in, including Deshah.

Muhammed smiled as he gazed at his army because he knew that these men would fight to the last man. He knew that they would all give their final breaths to their cause. There might be five commanders in this camp, but there was only one true leader, and Muhammed knew that it was a precious gift to own. And he would not squander it today. He would lead this mighty and holy cause to the town and cleanse it through the holy spirit of war and blood. Because that was the only way to find absolution for their sins. That was the only way for them to be free.

44

*J*o stood around the table in Mike's office, his chair remaining empty, and she kept her head bowed. "It's dawn. He should have been back by now."

"We know that," Furst said, his tone snippy. "But he's not, which either means he's dead or he's hurt, or he's been captured by those fucking animals." He kept his arms crossed, his expression set in the glower of a child that was caught between the emotions of fear and confusion. "We don't have enough men to hold The Village."

"And we don't have anywhere else we can go," Jan said. "If we start running down the mountain, they'll just chase after us and pick us apart from one by one." She looked at Jo and then exhaled as she nodded. "We have a better chance at staying here and defending our position. It worked last time. It can work again."

"You said they're coming back with four times the amount of men," Furst said. "They'll wash over us like a tidal wave."

"We're wasting time," Jo said, and then pushed herself off

of Mike's desk. "We need to start setting mines along the tree lines. We'll focus the brunt of the mines on the north side where they would have the high ground."

Jo left the office, leaving the deputies to sort out the affairs for the fight, and then glanced toward the sky above. The morning was in full swing now, and the mountain was still quiet. She had always enjoyed those long walks through the woods in the morning, even before Danny died. It was so peaceful, so calm, that it made Jo wonder if there was anyone else in the world besides her. Because that's what the wild did to a person, it cut you off from the rest of society, isolating you from the rest of the world. And Jo wasn't sure if that was a good or a bad thing.

She suspected that it was like most things in life, it could be used for good and bad depending on how often it was used, and if it was something that was abused. Maybe that's what she had done over the past four years. Perhaps she took one good thing about this place and ruined it, not just for herself, but for her girls as well. But she had to keep them safe. It was the sole purpose behind everything that she had done, and if she failed now, then all of those sacrifices would have been for nothing.

Jo was near the bell tower when the bomb connected with Rusty's garage and plumed an explosion of smoke and fire and debris that sent Jo to the ground.

On her back, Jo shifted uneasily from side to side, blind to the world with nothing but white light and deaf from the din in her ears. The front side of her body was hot from the burning sun and the fire that had caught at the station.

Another whistle echoed from the sky, and Jo scrambled to her feet, a fear gripping her as she had no idea where the bomb would land. She ran as fast as she could toward the bell tower in the center of town and then ducked again when she saw one of the accountant offices explode from another direct hit.

It was hard for Jo to comprehend what she was seeing, but she knew there was nothing that she could do against this type of weaponry save for finding shelter. Or try and locate where the enemy was firing from.

Jo double-timed it toward the bell tower, knowing it would provide her the best vantage point in The Village, and she hoped that she would be able to pinpoint the exact location of where the blasts were coming from.

She burst through the church doors, and the ground rattled and shook when she reached the spiral staircase that led to the top of the tower. She shut her eyes, sending up the brief prayer that the doctor's office was out of range of the explosions as she quickly churned her feet up the steps.

The moment she broke through to the top, she glanced east and whimpered in relief when she saw the doctor's office still standing, but when her eyes fell upon the location of where the target landed, her heart sank. "No."

Mags' store was pluming smoke through a massive hole in the roof, the structure looking as though it was about to cave in on itself at any moment. She gripped the side of the tower to keep her upright, and all of that grief erupted into a rage as she turned her sights into the woods.

Jo planted her elbows on the edge of the bell tower walls and peered through the scope, thrusting her hundreds of yards into the woods. "Where are you? Where are you hiding, you bastards?" She scanned the rocky hillside quickly, probably faster than she should have allowed herself, but she wasn't going to stop until she found the source of the fire.

The crosshairs found nothing but rocks and trees, but when she moved farther north on the mountain, she saw a cluster of men in the woods, holding grenades. Jo smiled. "Gotcha."

She pulled the trigger and sent a bolt through the neck of the man caught in her crosshairs. She loaded another bolt and lined up another shot before the second man knew where the bolt was fired from.

Jo killed three before they had the sense to run for cover, but because of the tower's elevation, she had a bead on them even when they ducked behind the cluster of rocks that they thought would protect them, and she was going to send them to meet their maker.

But just before she squeezed the trigger, she heard the cries and screams from the fighters below. She turned her attention to the rush of fighters that had sprinted down the mountain, all of them armed with weapons and even through the trees, Jo knew that there was enough of them to slaughter every man, woman, and child that resided in The Village.

THE FIRST EXPLOSION that Stacy felt prompted her to run to the front of the doctor's office, and she peered out into the street, looking for the source of the explosion. But she was too far down to be able to view the carnage from her current position. She'd need to step out into the street to see it, and that would expose her.

The doctor joined her by the window and then quickly pulled her away. "If the glass shatters, it could hurt you."

Two more explosions rocked the earth, these two closer, the noise like clapping thunder from a thousand different lightning strikes, and it was enough to push both Stacy and the doctor away from the barricaded door.

"Christ, how the hell are we supposed to survive that?"

the doctor asked, his fear causing his voice to edge on the cusp of hysteria.

"Any way we can," Stacy said, and then quickly turned to the doctor. "Can you get to the roof from in here?"

The doctor looked at her with a questionable glance. "You can't be serious."

"I need the high ground if we're going to keep this building from being overrun by the enemy." Stacy stepped closer and lifted the rifle. "I'm not going to let anyone through that door. Now, can I get to the roof or not?"

The doctor finally nodded and then led Stacy toward the back of the building and into a supply closet. He grabbed a rope dangling from one of the ceiling tiles, and a ladder came down. "It leads into the attic, but there's another ladder on the backside of the building that you can get to through a window and ledge. It's unlocked."

"Thanks, Doc," Stacy said, and as she planted one foot on the first step he grabbed her arm, and she froze, looking at him.

The doctor lowered his voice and leaned in. "If they come inside, I won't be able to save your sister. Or myself for that matter."

Stacy shook her head. "They won't get in." She hurried up into the attic, having to duck as she walked toward the back window, which provided the only light source, and she quickly bent outside onto the scaffolding that the doctor had said was there then climbed onto the roof.

More hellfire rained from the sky and destroyed more of the buildings along the main street, and by the time she reached the front of the building, she saw the destruction that the bombs had left behind, and when her eyes fell to Mags' store, her cheeks flushed red, first from shock, and then from rage.

Stacy stared at the destroyed building, unable to look at anything but the crumbling roof where she had gone to pick up candy from the sweet woman that owned the store. She looked to the blown-out windows of the store, the glass shimmering on the black pavement beneath the sun, and she waited for Mags to walk out of the store in one piece, to wave her hands and let Stacy know that she was okay.

But the longer that Stacy stared at the entrance and saw nothing but the shimmer of glass, the more she knew that if Mags was inside, then she wasn't coming out until someone pulled her body from the rubble.

Tears clouded Stacy's vision. She heard the screams of men coming from the hill, followed by the thunder of feet that were coming from the woods, and slowly her grief turned from fear to rage. And she knew precisely where to focus that rage as she pressed her eye against the scope of the rifle and brought down her first kill.

* * *

DOZENS OF FIGHTERS flooded into the streets, easily breaking past the few guards that they still had in the woods, and they killed everything they touched. But the villagers resisted, and Jo saw Jan lead their group of fighters from the sheriff's station to make their stand.

Using the height of the tower to her advantage, Jo quickly picked off seven different fighters before any of them realized where the bolts were coming from. But when they did, a group of five fighters rushed toward the church, sprinting into the back door.

Jo reached for another bolt, but the crossbow was empty. Jo abandoned the weapon, and then climbed over the side of the tower wall, knowing that she'd be overrun by the enemy in the narrow staircase.

Jo dangled from the ledge. It was at least a twelve-foot drop, but when she heard the hurried footsteps of the enemy heading toward her, she let go, her stomach swirling as she dropped and then landed hard on the pitched roof. Her legs buckled and she rolled over, tumbling head over feet until she finally managed to plant her foot down, stopping her from skidding off the edge of the roof where she would have most undoubtedly broken her neck had she kept rolling.

But Jo didn't rest on her laurels. She couldn't, not with the enemy still bearing down on her. She moved to the edge of the roof and glanced down, getting a better look at what lay ahead of her at the bottom. Bullets rained from overhead and she lunged forward, flinging herself off instead of planning out the landing better, but despite the pain when she hit the ground, she knew that she couldn't stop, and it was all she could do to limp forward as the gunmen in the bell tower took aim at her from above.

The nearest spot for cover was the church's side annex building, but it was another twenty yards. She was less than a second away from death when she veered hard left, heading toward the woods, and the bullet that was meant to kill her skidded across the pavement on the path to the annex building.

Jo dove behind the building's wall and unholstered the pistol at her hip. She glanced east toward the doctor's office and saw the backside of the buildings along the main drag.

The last thing she remembered seeing when she was up top were the swarms of fighters heading in that same direction, and while she had faith in her daughter's ability to shoot, she knew that Stacy couldn't fight all of them off without help.

* * *

Muhammed watched from the pack near the artillery as his men swarmed the small village. If the woman survived the initial onslaught then he would kill her himself, but finding her corpse among the dead wouldn't be difficult, and her death would still be satisfying even if it weren't by his hand. Because he had won.

The other commanders smiled and pointed at the men as they slaughtered the infidels. Each of them had placed bets on how many of the villagers each of their units would kill, though Muhammed knew that there was no real way for them to keep track. It was nothing but a pissing contest, and they could have their fun so long as their men came out victorious at the end.

But while they were bickering about kills, Muhammed kept his attention focused intently on the field of battle. He wanted to ensure that no one escaped their grasp this time, and the only way for him to make sure that happened was to keep an eye on the edges. He figured that most folks would head south, and he had a clear view of that line.

However, a commotion near the north side of the battle brought Muhammed's attention to the bell tower, and it was there that he saw a woman climb out and then stumble to the ground, limping to the cover of a group of rocks where she paused to rest.

It was the woman from the cabin. He had seen her picture on the wall, and while she had aged some since the photo was taken, he knew it was still her.

Muhammed picked up one of the rifles and moved swiftly down the mountain. This could be his one chance to even the odds, and he wasn't going to miss it.

* * *

A PILE of shells rested at Stacy's feet, and for every shell casing that collected on the pavement, there was a body on the streets to match it. Twelve fighters had made their way toward the doctor's office door, and twelve bodies now lay still and quiet.

But despite the sight of their slain, the enemy wouldn't stop, and while Stacy was able to line her shots quickly enough, she knew that she was going to run out of bullets eventually, and when three more men sprinted toward the front door, she heard the click of the firing pin after her first shot.

Stacy reached for another magazine cartridge, only for her fingers to grope nothing but air. She glanced down and saw that she was out.

Down below at the door, three others had joined the two that Stacy hadn't been able to kill and started their assault. Stacy still had the pistol, but she knew that she wouldn't have much of a shot from her current position from above, so she rushed toward the back of the building and ducked back into the attic, able to hear the heavy knock from the bastards trying to break through the front door's barricade.

Stacy sprinted through the attic and then dropped into the supply closet, her feet hitting the tiled floor at the exact moment she heard the crash of glass at the front of the building. The terrorists were breaking through.

Stacy gripped the pistol with both hands and peered into the hallway and saw one of the fighters trying to squeeze his way in through the window. But at least the barricade on the door was still holding firm. And that would give her a chance.

If Stacy could limit their entrance through the one

window, then she could create a kill funnel for anyone that tried to get through. With the pistol's short range it would be easier for her to shoot them, and she could still keep a relatively safe distance.

Stacy hurried down the hall, passing the doctor's office on the left, and saw that the door was closed. She figured that the doctor was hiding, or maybe he already left. Stacy didn't get the idea that he was a particularly brave man, and she didn't think that he would be much help once the fighting started.

With the terrorist struggling to squeeze through the front window, he didn't see Stacy when she entered the front waiting area, and she ducked behind one of the couches for cover. She wasn't sure if it would stop the bullets from their automatic rifles when they started firing, but she needed to stay close to make sure that her aim was accurate enough to kill whatever made it through the window.

Stacy gripped the pistol, aimed, and then fired, shooting the terrorist in the gut. He slumped over the window sill.

Retaliatory fire immediately forced her back down behind the couch, and she ducked low to make herself as small a target as she possibly could. She heard the shouts of the men outside, and she knew that they were trying to get inside.

Gun still in her hands, Stacy crawled to the edge of the couch and peered around the side, only to be pushed back by more gunfire from the window as the men tried to move their dead comrade out of the way.

The bullets were relentless, and the couch was falling to pieces, her cover growing shorter and shorter until she didn't think that there would be anything left for her to work with at all. She was running out of time.

* * *

JO KEPT to the backside of the buildings on her sprint toward the doctor's office. Most of the terrorists had flooded the main street, and she saw the fighting in the streets between the enemy and what remained of her town. And while she saw dead terrorists, she saw far too many of her fellow mountain residents than she should have. It was a fight that they were losing.

Jo was three-quarters of the way down the row of buildings when gunfire erupted behind her, forcing her through the back door of what remained of Mags' General Store.

Once behind the cover of the back wall, Jo slowly peered around to see where the gunfire had come from, but the moment she revealed herself, another round of shooting forced her to retreat.

Jo gripped the pistol with both hands and drew in a breath, trying to focus what little energy that she had left in her mind. She stepped toward the back door, keeping low, expecting the enemy to still be farther back, but she collided into the terrorist, their guns smacking into one another.

Face to face with the enemy, Jo locked with his eyes, and she quickly grabbed his weapon, trying to pry from his grip, but in doing so sacrificed the hold on her own gun, which also dropped to the ground.

But with both hands free, Jo secured the rifle and ripped it from the man's hands, then threw it to the ground. She rammed the palm of her hand into the terrorist's throat, causing him to stumble backward a few steps, clutching his throat and gasping for air.

Jo found her pistol on the ground, but during mid-lunge, the terrorist tackled her, throwing the pair back into Mags' store, rolling three rotations before they stopped with the man on top of her, his hands around her throat.

"You will die for what you did to my brother," he said, his eyes and cheeks red, a sharp contrast to the black hair on his head. "This isn't a fight that you can win, do you understand me? This isn't a fight that you can win!"

With the air closing around her throat and black spots peppering her vision, Jo worked her legs up between herself and the terrorist and then pushed, loosening his grip until she could breathe, then thrust her knee into his groin as hard as she could.

The man cried out in pain, and he lost his grip on Jo's throat completely, and she rolled him off to the side as she gasped for air.

The noise from the fighting beyond the walls only added to the confusion and distraction as Jo struggled to get her bearings on where the weapon fell. She searched the ground, and when she spotted the pistol near the back door, she only made it one lunge before she was pulled back.

Jo glanced at her feet, the terrorist clawing at her pants and pulling her closer, that same maddening expression on his face as he tried to close his hands around her neck again.

"You bitch! You fucking bitch!"

Jo kicked her legs as hard as she could, but it did little to move the behemoth who doubled down, raking his fingers across her leg so hard that she thought he broke her skin even through the jeans.

"You will rot on the mountain which you love so much!" The man had one hand on Jo's neck, trying to get his second firmly on it, while Jo reached for the pistol.

Her fingertips grazed it by inches, but she couldn't move close enough to physically grab it. She stretched her arm as far as it would go, but when the man closed his second hand around her throat she was pinned down, unable to move any further.

"For my brother," he said, spitting the words out through a mixture of grunts and labored breaths. "Your death will mark the end of this mountain, the end of the resistance, and the true beginning of our conquest over your petulant little country."

The pain along Jo's throat was excruciating, and the pressure in her head grew so tight that she thought her eyes would pop from their sockets. She lazily and limply pounded her fists against his chest and arms, but it did nothing to avert his efforts.

And as the man on top of her clamped down harder along her neck, nearly crushing her windpipe, she felt her very life slipping from her fingers.

Jo had gone numb, but just before the world faded to black, three gunshots rang out and Jo saw blood spurt from the terrorist's chest.

The grip around Jo's neck loosened, and then the terrorist collapsed to his side. Jo removed the man's hands, gasping for air, and then rolled to her stomach. She glanced behind her to find Mags propped up by the cash register, shrapnel sticking out of her stomach, her trusty revolver gripped limply in her hand.

"Mags," Jo coughed and scrambled to her feet to get to her friend.

Exhausted, her throat bruised and starting to become swollen and turning into a red and purple blotch, Jo dropped to the ground by Mag's side.

"I'm sorry I lost Amelia," Mags said. "Tell her—" She coughed, more blood spilling over the front of her shirt. "I'm sorry."

Jo held Mags' hand. "It's okay."

And Jo sat there, holding her friend's hand as the fight raged in the street until the light went out in Mags' eyes, and Jo kissed Mags' palm. "Goodbye, Mags."

Jo forced herself to her hands and knees and then made her way to the front of the store, knowing that she still needed to get to her daughters.

Chaos greeted Jo when she stepped onto the street, more bodies than she could count. She stumbled along the storefronts, bullets flying, and picked off two more terrorists along the way, but heavy gunfire eventually forced her back into one of the buildings for cover.

And with the hail of raining gunfire attacking her and her strength failing her, Jo struggled to push on. But when she saw the band of men outside the doctor's office, trying to break inside, Jo forced herself forward until a bullet caught her leg and she collapsed on the pavement.

Her vision faded in and out, and the last thing she saw were a horde of men coming down the road, firing into the town, killing the terrorists at the doctor's door.

*J*o cracked her eyes open and was blinded with white light. She lifted her hand to block the brightness but stiffened when she felt someone's touch.

Panic struck Jo, but only for a moment, and then she was soothed by the reassuring sound of her daughter's voice.

"Mom, it's okay," Stacy said. "It's me."

The bright light disappeared, and the outline of Stacy's face replaced it. Jo opened her mouth to speak, but there was nothing but raspy gasps of air that escaped, and Stacy quickly placed her hand on Jo's shoulder.

"Don't speak," Stacy said. "The doctor said you have severe damage to your vocal cords. They'll heal, but you need to rest." Sensing her mother's questions, she nodded again. "Em's okay."

Tears were the only answer that Jo could provide, and when the quick emotional relief of her daughter's safety ended, she frowned in confusion, mouthing a one-word question. "How?"

Stacy smiled. "It was Mike." She tilted her head to the

side. "Well, it was Mike and a small army. He brought the forces up the mountain just in time, and it was enough to push them back. He saved us, Mom. He saved all of us." She looked at the door and then back to her mother. "You know, he's outside. He comes to check on you a lot. You've been out for three days. Do you want me to get him?"

It was the first time in Jo's life that she wanted to say yes, but couldn't. Both physically and emotionally. She knew that there would be time for all of that later. What mattered now was being with her family. Being with her children. Because they were alive. And that was enough.

* * *

ONE YEAR LATER

Jo closed her eyes, feeling the warmth of the sun break through the tree branches and warm her face. She had her hiking boots on, the pistol at her hip. She had come a long way from the woman she was last year, but the gun was one habit that she couldn't break herself out of.

She was nearing the end of her morning walk, but she stopped to bask in the silence of the mountain. It had been eight months since the area was deemed safe after the last of the insurgents were captured and killed, but even now, a year later, the effects of their actions were still being felt.

But today was the start of a new day. And it was one that she and everyone else on the mountain had been waiting for. If she lingered here too long, then she was going to miss it.

Jo returned to the cabin, finding Stacy and Amelia in the garden. It was good having Stacy home, but it would be hard watching her leave to go to college again in the fall. Classes were finally starting to begin again, another sign that life was returning to normal.

Stacy was reading, and Amelia was planting new seasonal flowers, but she took the time to break from her gardening when she saw her mother appear through the woods. "About time you showed up!" Amelia planted her trowel into the dirt and stood. "We're going to be late."

"Then you better go inside and change," Jo said.

Amelia groaned, but then sprinted inside, leaving the door open in the process.

"You sure you don't want to come?" Jo asked, looking to Stacy.

Stacy shook her head, still focused on her book. "Too many people."

Jo raised her eyebrows. "You do know who you sound like, right?"

"Hey, you're the one who keeps saying we're the most alike," Stacy answered. "I guess the prophecy has been fulfilled."

Jo kissed the top of her daughter's head, and then went inside to change. "I'll let you know if it works."

"I'm sure I'll be able to hear the cheers of joy from here," Stacy said.

Once both Jo and Amelia were cleaned up, they walked the path back to the road. While the signs were still up around her property, Jo hadn't reinstated the trip wires and alarm bells after she moved back to the cabin.

It wasn't because she didn't believe in being prepared anymore, it was just that she knew, deep down, that she wouldn't be staying at the cabin full time. The place nothing more than a beautiful retreat, somewhere to get away when the crowds got too big in town.

Jo had slowly been re-acclimating herself into the world, one toe at a time. It was hard at first, but it was getting more comfortable. She had a good support structure to help her.

"You think they actually did it?" Amelia asked once the town came into view through the trees.

"I do," Jo answered.

"Kind of crazy to think we ever depended on it so much," Amelia said. "I feel like everyone's gotten used to living without power."

"Maybe," Jo said. "But people always remember what it was like, and it makes them want it back."

Jo thought that it was kind of how she felt when it came to life and her own recovery. It had taken some time, but she was finally ready for a reset, a real reboot, to experience all of the things that she didn't allow herself to enjoy. Moments like this, with her daughter, and the people that she cared about most. Including Mike.

"There you are," Mike said, dressed in his uniform as they stepped onto the street. "I wasn't sure you were going to come."

Amelia smiled and then raised her arms, the universal gesture to be picked up. And while she was a little too old for that to still be a thing, Mike gladly scooped her up and planted a kiss on her cheek. "Mom took a long walk."

Mike smiled and then pulled one arm around Jo's waist. "She does like to take her time."

Jo slapped Mike's stomach, and he winced. "Watch it."

"Yes, ma'am."

The three of them walked toward Mags' store, which had been one of the first buildings in town that had been rebuilt. Jo made sure of that.

She looked up at the store's moniker, which still bore her friend's name, and an ache formed in her heart. "I still miss her."

"Me too," Amelia said.

"Me three," Mike said.

The store was now run by Jo and Amelia and was part of Jo's steps of reintegrating herself into the community. It allowed her to be put in an excellent position to help people stay prepared by ordering supplies for the town. It was the perfect job.

"So you gonna flip the switch or not?" Mike asked.

The crowd that had gathered were all eager to see if the power had been restored, and the store had been chosen as the testing ground, in memory of the woman who had owned it before her. Jo moved to the door and opened it, finding the light switch inside that would light up the sign above.

The power company had said that all lines would be restored today by ten o'clock all along the mountain. Jo reached for the switch but paused, thinking of the past year, thinking of all the events that led her here today and the sacrifices that it took. She shut her eyes, whispering a prayer that only she and one other could hear.

"I miss you, Mags," Jo said. "I'll do my best to take care of this place. Just like you did. I hope I'm worthy."

Jo opened her eyes and then flicked on the switch. The light in the window turned on, and the crowd cheered in triumph.

But their joy didn't come from the return of the power, or the fact that their lives could return to a little back to normal, it came from their perseverance. They had faced the worst evil that life could have thrown them, and they came out victorious on the other side.

And Jo smiled because of the people that were looking at her, because Amelia and Mike were here, and while she pretended to hide in the back, Jo saw Stacy had come too. This was a life worth living. And she was so glad to have survived to see it.

Made in United States
North Haven, CT
10 February 2025